SILVER SPARROW

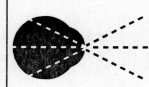

SILVER SPARROW

TAYARI JONES

THORNDIKE PRESS
A part of Gale, Cengage Learning

 GALE
CENGAGE Learning·

Detroit • New York • San Francisco • New Haven, Conn • Waterville, Maine • London

LIBRARY OF CONGRESS CATALOGING-IN-PUBLICATION DATA

Jones, Tayari.
    Silver sparrow / by Tayari Jones.
        p. cm. — (Thorndike Press large print African-American)
    ISBN-13: 978-1-4104-4013-6 (hardcover)
    ISBN-10: 1-4104-4013-3 (hardcover)
    1. African American families—Fiction. 2. Polygamy—Fiction.
3. African American teenage girls—Fiction. 4. Sisters—Fiction.
5. Mothers and daughters—Fiction. 6. Fathers and
daughters—Fiction. 7. Atlanta (Ga.)—Fiction. 8. Domestic
fiction. 9. Large type books. I. Title.
PS3610.O63S56 2011b
813'.6—dc22   2011018944

Published in 2011 by arrangement with Algonquin Books of Chapel Hill, a division of Workman Publishing Co., Inc.

Printed in Mexico
1 2 3 4 5 6 7 15 14 13 12 11

For my parents,
Barbara and Mack Jones,
who, to the best of my knowledge,
are married only to each other

A DAUGHTER IS A COLONY

a territory, a progeny,
  a spitting image
like Athena sprung

  from her father's head:
chip off the old block,
  issue and spawn;

a namesake, a wishbone —
  loyalist and traitor —
a native, an other,

  a subject, a study,
a history, a half blood,
  a continent dark and strange.
                    — NATASHA TRETHEWEY

■ ■ ■ ■ ■

PART I
DANA LYNN
YARBORO

■ ■ ■ ■ ■

1
THE SECRET

My father, James Witherspoon, is a bigamist. He was already married ten years when he first clamped eyes on my mother. In 1968, she was working at the gift-wrap counter at Davison's downtown when my father asked her to wrap the carving knife he had bought his wife for their wedding anniversary. Mother said she knew that something wasn't right between a man and a woman when the gift was a blade. I said that maybe it means there was a kind of trust between them. I love my mother, but we tend to see things a little bit differently. The point is that James's marriage was never hidden from us. James is what I call him. His other daughter, Chaurisse, the one who grew up in the house with him, she calls him Daddy, even now.

When most people think of bigamy, if they think of it at all, they imagine some primitive practice taking place on the pages of

11

National Geographic. In Atlanta, we remember one sect of the back-to-Africa movement that used to run bakeries in the West End. Some people said it was a cult, others called it a cultural movement. Whatever it was, it involved four wives for each husband. The bakeries have since closed down, but sometimes we still see the women, resplendent in white, trailing six humble paces behind their mutual husband. Even in Baptist churches, ushers keep smelling salts on the ready for the new widow confronted at the wake by the other grieving widow and *her* stair-step kids. Undertakers and judges know that it happens all the time, and not just between religious fanatics, traveling salesmen, handsome sociopaths, and desperate women.

It's a shame that there isn't a true name for a woman like my mother, Gwendolyn. My father, James, is a bigamist. That is what he is. Laverne is his wife. She found him first and my mother has always respected the other woman's squatter's rights. But was my mother his wife, too? She has legal documents and even a single Polaroid proving that she stood with James Alexander Witherspoon Junior in front of a judge just over the state line in Alabama. However, to call her only his "wife" doesn't really explain the full complexity of her position.

There are other terms, I know, and when she is tipsy, angry, or sad, Mother uses them to describe herself: *concubine, whore, mistress, consort.* There are just so many, and none are fair. And there are nasty words, too, for a person like me, the child of a person like her, but these words were not allowed in the air of our home. "You are his daughter. End of story." If this was ever true it was in the first four months of my life, before Chaurisse, his legitimate daughter, was born. My mother would curse at hearing me use that word, *legitimate,* but if she could hear the other word that formed in my head, she would close herself in her bedroom and cry. In my mind, Chaurisse is his *real* daughter. With wives, it only matters who gets there first. With daughters, the situation is a bit more complicated.

It matters what you called things. *Surveil* was my mother's word. If he knew, James would probably say *spy,* but that is too sinister. We didn't do damage to anyone but ourselves as we trailed Chaurisse and Laverne while they wound their way through their easy lives. I had always imagined that we would eventually be asked to explain ourselves, to press words forward in our own defense. On that day, my mother would be called upon to do the talking. She is gifted with language and is able to layer difficult details in such a way that the result is smooth as water. She is a magician who can make the whole world feel like a dizzy illusion. The truth is a coin she pulls from behind your ear.

Maybe mine was not a blissful girlhood. But is anyone's? Even people whose parents are happily married to each other and no one else, even these people have their share of unhappiness. They spend plenty of time nursing old slights, rehashing squabbles. So you see, I have something in common with the whole world.

Mother didn't ruin my childhood or anyone's marriage. She is a good person. She prepared me. Life, you see, is all about knowing things. That is why my mother and I shouldn't be pitied. Yes, we have suffered, but we never doubted that we enjoyed at least one peculiar advantage when it came to what really mattered: I knew about Chaurisse; she didn't know about me. My mother knew about Laverne, but Laverne was under the impression that hers was an ordinary life. We never lost track of that basic and fundamental fact.

When did I first discover that although I was an only child, my father was not *my* father and mine alone? I really can't say. It's something that I've known for as long as I've known that I had a father. I can only say for sure when I learned that this type of double-duty daddy wasn't ordinary.

I was about five years old, in kindergarten, when the art teacher, Miss Russell, asked us to draw pictures of our families. While all the other children scribbled with their crayons or soft-leaded pencils, I used a blue-ink pen and drew James, Chaurisse, and Laverne. In the background was Raleigh, my father's best friend, the only person we knew from his other life. I drew him with the crayon labeled "Flesh" because he is really light-skinned. This was years and years ago, but I still remember. I hung a necklace around the wife's neck. I gave the girl a big smile, stuffed with square teeth. Near the left margin, I drew my mother and me standing by ourselves. With a marker, I blacked in Mother's long hair and curving lashes. On my own face, I drew only a pair of wide eyes. Above, a friendly sun winked at all six of us.

The art teacher approached me from behind. "Now, who are these people you've drawn so beautifully?"

Charmed, I smiled up at her. "My family. My daddy has two wifes and two girls."

Cocking her head, she said, "I see."

I didn't think much more about it. I was still enjoying the memory of the way she pronounced *beautifully.* To this day, when I hear anyone say that word, I feel loved. At the end of the month, I brought all of my drawings home in a cardboard folder. James opened up his wallet, which he kept plump with two-dollar bills to reward me for my schoolwork. I saved the portrait, my masterpiece, for last, being as it was so beautifully drawn and everything.

My father picked the page up from the table and held it close to his face like he was looking for a coded message. Mother stood behind me, crossed her arms over my chest, and bent to place a kiss on the top of my head. "It's okay," she said.

"Did you tell your teacher who was in the picture?" James said.

I nodded slowly, the whole time thinking that I probably should lie, although I wasn't quite sure why.

"James," Mother said, "let's not make a molehill into a mountain. She's just a child."

"Gwen," he said, "this is important. Don't look so scared. I'm not going to take her out behind the woodshed." Then he chuckled, but my mother didn't laugh.

"All she did was draw a picture. Kids draw pictures."

"Go on in the kitchen, Gwen," James said. "Let me talk to my daughter."

My mother said, "Why can't I stay in here? She's my daughter, too."

"You are with her all the time. You tell me I don't spend enough time talking to her. So now let me talk."

Mother hesitated and then released me. "She's just a little kid, James. She doesn't even know the ins and outs yet."

"Trust me," James said.

She left the room, but I don't know that she trusted him not to say something that would leave me wounded and broken-winged for life. I could see it in her face. When she was upset she moved her jaw around invisible gum. At night, I could hear her in her room, grinding her teeth in her sleep. The sound was like gravel under car wheels.

"Dana, come here." James was wearing a navy chauffeur's uniform. His hat must have been in the car, but I could see the ridged mark across his forehead where the hatband usually rested. "Come closer," he said.

I hesitated, looking to the space in the doorway where Mother had disappeared.

"Dana," he said, "you're not afraid of me, are you? You're not scared of your own father, are you?"

His voice sounded mournful, but I took it as a dare. "No, sir," I said, taking a bold step forward.

"Don't call me sir, Dana. I'm not your boss. When you say that, it makes me feel like an overseer."

I shrugged. Mother told me that I should always call him sir. With a sudden motion, he reached out for me and lifted me up on his lap. He spoke to me with both of our faces looking outward, so I couldn't see his expression.

"Dana, I can't have you making drawings like the one you made for your art class. I can't have you doing things like that. What goes on in this house between your mother and me is grown people's business. I love you. You are my baby girl, and I love you, and I love your mama. But what we do in this house has to be a secret, okay?"

"I didn't even draw this house."

James sighed and bounced me on his lap a little bit. "What happens in my life, in my world, doesn't have anything to do with you.

You can't tell your teacher that your daddy has another wife. You can't tell your teacher that my name is James Witherspoon. Atlanta ain't nothing but a country town, and everyone knows everybody."

"Your other wife and your other girl is a secret?" I asked him.

He put me down from his lap, so we could look each other in the face. "No. You've got it the wrong way around. Dana, you are the one that's a secret."

Then he patted me on the head and tugged one of my braids. With a wink he pulled out his billfold and separated three two-dollar bills from the stack. He handed them over to me and I clamped them in my palm.

"Aren't you going to put them in your pocket?"

"Yes, sir."

And for once, he didn't tell me not to call him that.

James took me by the hand and we walked down the hallway to the kitchen for dinner. I closed my eyes on the short walk because I didn't like the wallpaper in the hallway. It was beige with a burgundy pattern. When it had started peeling at the edges, I was accused of picking at the seams. I denied it over and over again, but Mother reported me to James on his weekly visit. He took off his belt and swatted me around the legs and up on my backside, which seemed to satisfy something in my mother.

In the kitchen my mother placed the bowls and plates on the glass table in silence. She wore her favorite apron that James brought back from New Orleans. On the front was a drawing of a crawfish holding a spatula aloft and a caption: DON'T MAKE ME POISON YOUR FOOD! James took his place at the head of the table and polished the water spots from his fork with his napkin. "I didn't lay a hand on her; I didn't even raise my voice. Did I?"

"No, sir." And this was entirely the truth, but I felt different than I had just a few minutes before when I'd pulled my drawing out of its sleeve. My skin stayed the same while this difference snuck in through a pore and attached itself to whatever brittle part forms my center. *You are the secret.* He'd said it with a smile, touching the tip of my nose with the pad of his finger.

My mother came around and picked me up under my arms and sat me on the stack of phone books in my chair. She kissed my cheek and fixed a plate with salmon croquettes, a spoon of green beans, and corn.

"Are you okay?"

I nodded.

James ate his meal, spooning honey onto a dinner roll when my mother said there would be no dessert. He drank a big glass of Coke.

"Don't eat too much," my mother said. "You'll have to eat again in a little while."

"I'm always happy to eat your food, Gwen. I'm always happy to sit at your table."

I don't know how I decided that my missing teeth were the problem, but I devised a plan to slide a folded piece of paper behind my top teeth to camouflage the pink space in the center of my smile. I was inspired by James, actually, who once told me how he put cardboard in his shoes when he was little to make up for the holes in the soles. The paper was soggy and the blue lines ran with my saliva.

Mother caught me in the middle of this process. She walked into my room and lay across my twin bed with its purple checked spread. She liked to do this, just lie across my bed while I played with my toys or colored in my notebooks, watching me like I was a television show. She always smelled good, like flowery perfume, and sometimes like my father's cigarettes.

21

"What are you doing, Petunia?"

"Don't call me Petunia," I said, partially because I didn't like the name and partially because I wanted to see if I could talk with the paper in my mouth. "Petunia is the name of a pig."

"Petunia is a flower," my mother said. "A pretty one."

"It's Porky Pig's girlfriend."

"That's meant to be a joke, a pretty name for a pig, you see?"

"A joke is supposed to be funny."

"It is funny. You are just in a bad mood. What're you doing with the paper?"

"I'm trying to put my teeth back," I said, while trying to rearrange the sodden wad.

"How come?"

This seemed obvious as I took in my own reflection along with my mother's in the narrow mirror attached to the top of my chest of drawers. Of course James wanted to keep me a secret. Who would love a girl with a gaping pink hole in the middle of her mouth? None of the other children in my kindergarten reading circle looked like I did. Surely my mother could understand this. She spent half an hour each night squinting at her skin before a magnifying mirror, applying swipes of heavy creams from Mary Kay. When I asked her what she was doing,

22

she said, "I am improving my appearance. Wives can afford to let themselves go. Concubines must be vigilant."

Recalling it now, I know that she must have been drinking. Although I can't remember the moment so well, I know that just outside the frame was her glass of Asti Spumante, golden and busy with bubbles.

"I am improving my appearance." I hoped she would smile.

"Your appearance is perfect, Dana. You're five; you have beautiful skin, shiny eyes, and pretty hair."

"But no teeth," I said.

"You're a little girl. You don't need teeth."

"Yes, I do," I said quietly. "Yes, I do."

"Why? To eat corn on the cob? Your teeth will grow back. There is lots of corn in your future, I promise."

"I want to be like that other girl," I said finally.

Mother had been lying across my bed, like a goddess on a chaise lounge, but when I said that she snapped up. "What other girl?"

"James's other girl."

"You can say her name," Mother said.

I shook my head. "Can't."

"Yes, you can. Just say it. Her name is Chaurisse."

"Stop it," I said, afraid that just saying my

sister's name would unleash some terrible magic the way that saying "Bloody Mary" while staring into a pan of water would turn the liquid red and thick.

Mother rose from the bed and got down on her knees so we were the same height. As she pressed her hands down on my shoulders, traces of cigarette smoke lingered in her tumbly hair. I reached out for it.

"Her name is Chaurisse," my mother said again. "She's a little girl, just like you are."

"Please stop saying it," I begged her. "Stop it before something happens."

My mother hugged me to her chest. "What did your daddy say to you the other day? Tell me what he said."

"Nothing," I whispered.

"Dana, you can't lie to me, okay? I tell you everything and you tell me everything. That's the only way we can pull this off, baby. We have to keep the information moving between us." She shook me a little bit. Not enough to scare me, just enough to get my attention.

"He said I was a secret."

My mother pulled me into a close hug, crisscrossing her arms across my back and letting her hair hang around me like a magic curtain. I will never forget the smell of her hugs.

"That motherfucker," she said. "I love him, but I might have to kill him one day."

The next morning, my mother told me to put on the green and yellow dress that I'd worn for my school picture six weeks earlier, before the teeth were lost. She styled my long hair with slippery ribbons and strapped my feet into stiff shiny shoes. Then we climbed into my godmother's old Buick, on loan for the day.

"Where are we going?"

Mother turned off Gordon Road. "I am taking you to see something."

I waited for more information, poking my tongue into the slick space where my nice teeth had once been. She didn't say anything else about our destination, but she asked me to recite my -at words.

"H-a-t is *hat;* b-a-t is *bat.*" I didn't stop until I got to "M-a-t is *mat.*" By then, we'd pulled up in front of a small pink school building trimmed with green. Down the road was John A. White Park. We sat in the car a long time while I performed for her. I was glad to do it. I recited my numbers from one to one hundred and then I sang "Frère Jacques."

When a group of children spilled out into the yard of the small school, my mother held up a finger to stop my singing. "Roll down your window and look out," she said. "You see that chubby little girl in the blue jeans and red shirt? That's Chaurisse."

I found the girl my mother described standing in line with a group of other little kids. Chaurisse was utterly ordinary back then. Her hair was divided into two short puffs in the front and the shorter hair in the back was held down in a series of tight braids. "Look at her," my mother said. "She hardly has any hair. She is going to be fat when she grows up, just like her mammy. She doesn't know her -at words, and she can't sing a song in French."

I said, "She has her teeth."

"For now. She's your same age, so they are probably loose. But here's something you can't see. She was born too early so she has problems. The doctor had to stick plastic tubes down her ears to keep them from getting infected."

"But James loves her. She's not a secret."

"James has an obligation to her mammy and that's my problem, not yours. Okay? James loves you equal to Chaurisse. If he had any sense, he'd love you best. You're smarter, more mannerable, and you've got better hair. But what you have is equal love, and that is good enough."

I nodded as relief spread all over my body.

I felt all my muscles relax. Even my feet let go and settled themselves limp in my pretty shoes.

"Am I a secret?" I asked my mother.

"No," she said. "You are an unknown. That little girl there doesn't even know she has a sister. You know everything."

"God knows everything," I said. "He's got the whole world in his hands."

"That's true," my mother said. "And so do we."

2
A SORT OF CREEPING LOVE

It was not love at first sight, at least not on my mother's part. She didn't meet my father and feel a shift in her personal chemistry or a change in the rhythm that connected her heart to the rest of her body. It was love, mind you, but not the lightning-bolt kind. She had that sort of love in her first marriage, which had lasted only nineteen months. What she had with my father was a sort of creeping love, the kind that sinks in before you know it and makes a family of you. She says that love like what she has with my father occurs on the God level, not of the world and not bound by the laws of the state of Georgia.

You can't help but respect something like that.

Gift-wrap girl wasn't the job she dreamed of, as she never really dreamed of jobs. My mother had dreamed only about marriage, and her brief acquaintance with it had left her disappointed. Coming up with another dream was more than a notion, and she had no idea where to start.

For most of her early life, she wasted her wishes on her mother. Flora, my grandmother, ran off when my mother was just three months old. For six days Flora wrapped her breasts in cabbage leaves to dry up the milk and then just up and left one Sunday before church with nothing but the clothes on her back and the money she got when her numbers hit. "No note, no nothing. Just gone." The tone of her voice when she told this story made me wish my mother had named me after my grandmother, the wild woman. Instead, she called me Dana Lynn, a sly wink at her own name. Gwendolyn.

By the time James walked into Davison's, my mother wasn't just motherless but fatherless as well. My grandfather had disowned her for leaving her husband, Clarence Yarboro. It wasn't just because her father worked for his and could certainly lose his job but because this proved that my mother was just like Flora. She tells me that when she looks back on it, the reasons she left Clarence were not good enough reasons to leave a marriage, but she doesn't think that she ever had a good enough reason to marry him in the first place. Mother says she married him because he was good-looking and rich — the youngest in a family of pretty undertakers — and because he had asked her to the eighth-grade dance. Five years later, she was his wife. Seven years later, she was divorced, living in a rooming house, and falling in love with a married man. Eight years later, I was born.

When my parents met, Dr. Martin Luther King Jr. was only one month dead, and there was a sort of grayness over everything. Mother had gone to see Dr. King lying in state over at Spelman College, but the line had been so long, and she didn't know what was to be gained from standing there, so she left. Back at the gift-wrap counter, Mother felt cheated somehow, that he was assassinated before she could settle her life down enough to participate in the miracle that the man had been. But whom could she blame but herself? She felt a little guilty, enjoying this good job up in gift wrap, the very first colored woman to hold that post. And even the year before, when she was working in ladies' hats, did she not place a lovely pillbox directly on the head of a colored woman? So yes, she knew how much things had changed, and she was grateful for it, Lord knew that she was thankful for these new opportunities. Still, she hadn't fought for them, and now the man was dead. It would have been difficult to explain her shame even if she had anyone to explain herself to. Her father wasn't speaking to her, and her husband was on the verge of remarrying, less than a year since she had moved into the rooming house on Ashby Street. Mother worked each day, looking her best in one of the three good dresses she'd bought with her discount and a small advance on her pay.

James approached the counter on an afternoon on which she was feeling particularly remorseful, not so much for throwing away her marriage but for having gotten married in the first place.

"May I help you, sir?" she said. He was wearing his chauffeur uniform with the hat clutched under his arm like an army officer. She called him sir because that is what they called all the male customers, and she went out of her way to let the colored patrons hear that word of respect there in Davison's. Was this not what Dr. King died for?

Mother was pretty; she knew this. Not Dorothy Dandridge or Lena Horne beautiful but lovely enough that people noticed.

She had what she considered to be an ordinary Negro girl's face, the kind of medium-dark skin tone that no one called anything but "brownskin." Her eyelashes, in her opinion, were her best feature; she gestured with them, the way other people talked with their hands. Everyone else, she knew, would say that the key to her looks was her head of hair, long and thick, that reached past her shoulder blades. It was the only useful thing her mother left her. Willie Mae, the girl who roomed next door to her in the boardinghouse, made good money every two weeks pulling it straight with a hot comb and twirling it with irons. At that time of her life, Mother liked to think of herself as an honest person and told anyone who asked that her hair wasn't naturally good.

When James slid the electric carving knife across the counter, Mother noticed the flash of his wedding band and thought of Willie Mae, who had no problem spending time with men who were married — as long as they swore they were not happy. As my mother asked my father what sort of wrapping he wanted for the carving knife, she decided that he wouldn't do for Willie Mae, as she was a sucker for pretty men — bright-complected, with light eyes and wavy hair.

"You would have been crazy for my ex-husband," Gwen told her once, as Willie Mae pulled the straightening comb, sizzling with grease.

"Is he still available?"

Mother chuckled and took a drag from her cigarette, catching the smoke with a damp towel. "He was available the whole time I was married to him."

"Girl," Willie Mae said, "I am not telling you how to live your life, but you must be one high-minded lady to leave a perfectly good man just for chasing a little tail."

"It wasn't just that," my mother said. "And who's a lady? Not me. Just ask my daddy. According to him, I stopped being a lady the day I walked out on my husband."

"At least you had a husband to leave," Willie Mae said.

The man before my mother with the carving knife said, "Can you wrap it in anniversary paper?"

Mother said, "Wedding anniversary?"

"Yes, ma'am," he said.

She had to smile at the "ma'am." "Who's it for?"

"My wife."

Mother laughed and regretted it immediately. The man in front of her looked embarrassed, and there were white people in the line behind him.

"W-what?"

"Forgive me, sir," she said, and she really was sorry. "It's just that most men buy their wives something a little bit more romantic. Like perfume."

He looked at the carving knife. "This is a g-good present. It cost twenty-three dollars."

"Yes, sir," she said. "Let me wrap it for you. We have a nice floral paper that just came in."

"Wait." He took the knife back. "I ch-changed my mind." He headed toward the escalator, with his hat still clamped under his arm.

The next customer in line was a white woman who had purchased a set of baby's pajamas for her pregnant sister.

"Men," the customer said. "Who can understand the way their minds work?"

Mother knew what the white lady was talking about, but she couldn't laugh at a black man with her, even though she was only laughing at him for being a man.

James returned more than two hours later as the store was closing and my mother was tidying up the gift-wrap counter, throwing away bits of string, lining up the tape dispensers, and counting the shirt boxes. He handed her the carving knife again.

"It's a good knife," my mother said, tearing a rectangle of floral paper from the roll. "I didn't mean any harm."

He didn't speak, but she noticed his neck bulging as she squared the corners and rolled the tape to make it sticky on both sides.

Mother handed him the box, so pretty now with a double bow, wondering if she hadn't overdone it. She imagined his wife undoing the ribbons, assuming the contents were as lush as the wrapping, but she decided that it was not her concern.

"And this," he said in a rush of air, handing her a small box containing a compact of solid perfume.

"Your wife will like this," Mother said. "She'll love pulling it out of her purse in front of her friends." She felt like she was speaking too much, but this odd man was staring at her, and she felt that someone should do the talking. She wrapped the compact in a saucy red wrapper and used a simple gold tie. "Look at that. It's got a little cha-cha."

She slid it across the table to him and he shoved it back.

"I-i-i-t's . . ." He paused and tried again.

"Th-th-th . . ." He stopped.

"Is there something wrong? Do you want me to put them both in the same paper?"

His shoulder jerked in a little spasm, and he said, "It's for you."

Mother glanced at her left hand, where she wore her own wedding ring, although her husband, Clarence, was a year behind her and already engaged. She wore the ring to say that she believed in certain things.

My mother read *Life* magazine every week, so she knew that the rest of the country was enjoying free love and unkempt hair, but she didn't admire the young people who let themselves go. She pictured herself more like Mrs. Parks or Ella Baker. Dignified and proper, like a strand of pearls.

"Take it please," he said, nudging the red-wrapped present her way again.

And she did accept it, not only because it was a lovely gift; she'd admired the golden compact several times, sneaking her finger in for a sample to dab at her temples. Mother says she appreciated his effort, that he had won a fight with his stammer to give her this present. "Thank you, sir."

"Don't call me sir. My name is James Witherspoon. You don't have to be scared of me. I just wanted to give you something."

My mother spent the next week and a half

36

expecting James Witherspoon to emerge at the top of the escalator. She agreed with Willie Mae, who pointed out that men do nothing without a reason. That compact was more expensive than the carving knife. If he spent more money on her than on his wife, he'd be back.

"Some men," said Willie Mae, "would be back if all they bought you was a Peppermint Pattie. Money is for buying company, and they know it."

(Lovely Willie Mae, whom I called Auntie, stood up for my mother at her illegal wedding to my father, four months after I was born. She was my godmother, sweet to me when I was just a little girl. She died right after everything happened, shot to death by her boyfriend, a pretty man named William. I miss her very much.)

But Mother didn't feel that James Witherspoon was trying to buy her. She thought that, for some reason, he just liked her. It was a nice idea, being liked. There was no harm in being liked by a married man. There was no harm in liking one back if all you did was like.

By the time a month had passed and he hadn't returned, Mother regretted not having been more encouraging when he handed her the compact with its cha-cha wrapping, colored to look like a French bordello. She was sorry for staring so long at his wedding ring, a simple gold band, etched with vines, and she felt silly for wearing her own ring — just the band, as her ex-husband had taken back the stone; it belonged to his mother, and she couldn't expect to take it with her. And she wondered, now, why she kept on wearing it.

She also wondered why she wasn't able to care more about the important things happening in the world. There was the Vietnam War. She knew boys who had died, and there was always Dr. King, cold in the ground. Even though Willie Mae hadn't been bitten by a dog, she had been in Birmingham when the German shepherds were let loose. And where had Mother been when all of this was going on? She was busy learning to be a wife.

At the end of the summer, she was at work, just where James had left her three months ago, when he finally came back for her. "I came to say hello."

"You did?" My mother felt ashamed to be grateful for such a small gesture.

"Would you like to have coffee with me?"

She nodded.

"I'm m-married," he said. "I'm m-m-married. All I'm asking for is c-coffee. It's a long story. My life is a long story."

"Mine is, too."

She agreed to meet him at the end of her workday. She petted the hair at her temples, which had kinked up with sweat. It was time for Willie Mae to see about her, so Mother bound her hair into an oily bun at the nape of her neck. She would spend the evening saying to him, "Please excuse the way I look." And he would assure her that she looked fine. She liked that he said that she looked only fine and didn't pretend that she was beautiful on this day. She liked the truth of that, and the truth came without insult. She was fine; she would do; it was enough.

My mother stood on the curb at Peachtree Street, where five roads came together, near the plastic shed where she was accustomed to catching the bus. Willie Mae, who typed for an insurance company, would already be onboard, sitting right behind the driver, because she was from Alabama and had walked to work all that year to support Mrs. Parks.

Mother didn't recognize the limousine as her ride when it pulled up to the curb beside her. She stood there, her eyes trained over the roof of the double-doored Cadillac, looking for James. She wondered if maybe she shouldn't cross the street, so he could more easily find her. She glanced at her watch as he emerged from the driver's seat and tipped his hat.

"Oh," she said. "It's you." She laughed. "I didn't think —"

By now he had reached the backseat door and opened it. He smiled, but didn't speak. Mother touched her dirty hair, smoothing the edges again. She glanced up the road, looking to see her bus coming around the corner with Willie Mae perched on the first seat, but there was only the ordinary traffic of Studebakers, Packards, and other buses. She took a dainty step toward the open car door; the interior was velvet-looking, a warm tan, the color of peanut butter. She sat carefully on the seat and tugged at her skirt so that it lay smooth over her hips. "Thank you," she said.

"Madame," he said. Then he got into the driver's seat and pulled away.

My mother studied the back of his head, his orderly hairline made straight in a barber's chair. Classical music crackled out of the speakers, the zip of the violins making her feel anxious.

"Would you like to go to Paschal's?" he asked her.

40

"No," she said. "I can't go there. If it's okay, I don't want to go there."

"It's up to you," he said.

The car was heavy with the scent of the solid perfume he had given her; if he recognized it, he didn't say.

"Tell me about yourself," he said.

"I don't know," Mother said. "I don't know what to say."

"You can say whatever you want."

It was strangely comforting to talk to the back of his head like this. It was what she imagined talking to a priest would be like. Willie Mae went into the confessional every week. Mother was tempted to join her, but she didn't want to have to pretend to be Catholic. She didn't like to lie.

"I was born here in Atlanta. I used to be married, but I'm not married anymore." He didn't say anything, so she kept talking. "I'm twenty years old. Did I tell you my name? It's Gwendolyn, but people just call me Gwen. Oh, I don't know what else to say. I never knew my mother. And I didn't march with Dr. King. I went to Spelman to see him lie in state, but the line was so long and I had to go to work. I live in a rooming house because I don't have a lot of money."

He kept driving, but my mother didn't say anything else. She wanted to get out of the car. That would be the good thing about talking to a priest, how you said what you had to say and then you got to leave. But she was trapped here in this Cadillac, getting sick from the smell of her own perfume. "I think I'm ready to go now."

Without turning toward her, James said, "B-but we didn't have coffee yet."

"I don't feel well."

"I know that I'm married," James said. "I am not asking you to do anything that would make you feel low. I just want to have coffee with you. I have never b-b-been out for coffee or for dinner with a woman be-before."

"Except your wife," Mother said, regretting immediately the note of sarcasm in her voice. "It's not my business. Sorry."

"N-n-not even with her," he said with a sadness that was palpable. "It's a long story."

"My life is a long story," my mother said.

"Mine, too," said my father.

Then they both chuckled that the conversation had come round again. She imagined it like a circle, a child's ball, or even the whole world.

And this is how it started. Just with coffee and the exchange of their long stories. Love can be incremental. Predicaments, too. Coffee can start a life just as it can start a day. This was the meeting of two people who were destined to love from before they were born, from before they made choices that would complicate their lives. This love just rolled toward my mother as though she were standing at the bottom of a steep hill. Mother had no hand in this, only heart.

3
Notes on Precocity

Even though my father was a bit on the short side and wore glasses thick as a slice of Wonder bread, there was an uprightness about him that inspired a brand of respect. Even after everything that happened, he never lost this. Much of the esteem he enjoyed had to do with being profiled as a local entrepreneur once in the *Atlanta Journal* and twice in the *Daily World.* Witherspoon Sedans was a small fleet — three cars and two drivers: himself and Raleigh Arrington, his adopted brother and best friend. I could probably count the times that I have seen my father dressed like a regular person and not like a driver. There was no shame in it, however. After all, he was his own boss. When you have to wear dress blues and a hat and you work for white people, you're wearing a costume. You're no better than the monkey decked out in a red jacket with gold braiding. But when it's your own company and you picked the uniform yourself out of a catalog, when it was ordered in just your size and didn't need to be hemmed or let out, well, that was different.

It's no coincidence that he was wearing his uniform when my mother met him that famous afternoon in Davison's. It's remarkable, the way he seems almost fused with his clothing. It made him more confident, and when he was confident he stuttered less. And when he stuttered less you hardly noticed his heavy glasses; he seemed taller.

James was an easygoing man, master of his emotions. "The key to life," he told me once, "is to avoid the highs and the lows. It's the peaks and valleys that mess you up." He liked to behave as though his uninflected disposition was because of some philosophical leaning, but I knew it was because passion of any sort brought out the stammer and turned him into a freak. Anyone who has ever seen James when the stammer rode him could tell how much it hurt him. His face and neck seemed to swell as though the words were trapped in there, painful and deadly like sickle cells. And finally, with a jerk, spasm, or kick, the sentence would break free, unfettered and whole.

■ ■ ■ ■

My parents didn't really fight. The most they ever did was "have words," which was my mother's expression. Their disagreements were rare because of James's little-from-the-left-little-from-the-right disposition and also because there was no time for bickering. James ate over at our house only once a week, and once or twice a year he spent the night. When we received him in our apartment, seated him at our table, we treated him like the guest he was. We poured Coke with the meal, said grace like it was Sunday, and even let him smoke in the living room. My job was keeping him in clean glass ashtrays. He said his wife, Laverne, made him stand on the porch with his cigarettes, even when it rained.

Most children probably remember their parents' arguments with a stone-in-the-stomach ache. In the seventh grade, I read a novel called *It's Not the End of the World,* about divorcing parents. My teacher gave it to me, quietly, in a plain brown sack, after my mother explained to her that she and my father were separated but possibly reconciling, the perfect falsehood to explain his inconsistent presence in our lives. The book was about a girl who was torn apart by her parents' fighting. I thanked my teacher for the gift, but my feelings could not have been further from those of the traumatized heroine of that Judy Blume book. When my parents argued, it was over me; for the brief duration of their spats, I was at the center of something.

Mother never argued on her own behalf. It was "always about Dana Lynn." My father, before he refused to accommodate her demands always, first, insisted that he loved me. There was a time in my life when that was almost enough.

"This is about fairness, James," my mother would say, indicating to me that what was once a conversation had now morphed into "words." I could watch my father's neck bloat a little, as his defenses gathered there.

I am not a particularly graceful individual. I'm no klutz, but a person doesn't see me move and think, "Those hips were made for swaying" or "Those toes were born to pirouette." I am not putting myself down. As my mother would say, "Self-deprecation is not attractive." And as she wouldn't say, people in our position cannot afford to make themselves look bad. So when I say that I wasn't meant to be a dancer, I am just telling the basic truth. But that didn't stop my mother from saying to James, "I think that Dana should enjoy ballet lessons, just as your other daughter does." She loved that word, *enjoy,* and I had to admit that I liked it, too.

Turns out, I didn't literally *enjoy* the ballet lessons. When I'd envisioned myself as a ballerina, I saw myself in a lavender tutu with pink ribbons laced up my calves. Instead, I ended up in a hot upstairs room at the YWCA, crammed into a leotard the color of bandages, forcing my bare feet into impossible positions.

When I was about ten, my mother started lobbying for me to take extra classes in science. I was in favor of this, as I liked biology, but at my school we didn't get to do any experiments. On the last day of the school year, my teacher handed out flyers advertising the Saturday Science Academy at Kennedy Middle School. My mother said that she'd ask my father for the thirty-dollar deposit after dinner on Wednesday. To prepare, I brushed my hair around the edges and put on a short-sleeve collared shirt that I thought made me look smart. I stuck a pencil behind my ear.

We ate dinner that night as we always did, at the kitchen table. My mother invited

James into the den to watch *Tic Tac Dough* and enjoy a spot of cream sherry. He smiled and thanked my mother as she handed him a pretty glass.

"James," she said, "I want Dana to enjoy the benefits of extra tutoring in science."

James took a small sip of the sherry. His throat worked to swallow it down.

"Science is very important," my mother said. She talked as she walked to stand in front of the television. "There are a number of programs in the city that are open to exceptional children. Don't you think Dana is exceptional?"

James said, "I didn't say she wasn't exceptional."

"Good," my mother said. "Because she is."

I sat at his feet with my pencil behind my ear and tried to sit up exceptionally straight.

"That kind of thing costs money," James said.

"She has two working parents," my mother pointed out.

James didn't say anything. My mother sat down beside him on the sofa.

This she said softly: "The Saturday Science Academy makes allowances for female heads of household, you know."

I had not known about this, and it puzzled

me. If she could get me in free, why were we even bothering to involve my father at all?

"James," my mother said in a voice that was pleasant on the surface, "why are you so quiet?"

Sitting at his feet, I could feel his legs jerking at my back. The stammer could be like that, the words squirming through his body. With great effort he said, "You know I love you, Dana."

I gave my mother a sharp look. "Love" meant I wasn't going to be able to go. "Please," I said in a voice that was only a squeak.

Mother touched her lips to tell me to be quiet, that I should let her handle my father "Why not? Is it because she's a pretty girl? I have read that parents don't make the same investment in the minds of their good-looking daughters. Dana is an intellectual, you know."

I nodded, hoping that this didn't count as getting into the conversation.

"Dana, go and get the brochure and show it to your father."

I pushed myself up from the floor and found my feet. I didn't even get out of the room before he said, "Ch-ch-chaurisse is taking c-c-classes at the Saturday Academy."

"I see," my mother said.

But I knew that she had known all along. If Chaurisse was going, then I wasn't going to get to go. This was one of the basic rules of being an outside child. I thought about the flyer posted on my bedroom mirror. The kids in the pictures held beakers over Bunsen burners.

"Well, I am sure Chaurisse will enjoy herself this summer."

Carol Burnett was on the TV, and if anyone could see us, I bet we looked like a regular family.

"I don't need your permission to enroll her, James," my mother said. "This is not a threat. It's just a fact."

"St-t . . ." My father struggled. I felt sorry for him sometimes, even at a moment like this.

"Dana needs to know science, too."

"Gw-w-wen," he said, "why do you k-k-keep doing this? I try to be a good man. You know I am doing everything I can."

Mother said, "There are several programs for gifted children who excel in science. I've done some research."

I looked over at my mother. "Do they have Bunsen burners?"

She shushed me with a subtle movement of her hands. I knelt at my father's feet, letting my weight settle back on my heels.

"I can't afford any more payments," James said. "You know I am stretched real thin." This was said to my mother. Then he turned to me, "I love you, baby girl."

I was ready to tell him that it was okay, that I didn't have to go to science lessons. He seemed so sad and sincere. My mother touched her lips again, and I didn't say a word.

"It seems, James, that you have money for what you want to have money for." She didn't raise or lower her voice. "If you don't have money to pay for her to go to another program, then I will just have to send her to the Saturday Academy, where she can go for free. It's just that simple."

"Ch-ch-chaurisse is already going to that program. You know that, Gwen. Why d-d-do you have to go through this with everything? You know I am doing the best I can."

"Are you doing the best you can for Dana? That's what I want to know. I am not asking you to buy me a fox fur, although I saw your wife, and she looks quite lovely in hers."

"Y-y-you s-s-saw Laverne?"

"I'm not blind," my mother said. "I can't help who I run into in the grocery store, Like you always say, 'Atlanta ain't nothing

52

but a country town.' "

"St-t-tay away —"

"Nobody is interested in your quote-unquote family. I only brought up the matter of the fox fur to let you know that this is not about competition. This is about opportunity for Dana Lynn."

"D-d-don't you —"

"Can she at least go to the Fernbank Planetarium? I have a brochure, and I have enough money for half."

James continued to fight with his throat to release the words jammed there. With a sudden kick of his right leg, barely missing my shoulder, he said, "Stay the hell away from my family."

But by then he was slumped and exhausted. Although his words were sharp and direct, his rounded shoulders showed that he was beaten.

"Calm down," my mother said, rubbing his neck. "Don't curse like that in front of Dana. Do you want her to grow up attracted to violent men?"

I couldn't turn around and look at him. The planetarium didn't have anything to do with Bunsen burners.

"Tell your father thank you, Dana," my mother said.

"Thank you," I said with my back still facing him.

"Dana," she said, "what kind of appreciation is that?"

I turned to him and said, "Thank you. I really want to take the science lessons."

"You're welcome," he said.

"Yes, sir," I said, and then I couldn't help adding, "It's not fair." Looking up at him, I wanted a hug. That was the full extent of my ambition. I knew he wouldn't say that I could go ahead and go to the Saturday Academy, even if I promised not to bother Chaurisse. But I hoped he would hug me and tell me that he was sorry that I had to get second pick for everything and that he was sorry that my mother couldn't wear a fox-fur coat and that I couldn't tell anybody my daddy's real name. But he didn't say anything and his neck wasn't twitching so I knew that he wasn't stuck. He just didn't have any *sorry*s to say.

Since Mother was reared by her father with no mother in sight, she believes herself to be an expert in the ways of gentlemen. She says she knows how to hear all the things they leave unsaid. Some nights, after she kissed me good night, she would add, "Your father wishes you sweet dreams." I asked her once why he couldn't call and tell me himself. "He's your father, but first he is a man. A man is just a man, and that's all we have to work with."

After the Saturday Science Academy incident, just after James left our apartment for his house on Lynhurst, my mother sipped from his abandoned glass of sherry and said, "He'll be back. And I bet there is a fox fur involved." And she was almost right.

Less than a month later, I was up late, watching *Saturday Night Live,* and my mother was asleep on the couch. I turned the volume down low so she wouldn't wake up and make me go to bed. My face was pressed to the felt-covered television speaker, leaving me to feel the jokes when I couldn't really hear them. On the coffee table near my passed-out mother, the ice in her glass popped as it settled.

James didn't knock; he used his key to open the burglar door and the wooden door. My mother sat up with a start. "James?"

"Who else could it be? You got another man you didn't tell me about?" He laughed, following her voice into the den. "Dana!" he called, angling his voice toward my closed bedroom door.

"I'm in the den, too," I said.

"Glad I didn't wake anybody up."

James wasn't wearing his uniform. This

evening he was wearing jeans and a crisp blue shirt. In his arms was a large white box. He grabbed my mother around the waist and kissed her. "I love me a woman that can appreciate a cocktail. What you been drinking?"

"I was about to ask you the same thing," my mother said.

"Cuba Libre."

"I can't believe you are running the streets this time of night." Mother was smiling while they talked. We both acted like we didn't notice the big white box.

"Can't I come over any time I like because I miss my woman? Can't I deliver a special gift for my baby girl?"

I perked up. "That box is for me?"

"You know it is."

"James, I know you haven't been shopping at this hour."

"Who said nothing about shopping? I been playing cards, and I been playing well." He pulled off the top of the box with a flourish, revealing a waist-length fur jacket, junior size 7 — too big, but I'd grow into it.

"James," my mother said, feeling the soft fur, "tell me you did not win this in a card game."

"Yes, I did. My buddy Charlie Ray was playing so bad; all his money was gone so

56

he put this coat on the table."

My mother said, "James, you have to take it back. That coat belongs to someone."

"You are absolutely right. It belongs to me. And soon as she comes over here and gives me some sugar, it will belong to Dana. Come on, baby girl, p-p-put this on, and let your daddy see how p-p-pretty you are."

I paused for a second at the hitch in his voice, but he smiled and I knew that it would be okay.

The coat was piled on the floor beside him, and he held his arms outstretched. Feeling like I was in a movie, I hugged him around the neck and kissed him loudly on the cheek. James smelled sweet, like liquor and cola. To this day and for the rest of my life, I will always have a soft spot for a man with rum on his breath.

I think about the world and the way that things take place and in what order. I am not one of those people who believe that everything happens for a reason. Or, if I am, I don't believe that everything happens for a good reason. But the first time that I encountered my sister, Chaurisse, when I wasn't under the careful supervision of my mother, was at the Atlanta Civic Center in 1983. There's only so much that you can chalk up to coincidence. I believe in the eventuality of things. What's done in the dark shall come to the light. What goes up comes down. What goes around comes around. There are a million of these sayings, all, in their own way, true. And isn't that what's supposed to set you free?

The citywide science fair was held on the day of my fourteenth-and-a-half birthday. This was my own private holiday that I celebrated each year. My real birthday, the ninth of May, was really my mother's day. She made a big deal of it, forcing me to dress like a pageant queen for a special meal at the Mansion restaurant on Ponce de Leon Avenue. The waiters brought food I couldn't identify and my mother would say, "Isn't this nice? Happy birthday! You're growing up." Mother's attempts to make it special for just the two of us only reminded me how isolated we were. She and James were suspicious of outsiders, worried that someone might know someone who could expose us. You know what they say about southwest Atlanta.

On my fourteenth-and-a-half birthday, I set my alarm for 5:37 a.m., the precise minute of my birth, and shuffled a deck of playing cards. I'd heard that there was a way you could use an ordinary pinochle deck to

58

divine the future. The first six cards I dealt were hearts, and I hoped that this meant that there was love in my future. My mother laughed and sang a chirpy Sam Cooke song about how a girl of sixteen is too young to fall in love. And I told her that I may not know what love is, but I did know what exclusivity was. Now that really surprised her, me using that word. I learned it in school, not in English class, but in the guidance counselor's office. Miss Rhodes was her name. I'd been sent to her because I had been caught exchanging kisses with three different boys in six weeks. "There is something to be said for exclusivity, little girl."

High school was difficult for me. Any guidance counselor worth her salt should have understood that something heavy and barbed was behind the hostile attitude I adopted whenever I was called into her office. In my heart, I was a nice girl, and a smart one, eager to study biology. During my last year in middle school, I'd studied endlessly to pass the exam to be admitted into the math-and-science magnet. I crammed each night, memorizing the names of the noble gases and the quirks of various isotopes. I studied hard even though I was sick with fear that I would not be allowed to accept an invitation if Chaurisse decided that she wanted to go to Mays High School.

James and Laverne lived on Lynhurst Road, just a half mile from Mays, which had just been built as the flagship high school of black Atlanta. Because of her zip code, Chaurisse was entitled to enroll, even if she wasn't accepted into the magnet program. My mother's apartment was only three miles away, but we were in the district of Therrell High, which didn't have a magnet at all. I received my acceptance letter in June, but I had to wait another month to find out that Chaurisse was accepted to Northside High School, which specialized in the performing arts. Apparently she was somewhat gifted with woodwind instruments.

It would be too easy to say that I rejected high school before it had a chance to reject me, but even now, when I drive down I-285, I feel a stirring in my stomach when I see Mays High School on the right side of the expressway, not so modern now, but still imposing against a backdrop of kudzu and pine trees. I remember how it felt to be a student there, feeling like a trespasser, afraid each day that Chaurisse would change her mind about Northside High and the piccolo, deciding instead to claim my place.

About two weeks into the ninth grade, I decided that having a boyfriend, a real one, an exclusive one, would tether me to my school. That was the purpose of all the kissing that caused me to be banished again and again to the guidance counselor's office.

The reason that there were so many boys in such a short time was that I'd catch each of them passing notes to, looking at, or even talking to some other girl within days of making an overture toward me. I couldn't bear it. I dumped them and set out again. I would give any boy a chance if he seemed interested — I felt I couldn't afford to be particular — but again and again I was disappointed.

Not even the nerdy boys could be trusted. Just a month before my fourteenth-and-a-half birthday, I'd gotten tangled up with Perry Hammonds. He was tall and lanky and styled his hair into a high-top fade that was always in the need of a good mow. I picked him because he liked science, just like me, and because he seemed to be too weird to have other girls to cheat with. He was in the eleventh grade and had never kissed a girl before. (I liked the idea of historical exclusivity.) So, while working after school on our biology practicum, I let him kiss me. What I didn't realize was that there was a difference between *opportunity* to cheat and *will* to cheat. Perry didn't actually get together with another female human being during the course of our brief relationship, but I came into the practicum room to check on the germination of my project, and there was Perry, all crushed out on a substitute teacher. I knew he was serious because he had trimmed up the sides of his hair with a razor. The skin there was smooth, white, and nicked with tiny cuts.

Perhaps I overreacted. Maybe this is what my father was talking about when he warned me to stay away from emotion and all of its messy extremes. But I couldn't get over Perry. While he was running errands for the substitute teacher, a fully grown woman who would never kiss him in the band room, I used an eyedropper to add bleach to his tanks of brine shrimp. I didn't put in enough to kill all the ugly little creatures, but just enough to confuse his research. My mother had been right. I was a precocious child. A bitter woman at age fourteen.

A little bit of justice was meted out. Perry's project failed to qualify for the city-wide fair, and I was tapped to go. My work, "The Effects of Acid Rain on the Germination of Some Selected Seeds," would represent the ninth-grade class of the Benjamin E. Mays Academy for Math and Science. Perry moped in the practicum room as the magnet director encased my project in Bubble Wrap to get ready for my big day. "I just don't understand it," he said, thinking of his brine shrimp and maybe thinking a little bit about me and why I wouldn't talk to him anymore. I didn't say anything, although I think it would have given me some satisfaction to explain myself. But I lived in a world where you could never want what you wanted out in the open.

My session with the judges was not challenging. They seemed mostly concerned with whether or not I had done the work myself, trying to confuse me by quizzing me about the procedure for blending chemicals. They didn't even ask me what I thought about the issue of acid rain and whether I thought it was going to destroy the whole world.

Irritated, I tossed my hair around while answering the questions. Girls my age would hem me up in the bathroom for flaunting my excellent head of hair, but the men on the committee fidgeted in their chairs as I shifted my curls from one shoulder to the other. Against my mother's advice, I had applied a coat of liquid eyeliner, electric blue, to the pink rim above my lower lashes. It burned like crazy, but I just wet my lips and tried to look bored as tears leaked from my irritated and iridescent eyes.

One of the judges, a heavyset man with processed hair, said, "How did a pretty girl like you get so interested in science?"

The woman judge said, "Michael, that's out of line."

The other male judge said, "Michael, that's a misdemeanor."

I said, "I care about acid rain. It's going to destroy the world."

The three judges exchanged glares while I pulled on my rabbit-fur jacket.

"Nice coat," the woman judge said.

"My daddy won it for me in a poker game," I told them, rubbing my eyes with the backs of my hands.

I knew I wasn't going to win a gold key. I could tell by the way that the judges looked at one another as I was leaving the small room. I searched the hallway for my sponsor, but she was nowhere to be found. The civic center was swarming with kids, all excited about the competition. Everyone from Mays High had to wear baby blue and gold shirts. I wore mine, as it was the only way I could participate, but I kept my rabbit-fur jacket buttoned and belted even though the building was warm.

I felt a hand on my shoulder and turned around to see the woman judge.

"You put together a good project," she said. "But you really need to work on the way that you present yourself."

I raised my penciled eyebrows.

"Don't get defensive, dear," she said. "I am telling you this for your own good. Woman to woman."

I didn't say anything. She gave my coat a little pat as though it were a pet and then she walked away.

I went out and stood in front of the civic center, holding a pencil to my mouth as though it were a cigarette. It was a goofy habit, a little tic I had picked up from James. He was always taking short breaks from whatever he was doing to smoke one of his Kools. Even though my mother let him smoke in the house, he sometimes stepped outside to light up, and I often went with him, standing on the patio and watching him hold the match behind his cupped hands. When he did it, it was like the only thing that was happening in the world was taking place just inches in front of his face.

It was November and freezing already. Spending my fourteenth-and-a-half birthday this way couldn't have been a good sign for the year to come. Since I was hidden behind a white pillar, I went all the way and ground out my little golf pencil on the heel of my penny loafer. Commingled with the noise of cars zipping down Piedmont Avenue, was the sound of mewing. Peeking out from behind the pillar, what did I see? Chaurisse Witherspoon standing right in front of the glass doors, crying like her heart was breaking.

I wasn't exactly shocked to encounter her at the civic center. All the public schools sent a few students to the fair. As my mother would say, "People are going to see people." So the sight of her wasn't what had me all discombobulated. The thing that set off twitches at the corner of my mouth was the fact that Chaurisse was wearing a waist-length rabbit fur, too.

Shivering behind the column, I tried to think of a story that would let me believe that my father hadn't lied to me when he gave me the coat. Why James would go to so much trouble to deceive me this way? It wasn't like I hadn't known all my life that I wasn't his main daughter. If he had just admitted to buying the damn jacket in a store, I would have been prepared, in a way, for the possibility that there was one for

Chaurisse, too. Why had he burst into my home in the middle of the night, letting me believe that he had seen this coat on the poker table, spread over a pile of chips, and thought of me, and only me?

It's funny how three or four notes of anger can be struck at once, creating the perfect chord of fury. I thought about my father kissing my cheek with his rum breath. I thought about the guidance counselor and her smug talk about exclusivity. And who was the female judge to tell me anything about the way I handled myself? I looked out again at Chaurisse. The coat looked terrible on her, as it was my size, not hers. She couldn't even button it up around her round middle.

I emerged from behind the pillar still woozy with rage, but I only planned to look at Chaurisse. I was just going to fill my eyes with her as I walked through the double doors. This was all I had in mind. Who would believe me, but this was all I had planned to do. No talking, no touching, just a good look.

This, I now know, is how people go crazy and do things they regret. Look at the woman who almost killed Al Green. I am sure she cooked those grits, fully intending to eat them for breakfast. Then he did something that set her off. After that, she probably picked up the pot, just to scare him a little bit. Next thing she knew and the boiling grits were all over his face. There was a name for that kind of thing. "Crime of passion." It meant that it wasn't your fault.

Chaurisse stood in front of the civic center looking anxiously toward Piedmont Road, bouncing on the balls of her feet. She had quit crying but was sniffling and wiping her nose with the back of her hand. She looked over her shoulder and said, "Hi."

I said hi back, while taking in the details of the jacket. It was the very same garment, right down to the crystal buttons on the sleeves. This was my sister. As I understood from biology, we should have fifty percent of the same genes. I took her in, searching for something common between us. James was all over her face, from her narrow lips to her mannish chin. I looked so much like my mother that it seemed that James had willed even his genetic material to leave no traces. I stared hard until I found something that proved that we were kin — stray flecks of pigmentation on the whites of her eyes. My own eyes showed the very same imperfection.

I must have lingered a little too long,

because Chaurisse felt the need to explain herself. "I left my graphs at home. I'm so stupid."

I shrugged. "It doesn't matter. It's just the science fair."

Chaurisse shrugged back and said, "I worked hard on my project."

Then a black Lincoln with tinted windows pulled up to the curb. I fondled the golf pencil in my pocket as Chaurisse clasped her hands in front of her. The driver of the car blew the horn with a reassuring little toot. My pulse quickened, and I was warm inside my coat despite the winter weather. My scalp tingled underneath my hair. I guess I knew on some level that it was only a matter of time before James discovered that my mother and I had not abided by the stern order to "stay away from my family." But who would have thought it was to happen like this, utterly by accident? My heart flopped around in my chest, and I felt my blood racing through my body. In a way, I was glad that it was happening like this, that James and I could discover each other's deception at the same time. I only wished that my mother had been there.

My intention was to stand brave and defiant. I wouldn't say a word; I'd just stand beside my sister wearing an identical coat, letting spectacle do all the talking. Maybe his words would ball up in his windpipe and choke him to death. I was so furious that I didn't know that I was scared, but my body knew, and when the door to the Lincoln opened, my frightened neck turned my face away.

I heard Chaurisse call out, "Mama! Did you find it?"

I looked just in time to see my sister clap her hands together like a seal.

Chaurisse's mother, Laverne, was nothing like my mother. She was round like her daughter and had that sort of let-go look that beauticians have on their days off. Her red-dyed hair was pulled back and fastened with a plain rubber band. A T-shirt that had probably been black at one time, was tucked into what looked to be a pair of pretty satin pajama pants. She seemed relaxed, silly even, as she waved the orange folder over her head. She did what she did without thinking it over first.

"You mean this folder?" she said. "What's it worth to you? I was going to take it to the flea market and sell it."

"Mama," Chaurisse said, "you are embarrassing me." And then she sort of angled her head in my direction.

"Hello," Laverne said. "You got yourself a

nice coat. You girls are matching."

I nodded. Laverne wasn't pretty or showy in the way that my mother was, but she seemed more motherly to me. Her hands looked like they were born to make sandwiches. Not that my own mother didn't take care of me. She laid out my clothes each night until I was in the fifth grade but never looked quite at home doing it. There was always the feeling that she was doing me a favor. Laverne was the kind of mother you never had to say thank you to.

"My father gave me this coat," I said.

"Mine, too," Chaurisse said. She reached out and stroked my sleeve and her touch was charged.

Twisting away from my sister, I said, "He won it for me in a poker game." I said this to Laverne and it sounded like a question.

With a little slackness in the jaw, Laverne said, "Come again?"

I didn't say anything, because I knew that she'd heard me, and I could tell that what I said meant something to her. Her face creased and she looked a little less plump and satisfied. To my mind she always looked like a baby that had just been fed, full of milk and content.

Laverne said to Chaurisse, "Okay, kiddo. Good luck. I got to run errands."

Chaurisse said, "Okay, thank you," and ran toward the building.

I stayed out front until Laverne got back into the Lincoln. I couldn't see her face through the tinted glass, but I could imagine it, her looking at me and my coat. She knew that this moment was important; I had seen it in the set of her mouth as she got back in the car. I turned away, not wanting her to memorize my face just yet. This was just the beginning. Some things were inevitable. You'd have to be a fool to think otherwise.

4
GRAND GESTURE

My mother has proposed marriage to two men in her life. The first was Clarence, the undertaker's son. On the evening of the Sadie Hawkins dance in 1966, Clarence asked my mother if she would go to Paschal's hotel with him. "If it's good enough for Dr. King, it's good enough for us." He laughed when he said it, which Mother didn't like so much. Although everyone knew that Dr. King, Andy Young, and that whole Morehouse crowd frequented Paschal's restaurant for its legendary fried chicken, Clarence was talking about what went on upstairs in the narrow rooms behind the blackout curtains.

"It's a joke, Gwen," Clarence said.

"I'm thinking about it," she said.

"We've been going out serious like this for two years," Clarence said.

"I know."

"So it's a special night."

My mother looked at him, so handsome in his blue suit, always blue, never black. Black was for his working hours, when he hovered behind his father, as the undertaker's understudy. Her pale yellow frock with puffed sleeves and an empire waist had seemed elegant on the pattern envelope. She didn't care much for the finished product, but having spent too much time tracing the pattern and reinforcing buttonholes, she couldn't just throw it away because of a puckered neckline and an unflattering cut.

Shifting her eyes, she noticed a red carnation on the car seat beside Clarence. "You lost your boutonniere." She picked it up and pulled the hat pin from his lapel and busied herself reattaching the flower. On the radio, Smokey Robinson complained that "a taste of honey is worse than none at all."

Clarence grabbed her wrist, not too hard, not like a threat, but firm. "I already paid for the room."

"You did?"

"I wanted us to be together someplace nice."

My mother said, "You sure are taking a lot of liberties for this to be Sadie Hawkins Day."

"Sadie Hawkins means that ladies get to ask the fellows out on a date, but it doesn't mean the fellows just sit around twiddling their thumbs." He smiled. His teeth were pretty and white like marble headstones.

"Well, let me have my Sadie Hawkins Day," Mother said. "Let's get engaged and then we can go to Paschal's."

"What are you saying?"

"Will you marry me?"

Clarence let go of my mother's wrist, literally giving back her hand, and rubbed his chin and the soft whiskers that were just starting to grow there. He looked out the window. My mother started getting nervous, wondering if she had overplayed her hand. There was much at stake besides just her heart and her pride. Her father worked for Clarence's father and her relationship with Clarence had put her own father in a good position. And besides, if she didn't marry Clarence, who would she marry? She was already a senior in high school.

"Don't you want me?" she whispered.

Finally Clarence spoke. "Hell yeah, I want you. This just isn't the way I thought this was going to happen. But okay, we can get engaged. We're engaged right now. Okay?"

My mother nodded, limp with relief.

Clarence started the car and they drove toward Paschal's.

Now, Clarence was long gone and she was again wearing the same homemade yellow dress, not because she had come to like it but because the empire waist accommodated her changing figure. She was afraid to tell my father that she was four weeks late. Everyone knows that this is the hardest thing that you can ever tell a man, even if he's your husband, and my father was someone else's husband. All you can do is give him the news and let him decide if he is going to leave or if he is going to stay.

My mother was too frightened to speak the words, so she wrote them on a scrap of paper like a deaf beggar. As he read, the stutter raised in him so badly, he couldn't even get out the beginning of his response. My mother reminded him how much he wanted a baby. Laverne had been lying beneath him for a full decade, but she had not been able to give him what he most wanted. It had taken my mother only a few months. This baby was determined to be born, conceived despite all their caution. My mother told him that I was destiny.

At last he said, "You're giving me a son."

James sat on the porch swing at the rooming house and thought it over. She could see him processing it, going over it all in his head. He would think a while, and then look over at her — not at her face, but at her stomach, looking at me. Mother admits to feeling a little jealous. All he was thinking was that he could finally get to be a daddy, that he was going to get himself a junior. He and Laverne had had a baby boy a long time ago, when they first got married. The baby was born feet-first and didn't even live long enough to take his first breath. James rocked on the porch swing, thinking that here came his second chance.

While he was celebrating the idea that he could finally be a daddy, saying that he couldn't wait to tell his brother, my mother popped the question. She said it in a playful tone, like she was inviting him out for an ice-cream soda. "James," she said, "let's go get married. Make an honest woman out of me."

Just moments earlier, he had been all motion, but now it was like somebody had pumped him through with embalming fluid. Finally he came out and said, "I am not leaving Laverne."

Mother knew he was serious because he called his wife by her name. It made her remember her own father. When she had left Clarence, she knew her father was through with her because he said, "You're no better than Flora."

When James said he wasn't going to leave Laverne, Mother tried to act like he had misunderstood her, like she hadn't been suggesting that they run away together and live life like normal people, giving me a chance at ordinary life.

"Who said anything about leaving anybody? Marry me, too. Let's drive to Birmingham, get married in Alabama." Of course she knew the marriage wouldn't be legal, but it would be something, better than nothing. Even an illegal marriage would save me from being a bastard. This was all she was thinking. Mother says it was Willie Mae who pointed out that getting him to marry her, making him a bigamist, a criminal, would give her something to have up her sleeve. But when Mother popped the question, she wasn't angling. She was just thinking about love and about me.

He sat, staring at her from the neck down, and he tried to say something. The stammer was really bad back then. He bucked around like he was having a seizure or something and then he said, "For once in my life, I want to marry a woman who isn't already pregnant."

My mother laughed at him. She couldn't help herself. After all they had shared, he wanted to get all prissy, like he didn't get to be a June bride. She said, "Well, you need to stop lying down with women you are not married to."

The entire conversation took place on the screened-in porch of the rooming house. She should have taken him somewhere more private, but where did she have to go?

When he walked away, all the other girls watched from the windows. She could see them lifting corners of the shades and looking out.

Mother says it was like a slap in the face, but I don't correct her. Abandonment doesn't have the sharp but dissipating sting of a slap. It's like a punch to the gut, bruising your skin and driving the precious air from your body.

After my father drove away, Willie Mae walked out onto the porch and sat beside Mother on the swing. Mother knew then how disadvantaged her situation was, pregnant and by herself. And she knew how unequal life was that she was the one who got caught. James returned to his two-story house with a heavy heart, to be sure. My father is not a monster, but he still had a home to go to and a woman there to fix his plate for dinner.

My mother's former mother-in-law had given her a box of writing paper as a wedding gift. The stationery was lush rag cotton and engraved with my mother's new monogram. The gift was two-handed; my mother understood immediately the spirit of it. The monogram was a genuine welcome — my mother was now a Yarboro. (When she left the marriage, she returned the fifty-year-old diamond but not her married name.) The second message of the gifted paper, clean in its cardboard box, was that she was now a woman of some stature, and such women wrote thank-you notes. Mother had already known this, as she had done well in home economics, where she had also learned how to determine, while at dinner, the worth of a set of china.

She had written letters of gratitude for the wedding gifts — lush linens, silver-plated spoons, and cast-iron skillets that had taken the duration of her marriage to season. But she didn't use the Crane stationery; instead, she rebelled with floral patterned sheets purchased at Woolworth's. The monogrammed paper went with Mother, unused, to her new life on Ashby Street.

Sitting alone in her room, my mother

took the box of paper down from her closet shelf.

My mother's father, my grandfather, was only about five miles away from Ashby Street. He lived off Edgewood Avenue, under the watchful eyes of the church women who pitied him for first being abandoned by Flora and then having poured so much of his life into a daughter who could be no more decent than her mother had been.

When my mother didn't receive a response to her letter by the first of the month, she suspected that the church women had destroyed it. All her life, she had been uneasy with these surrogate stepmothers, dutiful and loveless. When she was about twelve, she accused them of intercepting Flora's letters and birthday telegrams. Of course, the women denied the charges, and Mother finally understood that Flora had simply abandoned her. The church women were rigid but not cruel.

Although the letter that Mother scratched onto her wedding stationery was short enough to fit easily on a postcard, it had taken four drafts to perfect. (The papers ruined with her false starts still rest in the box with the remaining sheets.)

Dear Daddy,
I am having a baby, and I want to come home.

Love,
Gwendolyn B. Yarboro

The response came, finally, after nine days. The landlady handed it to my mother. She was a church woman herself, a deaconess at Mount Moriah. Not an unfeeling person, but she made it clear that she couldn't have pregnant girls living in her place. Mother could stay as long as you couldn't look at her and know what was going on. The same was true for her job.

"I hope this letter is from somebody doing right by you," the landlady said.

My grandfather had written back on lined paper, a little sticky at the top where it had been pulled from a notepad. He didn't address her or sign his name:

This is not your home. Wherever you are is home.

When James finally returned, my mother was a different woman. It wasn't just her body, inflated with me, that had changed. Her spirit was bloated and tender, too. She'd have to leave the rooming house in the next couple of weeks. Willie Mae had given my mother her life savings — rolled coins and folded-over bills. This money was hard-earned and smelled like it. My mother's own savings were meager, as she'd tended to spend most of her money at Davison's, opening her pay envelope right there in the store and paying down layaways. She could imagine herself out on the street without even proper luggage in which to carry all her pretty store-bought dresses.

When James rang, Willie Mae showed him up the stairs. This was against the rules, but Mother was soon to be expelled, anyway. She was lying in bed, still wearing her clothes from work. Only her feet were undressed. If Willie Mae didn't come in every night at nine and force her to put on a gown, she would have slept just like that. All those good dresses, straining at the waist.

James came in the room, trailing behind Willie Mae with his hat in his hand like he was paying his respects to the dead. Lord only knew what Willie Mae said to him on the walk from the front door to the little room. He was looking like someone had taken him out behind the woodshed and beat him.

And then right behind him came Raleigh, dressed the same as James. This was my mother's first time seeing Raleigh, and for a second she thought he was a white man, and she wondered what kind of trouble she had gotten herself into.

"This is Raleigh," James said. "We were brought up together."

When she looked at him close, she could tell he was colored. She could tell, too, that Raleigh was a good man. Kindhearted. Tenderhearted, to be honest. For one quick moment, lying there in the bed in her wool crepe suit and panty hose, she looked at Raleigh and wished that she had met him first instead of James.

James knelt beside her bed. Willie Mae's money rested in a cigar box wedged between my mother's body and the wall. Willie Mae's perfume, Charlie, collided with the butterscotch melting in Raleigh's mouth. James smelled of clean cotton, aftershave, and menthol cigarettes. And there was her own sweaty odor, which was the same as the money's.

"Gwen," he said, "listen. I have worked something out."

My mother didn't answer, turning herself toward the wall with her body curled around the box of money.

"Gwen," he said, "I'm trying to do what's right. T-t-turn your face and look at me."

My mother didn't turn over. She wanted to hear what he had to say without worrying about how her face might respond.

"Raleigh," James said, "come here."

Raleigh moved toward the bed and folded his long, narrow self until he, too, was kneeling.

It was the butterscotch scent that caused my mother to twist herself toward the faces of James and Raleigh. She could imagine how they had been as children — mischievous and inseparable and sometimes afraid. Gwen didn't know it at the time but my grandmother, Miss Bunny, treated the boys as though they were a single being, beating and praising them in tandem, no matter which of them had sinned or excelled.

"Willie Mae?" my mother called, wanting some ally. The connection between the men was like a living thing, like a fifth person in the room.

"I'm going to go downstairs," Willie Mae said. "I'll keep an eye out for the landlady. You don't want her to catch you with the fellows up here."

"Doesn't matter," Gwen said. "Don't go." But Willie Mae left anyway.

With Willie Mae gone, the room seemed to

be full of men. "Can you sit up?" James asked.

My mother, propping herself up against the pillows, looked expectantly at James and Raleigh.

"It's nice to meet you," Raleigh said. "I've heard good things."

My mother didn't know how to respond to this, so she just nodded.

James said again, "We worked something out, Raleigh and me. W-w-we . . ." He looked to Raleigh and nudged him.

Raleigh continued the sentence. "We sold the Lincoln, got a good price for it. It's in a check right here, made out to you. It's on my account, but it's from James. We just had to do it this way because of records, you know. But we are going to take care of you."

Take care of her! For a moment, she imagined herself to be like her former mother-in-law, whose only responsibility in life was to be beautiful and speak proper English. To be taken care of was to not worry about not having enough love, not having enough money. It was like James and Raleigh were offering her the chance to be someone other than herself.

My mother looked to James, who nodded. "W-w-we want to do the right thing."

Raleigh handed my mother the check. It was plain sea-foam green, the sort you get free with your checking account. Her name was neatly printed across the line at the top, and Raleigh's sharp, but not fancy, signature was on the bottom. The "For" line was blank.

By the time she told me this story, the memory had gone bad like meat left too long in the freezer. She couldn't remember the thrill she must have felt at having her prayers answered so quickly, for the Lord to work in a way that was not mysterious but direct and clear. Telling me in 1986, she said, "Be careful what you wish for." Now she can recall the tobacco odor of my father's breath and the tang of his kiss. She remembers that Raleigh's knees cracked as he was getting up. Wise with knowledge of the future, she wanted me to believe that she was apprehensive even then, but I knew she was lying. I envied her that moment. Who doesn't dream of being rescued? Who doesn't desire grand gestures?

At the hospital, Raleigh signed my birth certificate, to save me the indignity of being a bastard on paper. Four months after I was born, my mother, my father, Raleigh, and Willie Mae drove to Birmingham, Alabama, where they stood before a judge in a county courthouse. My mother was surprised at how little was required to become man and wife. Not once did anyone ask if either of them was married to anyone else. Raleigh signed as a witness, as did Willie Mae. I was present for the ceremony, dressed in my white christening gown, the lace train draped over Willie Mae's arms. On my mother's night table is a framed photograph. Picture me there, small and clean, proof that all that went on that afternoon was both holy and true.

5
HEART DREAMS

By fifteen and a half, I had become obsessed with my own heart. I dreamt about it several nights a week. Sometimes it took the form of a pear, bruised and slimy in the bowl of my chest. In another dream, it was anatomically correct, pulsing with regular contractions. The only problem was that the valves were faulty; thick blood oozed out with every beat. These were the nightmares. Other heart-dreams were bright as summer. In one, my heart was a red-velvet cake, served by Mother on beautiful plates of polished silver. In a dream that was neither happy nor sad, the heart was a wine goblet, wrapped in a handkerchief and crushed under my shoe with quick mercy.

I had a boyfriend, Marcus McCready, and he was the secret center of everything. He was eighteen and, technically, the things we did were illegal. I looked up the word *statu-*

tory in the dictionary, but I didn't find anything helpful. "Jailbait" is what he called me, his mouth sugary with Southern Comfort and ginger ale. "Who came up with the age of consent, anyway?" I asked him this, aware that the answer was unknowable and irrelevant. If I'd learned anything from my parents, it was that the law didn't understand anything about what passed between men and women.

To my mind, there was nothing not to love about Marcus. He was handsome and a little bit cocky sometimes, but I knew it was just an act. All the posturing, the pimp-dip in his walk, the arrogant up-jerk of his chin — that was just to cover up his shame about his age. Marcus started school a year late because he had whooping cough when he was little, and on top of that his birthday fell at the start of the year. That made him a little bit older than the rest of the kids in his class, but it didn't mean that he was slow. He was just born at the wrong time, which is something that could happen to anyone.

The McCreadys were a good family. His mother taught music to grade-schoolers and his father was a tax accountant. Marcus Senior handled my father's books, something I discovered quite by accident, but it gave me a thrill to be so close to James's real life. When Marcus's parents had renewed their vows at Callanwolde, my father drove the limousine at a reduced rate. His father called mine "Jim."

We snuck around a lot, Marcus and me. When I passed him in the corridors at school, he looked away. After a month, I learned to shift my attention first. It wasn't personal. It was just that Marcus had gotten into trouble the year before when he went to Woodward Academy, so he wasn't supposed to run around with underclassmen. I slipped easily into my role as unacknowledged girlfriend. When you already had one secret life, what bother was it to have another secret within that secret? I even changed my appearance to exaggerate the effects of my doubly double life. For my everyday self, I gathered up my hair into two Princess Leia buns over my ears and stopped lining my eyes. I asked my mother to buy me black saddle shoes like Olivia Newton-John wore in *Grease,* but they didn't make them anymore. I made do with penny loafers, wearing them with white socks, marveling at my chaste ankles.

"What is wrong with you?" my mother wanted know. "There is nothing wrong with fixing yourself up. Is this a phase?"

She took me by the shoulders and searched my face for answers. The deal was that we were to tell each other everything. She touched my forehead and then my ears. "Where are your earrings?"

"In my jewelry box," I told her.

"You never wear them anymore," she said sadly.

But I did. I wore them when I was with Marcus.

It wouldn't be right to say that Marcus changed me, that he took a sweet quiet girl who wanted to grow up to be a pediatrician and turned her into the freak of the week. I know that's what some people said about me behind my back, but that doesn't make it true. It was more like Marcus showed me new possibilities. I met him, of all places, in Kroger. My mother and I were there to stock up on canned goods — the weatherman had predicted up to four inches of snow and the city was going crazy. Mother had gotten home late and we had rushed to the store to see if there was any food left. She made herself busy snapping up whatever cans of soup remained and I was sent to find deviled ham. The store was packed with panicked shoppers, snapping up anything nonperishable, even oysters packed in brine. The deviled ham was long gone, but I did spy a few dented cans of Vienna sausages way in the back of the shelf.

I was cradling several cans in my arms when I felt a tug on my belt loops. I looked over my shoulder and saw Marcus. I knew who he was — there was no way you could go to Mays and not know Marcus Mc-Cready III.

Still holding me at the waist, he leaned toward me, resting his newscaster chin on my shoulder. His breath smelled of orange rind and something spicy like clove. "Hey, pretty girl. If you wasn't jailbait, I would ask you to give me a chance." His hand moved up from my belt to my back. I stood still and let him push his other hand into my hair. "You are some kind of pretty. Fine, too. Thick." I could envision my heart like the tiny jingling bell on a cat's collar.

I locked my knees, even though I knew that locked knees were how girls made themselves faint when they didn't want to dress out for gym, but still, I tensed my legs to hold myself upright. This was desire, pure and uncut. I knew the word from reading Judith Krantz, but still, trashy paperbacks hadn't prepared me for Marcus's fingers against my scalp and his potpourri breath. I leaned into his tug of my hair and he said,

"You like it."

Suddenly, he released me, and said in a brighter tone, "Hello, Mrs. Grant."

I turned to see a light-skinned lady pushing a cart piled high. "Hello, Marcus." I blinked my eyes, as though someone had just turned on a bright light. I looked at my feet, too embarrassed to face the shoppers all around us who had seen God knew what.

"Give me your number," Marcus said. "I could go to jail, but I don't care. Damn, girl. You look so good."

I didn't have paper, but I did have a pen in my fake Louis Vuitton. Marcus peeled the corner of the label from a can of tuna and I wrote my number in tiny but clear print. He folded the scrap until it looked like a spitball and tucked it into his pocket. I stood, unmoving, feeling my body expand and contract just under my skin until my mother rolled her cart down the aisle.

"There you are."

I gave her the Vienna sausages and unlocked my knees. I smiled like nothing was wrong, as though I was the same girl I was ten minutes ago. But in truth, I was different now, burning and anointed.

6
THINK ABOUT IT

Through Marcus, I found myself a best friend. Ronalda Harris. She was often at his house parties, not because she was part of his crew but because Marcus was always looking for more girls to even the numbers out. Ronalda lived right next door to him and, like me, didn't have a reputation to protect. Sometimes at the parties, Marcus called me his "girlfriend" and even kissed me in front of everyone. I'd sit on his lap and drink from his cup. Other times, he just acknowledged me with secret winks and smiles over the heads of his guests.

When Marcus didn't have time to talk to me, I'd hang with Ronalda. She was the new girl and so different from everyone else that she could have been an exchange student. She had tried to give herself a relaxer and as a result she was nearly bald-headed so she wore huge earrings and sparkly eye shadow so everyone could tell she was a girl.

On top of that, she had a curious accent; it wasn't so much in her pronunciation but the way she grouped words together. For emphasis, she would repeat a word three times. "That test was hard, hard, hard." She said "make groceries," like she was from Louisiana. Her face was ordinary as a loaf of bread, but she had a boyfriend who was a grown man. He was in the army and picked her up sometimes in a navy blue Cutlass Supreme. On a few occasions, I rode in the backseat, staring up at the shiny yellow fabric covering the ceiling, held in place by a dozen feathered roach clips. I thought she was fascinating, but Marcus thought she was weird. "Bama," he said, and "ghetto."

"Ghetto," Ronalda said she could live with, but she didn't want anybody to call her "Bama." "How can somebody from Georgia call somebody else a Bama?" She was from Indy, a real city and it was Up North. "North enough that we don't lose our minds over a couple snow flurries. Marcus and them may be bourgie, but they are the ones that's Bama. Bourgie Bamas."

She explained this to me when I went to her house to tutor her in math. Her school in Indy had put people either on the college-prep track or the other track. Ronalda got stuck on the other track and this left her without the skills she was going to need at Mays High. She tried on her own for almost half a year, keeping her head down and paying attention when the teacher talked. The rest of us passed notes or made tentative lists of bridesmaids for weddings scheduled to take place the June after our twenty-first birthdays. The week before midterms, Ronalda even turned in her seat and said "Excuse you" to someone who made too much noise unwrapping a butter mint. But still, trigonometry was more than a notion when she hadn't even had Algebra II. Her father had pulled strings to get her admitted into the math-and-science magnet, and she was terrified that she would fail and get sent back to Indy.

I volunteered to help her not just because I liked her, although I did. New kids at the start of the school year are interesting enough, but new kids that drop in out of nowhere two months into the term — everyone knew there was a story there. And when it comes to having a story, takes one to know one.

Her house, a large ranch, was almost identical to Marcus's, but the McCreadys had a garage and Ronalda's family had only a carport. Still, it was a nice home with four bedrooms and two bathrooms.

"I like to work on the dining-room table," she said, placing her notebook on a smoky glass oval perched on a black pedestal. "Be careful, though. My stepmother gets mad, mad, mad if you scratch the finish."

We worked together about two hours. Ronalda caught on pretty quick, but she was still behind. We puzzled over sine, cosine, and tangent, but the class was already doing complex proofs. At the end of the session, I did my homework and let her copy it with her nervous handwriting.

"What time do you have to be home?" she asked me.

"No particular time," I said, "as long as I'm back before my mother gets home at seven."

"Do you want to see the basement?"

I followed her down the stairs into a laundry room, pausing at the luxury. My mother and I had to take our dirty clothes to the Laundromat and sit there for ninety minutes while our clothes spun in the coin-operated machines. James offered to help us buy a stackable set, but our apartment didn't have an outside vent for a dryer.

The dark-paneled basement was as large as the rest of the house, but it gave a different vibe. The upstairs was clearly Ronalda's stepmother's territory, bright with natural light and gleaming with crystal and mirrors. Pale blue china platters were displayed face out beside cobalt glassware. The basement, on the other hand, was a manly space, equipped with a Ping-Pong table, wet bar, and cable TV. The atmosphere was cool and damp like earthworms and smelled vaguely of strawberry incense.

Ronalda clicked on the heater that dominated the far wall, near the component set. It was painted green and was shaped to resemble a fireplace. It hummed on, and fake logs glowed orange. "It's nice, isn't it?" Ronalda said.

"Yeah," I said.

"Let me empty out the dehumidifier. That's one of my chores." She went to what looked like a small metal cabinet and pulled out a pan of water, which she emptied into the washing machine.

"My dad comes down here a lot," she said.

The whole place was decorated to show the world how much Mr. Harris enjoyed being a black man. On the walls were line drawings of men whose images I saw at school during Black History Week — Malcolm X, W. E. B. Du Bois, and other faces I wasn't completely sure, but I thought one of them invented the stoplight. Among these pictures was a just-born portrait of Ronalda's little brother, Nkrumah. On another wall was a poster of Hank Aaron hitting his 735th homerun. The one woman in this portrait gallery was half-naked. I kept staring at the poster, trying to decide if she was pretty or not. Her dark-skinned body shone with oil. Between her pointed breasts was a bullet-studded strap. Her thick afro was decorated with bullets and from her hips hung even more bullets, hiding her privates.

The image confused me. The very fact that she was splayed out naked meant that she was supposed to be sexy, but I had never seen a pinup this dark or this nappy. I imagined myself halfway between this woman and Marcus's favorite, Jayne Kennedy. Like Jayne, I had the hair, but like Ronalda's father's fantasy, I was dark as burnt brass. At the bottom of the poster, just under her knee-high leather boots, was a caption: THINK ABOUT IT.

I pointed to the picture. "I don't get it. Think about what?"

"All men like to look at pictures of naked women," Ronalda said. "My boyfriend, Jerome, you should see all the pictures he got."

I nodded as though I understood this, but the picture made me feel a sort of roaming sadness in my stomach. I wondered how James decorated his private spaces. He wasn't a back-to-Africa man, so I knew he wouldn't look at naked women with nappy hair. Maybe his fantasy women would sprawl on the hoods of limousines. Maybe they'd be inside the cars, resting their breasts on the steering wheel, wearing nothing but chauffeur's caps with yards of glossy hair tumbling out from underneath. I thought about it.

"You want to look around?"

I nodded again.

"This is my father's study." She opened a door and led me into a small room crammed with books and more illustrations of black men looking serious. She pointed to a dark-skinned man with a high forehead. "That's Kwame Nkrumah, who my little brother is named after."

"Who is he?"

"An African president. My daddy is really into Africa. Presidents especially." She sat in a leather desk chair and swiveled around. "Africa, Africa, Africa."

"What about your mother? I mean your real mother. Is she like that, too?"

Ronalda's mouth turned up at the corner and she mashed her lips together before she spoke. "My mother is dead. I don't want to talk about it."

"I'm sorry," I said, even though Ronalda didn't sound exactly sad. It was more like she was angry with me for mentioning it.

"Can you show me around some more?" I asked.

She opened another room, the same size as her father's study, but it was nearly empty. There were bookcases installed, but only one shelf held any books. There was a desk, but it wasn't cluttered with papers. In the corner stood an electric belt exerciser. My mother had one of those, too. You turned it on and it would jiggle the fat off of you.

"This is my stepmother's office," Ronalda said. "We can hang out in here."

"What do you call her?"

"My stepmother?"

"Yeah."

"Jocelyn. She never comes down here."

Ronalda opened one of the desk drawers, revealing eight strawberry wine coolers. "My secret stash. You want one?"

She gave me a bottle; I screwed off the top and handed it back to her. She handed me another. We each drank two coolers as quickly as the effervescence would allow. The taste was sweet and medicinal at the same time. We opened our third and proceeded with ladylike sips.

"That was good," Ronalda said.

"Ditto."

We were both seated on the wooden desk, as there wasn't even a chair in the office. The smell of our perfumes competed with the smell of the booze and the odor of our bodies. I thrilled at the confinement of it.

Ronalda said, "Can I touch your hair?"

I nodded and she reached out and gently stroked the hair covering my shoulder blades. Her touch was light, as though she worried she would hurt it.

Ronalda's had started to grow back at last. It was now long enough that it could be straightened and set with brush rollers. There wasn't enough to catch in a ponytail, but at least people had stopped calling her bald-headed.

"Your hair is so pretty," she said.

"I look just like my mother," I told her, so as not to seem conceited.

"Me, too," she said. "I look like she just spit me out."

"You have a picture of her?"

Ronalda shook her head. "I didn't bring anything with me from home. Just a paper sack with a change of clothes and a box of Kotex, but to look in my face, it's like seeing my mother. Except that I am a nice person."

I didn't press her, but I wanted to know more. I'd heard some stories from Marcus. His mother was friends with Ronalda's stepmother. Ronalda, said the stepmother, had been living like a wild child in Indiana. No adult supervision. None whatsoever.

"What is your mother like?" Ronalda asked me.

I wasn't sure how to answer. My mother was difficult to describe. Presently, she was at work, taking people's blood pressure, listening to their hearts. In a couple hours, she would be home, cooking dinner like a regular mother. I almost told Ronalda that my mother was like a superhero with a secret identity, but that wasn't really true. My mother's secret self was almost identical to her real self. You had to really pay attention to see when she shifted.

"My mother is named Gwen." I drank some more of the wine cooler. There was a tightness in my forehead and a pleasant vacant feeling below.

"Does she like Marcus?"

"She can't like what she doesn't know about." I laughed.

"My stepmother doesn't like Jerome. She says he's too old for me, just because he's in the service. I'll tell you exactly what she said. 'Although you may be mature physically, the mind can take a while to catch up.' I was looking at her like she had gone stone crazy and then she had the nerve to say that she was a virgin when she married my father. She said it with this little smile on her face."

I knew the little smile she was talking about. You see it on the faces of girls who were born to be somebody's wife. That virgin-smile was plenty annoying on the faces of tenth-grade girls, but on grown women it was infuriating. One good thing about having a mother like mine is that she never went and got all superior on me.

"You know her favorite word? *Inappropriate.* Seems like the only appropriate thing for me to do is to babysit."

"Does she pay you?"

"Yeah," Ronalda said. "I get allowance. But sometimes I don't want her to pay me. I want it to be like I am just someone in the family, but I don't want to get took advantage of, either. Next week, my stepmother is taking her nieces to see *The Wiz.* She asked me yesterday if I wanted to come along. I said yes at first, and then she told me that she was going to have to buy an extra ticket and I might end up sitting by myself in the balcony or something. So I told her I didn't want to go, that I don't like plays. But really I have never seen one before."

She looked so unhappy that I wanted to touch her, but I didn't know where to put my hand. I ended up stroking my own shoulder. "I would go to see a play with you if you wanted to see one."

"I don't want to see one," she said. "I just wanted to be invited somewhere."

"I go places with my mother," I said. "But not any place special."

Ronalda looked at me as though she couldn't imagine an unspecial mother-daughter outing. It was like I had told her that I had money, but not the kind you could spend.

"Really," I said.

Ronalda put her hand in my hair again. "Did you bring a brush?"

I knelt on the tile floor between her knees while Ronalda sat up on the desk pulling the brush through my hair. All my life people have wanted to play in my head. On the very first day of first grade, the teacher took me into the lounge and undid my ponytails. Ronalda wanted to know if I was tender-headed. I murmured that I wasn't, resting my face on her thigh.

"Tell me what you were about to tell me," she said. The bristles against my scalp felt

106

firm and good. I knew she was probably brushing out my curls, but I didn't ask her to stop. "Tell me. Tell me about your mother."

It was as though she had pulled the truth out of my head. "I'm illegitimate."

"Join the club," said Ronalda.

"No," I said. "It's worse. I'm a secret."

"Oh," Ronalda said. "You're an outside child?"

"Yeah," I whispered.

"That's okay," she said. "A lot of people are."

I let go of a breath I hadn't even known I was holding. This was what it was to have a friend, someone who knew exactly who you were and didn't blame you for it. I twisted to look at her, but if she knew something important had passed between us, her face didn't show it.

I asked her, "Was your father married to your stepmother when you were born?"

She shook her head. "No. They got together back when they were both living in Indy. He got her pregnant the night before he left to go to Notre Dame."

"At least he claims you. I wonder sometimes what would happen to me if my mother passed away. I wonder if my father would take me in."

She stopped brushing. The floor was cold under me, but I could feel the warmth of Ronalda's thigh through her jeans. I wanted another of the sweet wine coolers, but I couldn't ask for it because I had somehow forgotten how to speak.

"Don't cry," Ronalda said. "I have a secret, too. My mother's not really dead. I just tell people that. She's alive, she's just negligent." She pronounced the word carefully, as though she were reading it from a legal document. "The principal at my school called child services on her. She left me by myself for two weeks. While she was gone is when I broke my leg, trying to wear heels, and there was no one to come and pick me up at the school. The principal put two and two together and the next thing I knew, my daddy drove all the way to Indy and carried me back to Atlanta with him. He drove all night and it was snowing bad, bad, bad."

"Where was your mama gone to?"

"I don't know. She even took the hot comb. I asked her when she was coming back and she said, 'Tomorrow,' but I knew she was lying when she started putting my little brother's stuff in a bag, too.

"She loved that little boy like nothing in the world. Before he was born, she used to drink, drink, drink! She even drank Crown Royal when she was pregnant with me. I'm lucky I didn't get born cross-eyed, retarded, or something. But after Corey, it was like she fell stupid in love with him. She cut out the drinking, stopped slapping people around. She even made hot cocoa a couple of times on Sundays. Before Corey, I thought that my mama just didn't like kids, but when Corey was born and I saw the way she carried on about him, I saw that it wasn't that she didn't like kids, she just didn't like me."

"She likes you," I said. "She's your mother. Everybody's mother likes them."

"I think maybe she loves me," Ronalda said. "I mean, she kept food in the fridge and a roof over my head. But she never liked me. Now, my little brother, she could just eat him up. That's why she took him with her when she left."

"It's not like that," I told her. "You get equal love."

"Do you have a brother?" Ronalda asked. I said no.

"If you have a brother, it's the worst thing. If your mama has a boy to care for, she will show you the kind of love she is capable of. And once you see that, you will never get over it. You will be lonely for the rest of your life."

I had no response for her. I didn't know how my mother would react to a boy in our lives, but I knew that my father always wanted a son. James was at our apartment when Laverne went into labor with Chaurisse, six weeks early. Raleigh came to the house, and James stood up from my mother's table, leaving his pound cake half-eaten. My mother tells me that she fell on her knees beside my bassinette and prayed that Laverne not give birth to a boy. "A healthy daughter is what I asked the Lord to give. That wouldn't put too much pull on his heart."

"My father has another kid, but a girl," I said. "With his wife."

"Count your blessings," Ronalda said. "And hope they don't have any more kids. You don't want to go through what I been through."

I tried to tell myself that she was right, that I was lucky. But second best is second best, no matter the reason why.

To Ronalda I said, "Let's have another cooler."

She opened the drawer and we took the last two, putting us at four each, which was about a cooler and a half too many. This we

110

knew even as we let the warm sudsy drink foam into our mouths. We stumbled out of her stepmother's study into the rec-room part of the basement. Ronalda looked through her father's records and decided to play Richard Pryor just to hear him cuss.

"How do you feel?" Ronalda stretched herself on the carpet in front of the imitation fireplace.

"Sick."

"It's a secret, all right?" she said. "Everything about my mother is a secret."

"Same for mine."

7

I DARE YOU

My mother worked very hard for a living.
This was no one's fault. Even women who
were wives had to do their part to keep the
family fed. When I was small, she took a
few classes to learn travel-agenting — thinking she could work from the apartment, using our telephone — but sometime in the
midseventies she got sensible and took night
courses at Atlanta Junior College to become
a licensed practical nurse. For the most
part, Mother was fortunate in her schedul-
ing — seven to three — but sometimes she
was assigned eleven to seven, and on holi-
days she pulled doubles. When she came
home those mornings while I was eating my
breakfast, she soaked her feet in a pan of
saltwater and rubbed the red bites on her
neck where the stethoscope pinched her.

Hers was a good job with benefits that
included more than health, eye, and dental.
Mother had daily access to doctors. As she

assisted them by performing the tasks that were beneath them, she asked them about their daughters. What lessons did they take, where did they buy their clothes, and where did they plan to go to college? Every now and then, she would chat with the doctors' wives, mining for personal information, like where they stood on issues like contraception and sex ed in schools (testing out her theory that rich people put their girls on the Pill at twelve). On her break, she took careful notes on a small pad she kept in her locker. For six weeks in the early 1980s she got to work alongside a woman resident who was even engaged to another doctor. She owed everything, this lady said, to Mount Holyoke, a college in Massachusetts. My mother pressed down hard on the notepad and underscored the name of the state. In parenthesis she wrote: *Kennedy, etc.* A doctor married to a doctor! Mother called it the "the trifecta," even though it was only two things.

Such information was worth the sometimes-odd hours. When Marcus and I first started going together, she worked eight to four in a pediatrician's office and then looked after private patients from seven thirty to midnight. It was just a temporary arrangement for November since Christmas was right around the bend. At six fifteen when she was heading out, fresh and pretty in white, I promised her that I would spend the evening doing SAT drills on the new Commodore computer that she had bought with her "own money." I didn't like it when she used this phrase, sounding like a child, bragging about what she had done with her babysitting pay. She meant that this gift had come from her, without any contribution from my father. She'd paid for it with the labor of swollen legs and stiff fingers. I didn't use the computer, but I did appreciate the gift, the thought of it. I didn't have anything against the machine or the SATs; it was just that the only opportunity I had to see Marcus was when my mother was at work, late at night, between the hours of seven thirty and midnight.

On one particular night, Marcus and I were going to go to Acres Mill to see a movie with a bunch of his friends. I took extra time with my hair and makeup because I knew that Marcus wanted to show me off. I loved being displayed on his arm, held up for everyone to see.

I looked out of my bedroom window, expecting to see Marcus's two-door Jetta, but instead I found the good Lincoln, the newer one that was really navy blue if you looked at it close-up. With much agitation, I tiptoed into the living room and through the picture window saw James let himself out of the passenger side. Raleigh was driving. I can remember very few times in my life that I have been alone in the house with my father. If my mother wasn't home, he always brought Raleigh with him, like I was someone else's daughter and there was a need to make it clear that everything was aboveboard.

James and Raleigh walked up the sidewalk to our apartment. The buzzer rang, and I knew that it was Raleigh who had pressed it because James liked to use his key.

"Who is it?" I sang.

"Raleigh here. And James."

I twisted back the deadbolt and undid the chain lock. Seeing them framed there in the doorway, they looked like a comedy duo. My father was shorter than Raleigh but cool-looking. His hat was sort of turned to the side, Detroit-style, so I knew they had been over to the Carousel for a nip. Not enough to be stumbling but just enough to have a little buzz. Raleigh, behind him, was flushed in the face. When Raleigh drank, he loved every person in a three-mile radius. Whereas when James had one leg in a bottle, he just fell deeper into whatever

115

mood he was already in. I didn't know how he was feeling when he walked into the Carousel, so I didn't know what was rattling around in his head when he walked out.

I stood in the doorway, hoping they had just come over to drop something off. "Hi," I said.

"What's going on?" Raleigh laughed. "You're not going to let us in? Why you blocking the door?" He bumped my father with his chuckle, but James didn't join in.

"Come in," I said, hoping to sound relaxed like my mother, standing to the side. She was so good at making them feel like special company and old friends at the same time. She greeted my father with a fast kiss on the lips each time he walked through the door. For Raleigh, she got on tiptoe and hugged his skinny neck. I just stood by at those times and let her do the welcoming. When I was alone like this, I never quite knew what to do. Without my mother, I was as useless as a single shoe.

"Do you want something to drink?"

"What do you have?" James wanted to know.

I opened the refrigerator wide. My mother had just been to the store, and I was proud of the full produce drawers, the two dozen eggs safe in their holders, and the glass bottles of juice. "We have Diet Coke."

James made a face.

"Cucumber water?" This was my mother's concoction; a doctor's wife had told her that they serve it at day spas.

"Just ice water is fine," Raleigh said.

"Go on in the living room," I said. "I'll bring it out."

James headed in the direction of the living room, but Raleigh looked over his shoulder.

"My mother's not home," I said.

He gave a disappointed little nod and followed my father.

Both James and Raleigh preferred my mother's company to mine, and I couldn't quite blame them. They belonged to her. All three of us did, really.

In the summer, the four of us enjoyed small parties on our patio. Knowing the neighbors never complained about the music when James's wax-slick car was out front, my mother cranked up the console stereo in the living room, so the sounds of Harold Melvin and the Blue Notes streamed through the dusty screen door, mingling with James's cigarette smoke, which kept mosquitoes away. My mother would try to dance with James first, knowing that he wouldn't. She might twirl around shaking her pretty shoulders and gorgeous hair, calling his name, until James would say to Raleigh, "Dance with this beautiful woman for me."

My job was to keep the glasses filled with ice and to mix the gin-and-tonics. With a paring knife, I carved perfect twists of lime. When I dropped the curving rind into my father's glass, he would kiss my fingers.

While my mother was dancing with Raleigh, she kept her eyes firmly on James. When Raleigh held her waist, she let her torso fall backward, her hair leading the way, laughing until she righted herself quickly. She and I had the same hair, but I hadn't learned yet to make it move for me. When the music stopped, Raleigh let my mother go, his arms falling to his sides. I kept my eyes peeled for that moment, so I could be there, ready with an icy glass for his empty hand.

Mother would leave the dancing area — just a small space between the rusting railing and the wire patio set — to sit on James's lap and wrap her arms around his neck. Raleigh usually sank to the concrete floor where he had just been dancing and leaned himself against the railing, not caring about the rust marks on his shirt. I would sit beside him, leaning my head on his chest. My mother, taking a big drink from James's gin-and-tonic, would look over the rim of the glass and say, "Raleigh, you may be white on the outside, but when the music starts you are one hundred percent American Negro."

Then Raleigh would blush as red as my mother's shiny toenails and I wondered what it felt like to live inside such disloyal skin.

The last song was always Bobby Caldwell. When he sang, "Makes me do for love what I would not do," my mother would close her eyes, and James would touch her eyelids. On those summer nights, my parents lived in a space all by themselves, breathing only each other's air. I sat beside Raleigh, breathing normally, and he sat beside me, so still, as though he were taking in no air at all.

But on the evening that my father came to talk to me about life, my mother wasn't home, so Raleigh sat on the vinyl couch, drinking water and fooling with the 35mm camera strung around his neck with a red strap. This was before he was serious, when James encouraged his photography because it was a good tie-in for the limo business. They could offer marrying couples a package: photos and a ride.

"Can I get you something else?" I said,

hoping James would drink his ice water and leave before Marcus came to pick me up.

"No," he said. "Not unless you want something for yourself."

"No," I said, "I'm fine. What about you, Raleigh? You need something?"

"I need a tripod."

"Sorry," I said. "No tripods today."

My father said, "Just sit down. I want to talk to you. You don't mind if old Raleigh is in here when we talk, do you?"

"Is there something wrong?"

I can't say for sure if the talk that came next was prompted by the little circle of skin showing below my collar bone or if he had visited for the very purpose of explaining to me the benefits of chastity, but he told me again to sit down. I did, with a glance at the clock and a certain busyness of breath.

"Sir?" I said.

"Don't call me sir. I feel like an overseer when you call me sir."

Raleigh chuckled. "You can call me sir whenever you want."

"You going somewhere tonight?" James asked me.

I knew I couldn't lie. The makeup I could have explained away but not the keyhole blouse. I shrugged. "Sort of."

"With who?"

"Some people I know. They have a car."

"Does your mama know about this?"

"Yeah," I said.

"Would you lie to me, Dana?" James said.

"No, sir," I said, leaning on the last word.

"Jim-Bo," Raleigh said, "lighten up." Then he said to me, "We've had a couple of drinks. Pour us a couple glasses of that cucumber water, whatever the hell that is. It doesn't have alcohol, does it?"

"No," I said. "It's just water mostly."

"Then we need that," Raleigh said.

I popped up from my chair, just to escape my father, who was staring at the keyhole like he'd only now noticed that I had developed into a teenager. I'd had my breasts for five years now and my period for four. I was past the embarrassment I had felt when things first started changing, when I wore a sweater well into the spring to hide my bra straps. At fifteen, I threw my box of tampons on the drugstore counter along with my packs of gum and nail-polish remover. But under my father's eyes that evening, I felt shy again and obscene.

"Sit back down," James said. "We don't need no cucumber water. What we need here is to have a conversation. Raleigh, you got eyes in your h-head. What we n-n-need to do is s-s-it down and talk."

Sitting back down, I faked a cough to give myself a reason to pat my chest and cover the keyhole with my palm.

"You're going on a date," James said. "Don't lie to me." His voice was turning angry. I looked over at Raleigh, who picked up a magazine from the coffee table and stared at the pages.

"It's not really a date," I said.

"It's something," James snapped back. "When did you start wearing so much makeup?"

The real answer was that I started wearing Fashion Fair when Ronalda and I figured out how to swipe the testers from the counter at Rich's. The eye shadows were fastened down to the displays, but a person could get away with the lipstick and blusher if she knew what she was doing.

James went on, "Look at that shirt you've got on."

I didn't speak to my father. I told myself to be calm, that he would start to stammer soon, that whatever conversation he seemed bent on having could never take place.

"Where did you even b-b-buy that top? Y-y-y-you're about to b-b-b-bust out of it."

"I was going to wear a jacket," I said.

"She's just growing up," Raleigh said. "Both the girls are growing up."

122

James shrugged Raleigh's hand off his shoulder. "That's easy for you to say. They're not your daughters."

I looked up at James. Had he ever spoken of me and Chaurisse in a single breath? It was like we were regular sisters, driving our dad crazy like the light-skinned daughters on *The Cosby Show.*

"Dana," James said, "I know your mama has talked to you about this already." He looked at me for confirmation so I bobbed my head a little bit, still smiling like a fool. "You're a good girl. I know you're a good girl. I love you, right? Your uncle Raleigh, he loves you, too. Right, Raleigh?"

"Of course, Jimmy," he said. "Both of us love you, Dana." He raised his camera to his face and snapped it at me.

"I love you, too," I said. "Daddy." Feeling brave, I repeated the whole sentence. "I love you, too, Daddy." The word tasted a little sharp, like milk about to turn, but still, I wanted to say it again and again.

Raleigh pressed the shutter once more, and it was like the Fourth of July. I blinked in the purple flash; the spots left in front of my face were like those little cartoon hearts around Popeye's head when he looks at Olive Oyl. My father loved me. He said it, right here, not to please my mother, but just

123

because he wanted it to be said.

My father licked his thumb and reached toward my cheek. There was a part of me that knew that his damp finger meant that he wanted to wipe something from my face, that he was probably aiming for my chocolate raspberry blusher. I understood this in the brain, but my body twitched. My shoulder rose to protect my face.

I should have been over it by then, but I cringed, jumping back the way I did whenever Marcus raised his hand, even if he was just reaching for the light switch to give us some privacy. "Don't be scared of me," he had said just the day before, when I ducked as he was adjusting the light in the top of his car. I told him I wasn't scared. I didn't want to get into it all over again. It wasn't like it happened all the time, and when it did, people had been drinking.

Twitching like that in front of James shamed me as much as the keyhole in the shirt. It wasn't normal, this aversion to being touched. Marcus let me know that other girls didn't behave like this, which only aggravated the situation. This flinching had become worse than a reflex; it was a stammer of the body.

I let my head hang heavy on my neck and

said, "I'll change my clothes before I go. I wasn't going to wear this, anyway." I got up and I glanced at the clock, carefully, not wanting to draw attention to my nervousness.

"Sit back down," James said. "Sit back down. What time is he picking you up? I want to meet him."

"Nobody is coming to pick me up," I said. "I am meeting the people over at their house. It's not a date. It's not just one person I'm going out with."

"So you wearing that top with all your business hanging out just to see what you can catch?"

"Aw, Jimmy," Raleigh said. "It's not fair to talk to her like that."

"I'm fair," James said. "I would be the same way with Chaurisse. I'm fair. Even-handed. Fifty-fifty in everything."

Raleigh said, "I didn't mean it like that."

"Speak for yourself," James said. "I am trying to talk to my child here. It's my duty."

I touched my earlobes, disturbing my earrings. My mother's mother had given them to her when she was born and when I was born, my mother gave them to me. She told me to give them to my daughter. I asked what would happen if I didn't have one, what if I had only a son, or no children at all. "In that case," my mother said. "You get to keep them and wear them in your coffin."

James wet his finger again and aimed for my brow bone. Again, I jerked away.

"Dana?" Raleigh said. "What's wrong?"

"Nothing," I said. "Nothing. Reflexes. Nothing." I kept repeating the last word, unable to stop myself.

"Dana," Raleigh said again.

"Are you scared of me?" James said.

"No," I said. "You're wrong."

"I'm not," James said softly. "You're scared of me. I've been a good father to you. You have no cause to be scared of me like that."

"I'm not scared," I said, pleading now. I knew the feeling was called déjà vu. "I'm not scared," I'd said to Marcus in the dark of his parent's bedroom. "I'm not," I'd said, balling my shaking hands into fists and stuffing them under my thighs.

That had been only two weeks earlier. I'd taken the 66 Lynhurst bus to Marcus's house. When the bus passed right in front of my father's house with its orange-sherbet bricks, I opened my mouth and swallowed air. The address was written out in cursive letters, SEVEN THIRTY-NINE, instead of just

126

numbers like regular people. The sign staked in the yard read CHAURISSE'S PINK FOX. After West Manor Elementary, I pulled the cord and the driver let me off. Marcus's parents, whom I had never seen, were away at a bridge tournament. The house was stuffed with kids, some of them from other schools. I went into the bedroom looking for Marcus but found only Angie, a wild girl who wore keyhole tops even to school. She lay on his bed, talking on the telephone, looking up at the poster of Jayne Kennedy mounted on the ceiling. When I lay on Marcus's bed, I always closed my eyes against the beautiful woman spread above me.

Wandering back into the living room, I found Ronalda who asked me what was wrong.

"Angie's in his room."

She corrected her eyeliner with her finger and frowned. "Are you going to leave?"

"I don't know," I said.

Ronalda gave a deep sigh like she had already seen everything in the world. "You know what my mama says? 'Your pride or your man. You can't have them both.'"

The guys came in then from the backyard, where they had been working on the barbecue grill.

"The coals are hot," Marcus said. He smelled dangerous, like lighter fluid.

"Hi, Marcus," I said, and waved. Maybe I sounded a bit too eager, because he tensed.

"Don't get carried away," he said. "It's not that serious, babygirl."

Everyone in the room laughed, except Ronalda.

Now I must have looked hurt, because Marcus approached me from behind, touching my waist and saying hello into my hair. He greeted me like my father greeted my mother, except we were in front of other people. "You look good," he said, pressing himself against my backside. I wanted to melt into him, but the laughter of his friends still hung in the air.

"It was a joke," Marcus said softly, still directing his words into my scalp. "A joke. Why do you have to be so serious all the time?"

"I'm not mad," I said.

"It wasn't funny," Ronalda spoke up from the couch.

Now all his friends laughed at him, although Ronalda hadn't even made a joke.

"Bald-headed bitch," Marcus said, but if Ronalda heard him, she didn't react.

It wasn't like on television. It wasn't *The*

Burning Bed. I wouldn't even call it violence, really. Sometimes it was like a shove with a bit of a shake. Yes, there were slaps, but with a slap, the shock was in the sound more than anything else. It scared me, that was all. And I shouldn't have asked him about Angie. The two of them had known each other forever. They went to the same church. Their houses had identical floor plans. They were bathed together as babies. I needed to learn how to trust people.

My mother says that if a man hits you once, leave. But the truth is this — my father smacked my mother across the jaw when I was six months old. She stumbled out of the room, and he sat in front of my crib and cried. She says that was the first and only time. So it happens. But you can't go around saying that.

I went into the kitchen to pour myself some cucumber water. James and Raleigh followed me like bodyguards. According to the clock on the microwave oven, Marcus was ten minutes late already; for once I was grateful for his habit of rarely keeping his promises. There was even the possibility that he wouldn't show up at all. His life was busy, and he had many friends and obligations. That was just the way things were.

Love didn't always look and act the way you expected it to.

"So who's the boyfriend?" my father wanted to know. He turned to Raleigh. "She's too young to be going out this late at night, right?"

Raleigh picked up his camera and aimed it at my father's face. When James repeated himself, I heard the click of the shutter. Raleigh turned the camera toward me, and I felt myself straighten, improve my posture.

"Not looking like that, Raleigh. Don't take her picture," James said. "What's wrong with you?"

Raleigh lowered the camera.

I said, "I didn't even say I had a boyfriend." The lie reminded me of what Marcus had said on the night of the barbecue. *I am not your boyfriend.* The memory made my left arm tingle. It wasn't right for Marcus to talk to me like that, not in front of people, but I knew my father was a man to care only about what Marcus *did* to me, what I did with Marcus, or the things we did together. James stood before me with his fist throbbing like a human heart. He wanted to hit something. I took a step back.

"What?" James said.

"Nothing," I said.

James returned to the living room, sat on

the couch and the pillows gave a sigh. "Where is your mama?" he wanted to know. "Why didn't Gwen tell me about this boyfriend?"

I didn't respond, and the room was quiet except for the pop of Raleigh's knuckles. He was also a person longing to use his hands. I could tell that he wanted to turn the camera on James again. My father was sitting on the sofa hunched over like a mourning bear. "I would have thought your mother was raising you a little better than this."

"Don't talk about my mother," I said.

"He didn't say anything about Gwen," Raleigh said. "Dana, simmer down."

"My mother's at work. Not everybody can have a beauty parlor right in their own house. Not everybody can wear a fox-fur coat. Some people have to work."

This was the kind of thing Mother said late at night when we were here alone, when she was drinking. I used the tone she used at the best part of the night, when she played her Simon and Garfunkel and sang "Sail on, silver girl" until her voice grew tough and textured. This was the way she sounded just before she started to cry.

"She is a good mother," I said.

Raleigh murmured, "We know that."

131

James said, "Don't change the subject. Who is the boyfriend? How old is he?" He paced around the living room with heavy steps, making the picture frames rattle on the wall. Raleigh's fingers still fluttered on the shell of the camera, and I looked at the clock, not sure now if Marcus would show up at all and not sure if I wanted him to.

James turned to me. "W-w-w-what's . . ."

I waited.

He tried again, "I-I-I-I w-w-ant to know . . ."

Standing up, James folded his lips over on themselves and breathed through his nose. Deep breaths swelled his chest inside his cotton shirt. "The name. I'll k-k-k . . ."

I leaned forward just a little bit. He was going to do what? Kick Marcus's ass? Kill him? My mouth twitched into a little smile.

The words gave way with a swinging of my father's arm, and I ducked.

"I will kill him," my father said. "I will kill him. What's his name?"

"Marcus McCready," I said, and my father's face changed.

"I know his father," James said.

"The tax guy," Raleigh said.

James sat back on the sofa. "God damn it. How old is he? Isn't he out of high school yet?"

"He didn't get kept back," I said. "He has a late birthday."

Raleigh said, "Didn't he get in some trouble?"

"Is he going to college?" James asked me in a way that made it sound like he knew the answer.

"He's taking the year off," I said. "He's going to work and save up some money."

Raleigh patted James's arm. "Dana, Marcus isn't the kind of guy you want to even know your daughter's name, let alone . . ." He looked at the keyhole. "Let alone whatever else."

"He's a loser, baby," said James. "A pervert. He got kicked out of some private school."

"Something like that," Raleigh said.

Now my hands were pumping like a heart. "He's on his way here."

"I'll kill him," my father said again, but his voice wasn't so determined. His hands were not ready.

"No, you won't."

"I'm going to kill him."

"Who are you going to tell him that you are?" I asked. "The neighborhood watch?"

"Watch your mouth," James said.

Raleigh was looking at the window. "Does he drive a red Jetta?"

My father answered for me. "Yeah, that's his car. I helped his daddy pick it out."

We heard the horn. It was a queer sound. People weren't yet used to foreign cars.

"He's just going to blow the horn like that?" James said.

I shrugged. "Doesn't matter."

"I am not letting you leave this house," my father said. "I'm not playing, Dana."

I reached for my keys on their purple rabbit's foot.

My father said, "Put those keys down."

Marcus blew the horn again. Two toots this time.

I took my keys from the coffee table. "He's a nice guy."

My father took two steps after me as I headed for the front door.

"Watch out," I said, "or he's going to see you."

My father froze in his place. I stood in the doorway, longer than I needed to, waiting for him to spring forward like a superhero. I tugged the hem of my keyhole shirt. I pulled my fingers through my hair, and looked hard at myself in the oval mirror in the foyer. These were my mother's habits before leaving the house. I tamped my lips together and used my little finger to wipe away any eyeliner that may have smeared.

"I'm leaving now," I said to my father. "Lock the door behind you."

"Dana," my father said, "do not walk out of that door."

"Bye now," I said. I opened the door and walked through it, not closing up behind me. I was hoping to hear my father's feet behind me, but there was no sound from the house as I walked on the cracked cement driveway where Marcus waited, in the Jetta. The backseat was crammed with what looked like four other people, but the seat beside Marcus was empty, reserved for me. I was his girl, and tonight he didn't care who knew. I turned toward the house and made out my father's face shadowed in the doorway. I couldn't see his expression, but I knew he could see mine. I knew he saw the fire in my face, the challenge in my eyes.

Save me, James. I dare you.

8
FIG LEAF

At the start of my junior year, without
ceremony, without even a big breakup fight,
Marcus gave his class ring to a girl with four
names: Ruth Nicole Elizabeth Grant. She
had long hair like mine but not quite as full.
Her skin was like expensive china, pale and
so thin that you could see a network of lavender veins crisscrossing on her eyelids. I
would know that ring anywhere — the
garnet stone with the one-eighth-karat
diamonds on either side. I was sitting in
English when my eyes were drawn to Ruth
Nicole Elizabeth's already impressive add-
a-bead necklace, weighed down in the
center with the hunk of gold that was
Marcus's ring. I was so distraught that I
begged Ronalda to skip third period so that
I could spend some time recuperating in
the cool safety of her basement. As soon as
we arrived, I surveilled Marcus's house
through the slats over the corner window of

Ronalda's stepmother's study.

"Don't worry about it," Ronalda said. "You want to go with me to Fort McPherson? There are a lot of guys over there."

"No."

"You're just going to wait him out?"

"He'll explain. Love is complicated."

"Well," Ronalda said with sympathy, "here go something else my mama said. 'You like who you like and you can't help it.'"

The next day I found Marcus in the student parking lot. He was always there when classes let out even though he supposedly worked with his father from nine to five. I snuck away before the last bell so I could talk to him before all the kids swarmed out and underclassmen would be shaking his hand like he was the president. His middle finger looked naked without his giant ring. He once let me try it on but wouldn't let me keep it, even though I promised never to wear it to school. He had said it was too dangerous. "Evidence," he called it. It was okay for our friends to know about us, but at school, in front of adults, he had to be more careful. It made sense at the time, but Ruth Nicole was even younger than I was. If I was jailbait, she was super-jailbait.

As I explained this to him, Marcus told

me to lower my voice and calm down. Was I trying to get him arrested? He told me not to worry. Ruth Nicole's family knew his family. He rubbed my arm and spoke so gently that everything he said sounded like love. "Why do you care so much about that ring? It don't mean nothing."

I knew that I was supposed to be mad and I should have broken up with him. Ronalda, quoting more of her mother's wisdom said, "You gotta decide whether half a nigger is better than no nigger at all."

"Don't call him that."

"You got it bad," Ronalda said.

Down in the basement, we rifled through Ronalda's father's desk drawer and found what looked to be a nickel bag of weed. It wasn't the greatest quality, more seeds than anything, but we borrowed enough to roll a slender joint, which we shared in her step-mother's office after jamming a towel under the door. Ronalda took hard pulls, trying to get buzzed quick. No one else was home, but she was paranoid that someone would walk in on us.

"If they catch me," she said, "that's it. They'll send me back to Indiana."

"How can they get mad? You got it out of your father's drawer."

"It's his house; he can do whatever he wants."

"All right," I said, taking the smoldering wad. I put it to my mouth; it was damp from her lips. "I'll hurry up."

She took the joint back and took a hard drag. "I'll blow you a shotgun." I put my face next to hers and she blew the smoke right into my mouth.

"It's not that I don't want to go home," Ronalda said.

"For a visit, right?"

"I mean, I wouldn't mind going back. You know I don't fit in here."

"Yes you do," I said.

"Don't get all weird," Ronalda said. "All I mean is I wouldn't mind *going* back home. I just don't want to be *sent* back."

"It's the same thing," I said. "Gone is gone."

"No, it's not." She picked up the stub of the joint with her fingernails and lit it again. She held it to my lips.

"Your turn."

I pulled hard on the joint, trying to take enough in for the both of us. When she put her mouth to mine for the shotgun, I was going to push the words *Please stay* deep into her body.

"Don't cough," she said. "Coughing will

get you too high."

"I can't help it," I said, hacking until my throat burned and tears wet my face.

By Halloween, Marcus had started hanging out again but only late at night and without anyone else around. A temporary arrangement, he promised. Since he was working, he had more money in his pocket. Sometimes we went to the Varsity or J.R. Crickets and he paid for everything, leaving the waitress a big tip so we wouldn't get carded. Ronalda and I spent time together in the afternoons, doing homework, smoking dope, and watching Cinemax. It wasn't a bad way to live. At six o'clock, I would climb aboard the 66 Lynhurst, a little bit hungry and still a little bit high. This was why I preferred smoking to drinking. Liquor made me emotional while weed put a little daylight between me and my problems. It wasn't that I forgot my troubles, it's just that they didn't trouble me quite so much.

One afternoon, Ronalda had sent me on my way with a small paper bag filled with peanuts and jelly beans. I looked forward to shutting myself in my room and eating them by the handful. When I arrived at our building, the Lincoln was out front. Not the new one with the electric windows, but the '82 that Raleigh usually drove. I wasn't expecting my uncle on a Monday. He tended to drop by on Thursday afternoons, when James worked the line at the airport. On Thursdays, my mother fixed Raleigh a cold lunch before she pulled out the double deck of cards with which they played Tonk. I don't know if James was aware of these afternoon games, but they were never mentioned when I was around.

I used my key, trying to make myself seem sober, but I know I must have looked really confused to find James and my mother seated on the couch. Above them grinned a montage of photos, all of me. I had never really paid attention until Ronalda pointed them out, but now they seemed stupid, these pictures of me smiling the same way, every year of my life. I was older in each but nothing more. It was just my camera face, perfected by the time I started first grade.

"Hey," I said. "What's up?"

"Dana," my mother said, "I need to talk to you."

"Okay," I said. "Let me go upstairs and wash up."

James said, "You look clean enough to me."

I licked my lips. I knew the fragrance of

141

the marijuana had snaked itself into my clothes and hair. Even my upper lip seemed to radiate the odor.

"Okay," I said, remaining by the door, trying not to get any closer. I wondered what I looked like. I knew from television that parents can diagnose their kids with drug use by looking at their pupils, so I kept my eyes to the carpet. The paper bag of jelly beans and peanuts rattled in my hand. "What's up?"

"Where have you been, Dana?" my mother asked.

James's arms were crossed across the front of his uniform. When half a year had gone by after I'd dared my father to save me from Marcus, I'd been foolish enough to think that I had won something. Of course, six months is a long time on the calendar of a sixteen-year-old girl. For James, it was just enough time to collect his thoughts and get his game together. His round face, squished under his hat and hidden behind his glasses, shone with satisfaction.

"I was out," I said.

"You see, Gwen. This is what I was talking about."

When I was a girl, I would have been thrilled to know they had been discussing me, but now, I was just annoyed. Who was he to act like he knew me? From his righteous posture, I knew he hadn't told my mother about the time he'd let me leave the house half-naked at midnight, all because he'd been afraid to show his face. I would bet anything that he claimed to have found out through his connections, all the people he knows in such high places all over the city.

I moved toward the couch, wanting them now to smell me. I wedged myself into the thick of them. The couch was plenty big enough for three people, but neither of my parents moved as I forced myself in the space between them.

My mother sniffed my hair. "Have you been smoking grass?"

I laughed at her term, *grass*. I knew it wasn't funny, but at the same time it was sort of funny.

"So now Marcus McCready has you using drugs?" my father said.

I giggled again, as Marcus stayed away from weed. It would violate his probation. The whole thing was funny, my parents sitting here waiting for me at six in the evening as though it were three o'clock in the morning, as if they were regular parents, as if I were an ordinary girl.

"Gwen," James said, "if you can't control her —"

"If she can't control me, what?"

"She doesn't need controlling," my mother said. "She needs something else."

"Legitimacy," I said.

"You are legitimate," my mother said.

"What's in the paper sack?" James asked, reaching for it.

I clamped the bag down between my knees. "It's not your business. It's a present."

"Don't talk to me like that," James said. "Give it to me."

My mother was stricken. "What is it, Dana? Dana, honey, what is it?"

"It's mine." I felt like I was watching this whole scene happen, that I wasn't really me and these weren't really my parents.

"You used to like me," I said to James. "When I was little, you liked me."

"What are you talking about?" he said. "I like you now. I just need to know what's in the bag."

I looked to my mother. "Tell him to leave me alone. There is nothing in the bag. Tell him to trust me. Please. Make him leave me alone."

My mother looked at the bag. "What has happened to you, Dana? What happened to my little girl? We used to do everything together."

"It's not fair," I said.

"James," my mother said, "why don't you run on home? I need to talk to Dana in private."

"You can't send me away," James said. "You can't send me away like I don't belong here. She's my daughter. You're my family. I need to see what's in the bag."

"There's nothing in the bag," I said.

"There's something in the bag," James said. "Let me see it."

"Mother," I said, "tell him to leave me alone."

Her eyes flickered between the two of us. She looked a long time at the bag, trying to make a guess as to its contents. She took a deep breath, no doubt taking in the smell of the weed, my anger, and my sweat. She knew I had been up to something; I had no argument, no reasonable cover story, but I wanted her to stand up for me anyway. Isn't love when you defend someone when you know she's wrong? I didn't want her to stand up for what was *right,* I wanted my mother to stand up for *me.*

"Mama," I said.

"Dana —"

"Mommy?"

145

"Dana, baby, just show him what's in the bag. If it's nothing, show him that it's nothing. What has happened to you, Dana? What are you doing? You come home smelling like grass. You have this boyfriend, a delinquent. Don't ruin your life, baby. Just show your father what's in the bag."

Keeping my eyes on Mother, I opened the bag, turned it upside down, and poured the jelly beans and peanuts on the floor. They made a beautiful mess. Ronalda had gotten these jelly beans special, from Lenox Square. They were all colors, pink with brown flecks, purple, orange. The flavors had exotic names like Piña Colada and Fig Leaf. The sight of them there on the ugly brown carpet made me want to cry.

"Are you happy?" I said, not knowing for sure if I was talking to my mother or my father. I wondered if weed could make me emotional after all. I couldn't care this much about a bag of candy and nuts.

My parents looked at the mess on the carpet, and then they looked at each other. My mother worried her rings and my father bucked his head as he tried to free the words stuck in his throat.

"I told you there was nothing in the bag," I said. "You didn't believe me."

"From who?" James snapped. "F-f-f-from

146

M-Marcus McCready?"

What right did my father have to the details of my life? He squandered his chance to be the protective father. You can't come rushing to the rescue six months later. I wasn't a person to be saved only when it was a convenient time to swoop in.

My mother said, "This boy isn't good for you. He's not going to give you anything but a reputation."

James said, "I-i-if a-all you end up with is a reputation, you'll be lucky."

"Do you talk to Chaurisse like this?" I said. "I've seen her. She walks around looking like a streetwalker. I don't see you saying anything to her."

My mother looked at me sharply. We had gone surveilling at the JCPenney outlet the week before. Chaurisse was wearing a halter top that was too small for her.

"Don't talk about my d-d-daughter," James said. "You don't know anything about her."

"That's it," my mother said. "This is enough and getting out of hand. Dana, you go on to your room. You will not see the boyfriend anymore. That's that. And James, you need to go home and cool off."

We each did as she said. My father went to his car and blew the horn twice as he was pulling away, as though this day were like any other. My mother busied herself in the kitchen; I heard the dishes moving around in the cupboard as I lay on my bed, staring at the water spots on the ceiling. My mother called my name, but I didn't answer her.

"Dana," she said, "I know you are not asleep. Come here."

I made my way to the den, where she sat on the couch James had just vacated.

"Tell me what you're thinking," she said.

"You know what I'm thinking," I said.

"No, I don't. I don't know what's on your mind; you didn't even tell me about the boyfriend."

"Don't I have the right to some privacy?" I said. "Can't I have my own life?"

"Don't be ridiculous, Dana. This is the time in your life when you need your mother most. You're sixteen. One wrong move and you can ruin your life forever. Talk to me, Dana. Tell me what's on your mind."

"You took his word for what's happening, and he doesn't even live here."

"Tell me about the boy," my mother said.

"His name is Marcus, and James doesn't like him because Marcus's dad does James's taxes."

My mother's face bent to let me know that

James had left out this detail. "Your father said he was a hoodlum."

"He lives on Lynn Circle," I said. "Nearby to Ronalda."

"Your father said that he's twenty years old. That he isn't allowed around underage girls."

"Marcus isn't like that. And he's just nineteen."

My mother looked at me with her tired face. "Dana. I need you to tell me the truth here. Are you being intimate with him?"

"No," I said. "Nothing like that. We're waiting until we get married."

"I find it hard to believe that you two are just playing pinochle."

I was seized with a desperate need for her trust. "You can take me to the doctor. A doctor can look at me and see I haven't been doing anything."

"Is he a good guy, Dana?"

"Yes," I said. "He's so nice to me. He's so good to me. He doesn't cheat on me. A lot of girls like him, but I am the only one he goes out with. He loves me. He doesn't have a temper. He has never raised his hand to me." I could hear my own voice, shrill with lies.

"He's hitting you?" my mother said. "He's hitting you, Dana? Oh baby, come here."

She opened her arms to me, but I didn't walk into them.

"I said he's *not* hitting me."

"Dana, I am your mother. You can't lie to me."

"You can't read my mind."

"Baby, I made your mind."

"He's not hitting me."

"Yes, he is."

It was wrong the way she could browse among my secret thoughts. She says that it was motherly intuition, but this is not true. She and I have a connection. Today, the link is rusty, the current erratic, but there will always be something between us.

"So?" I said. "James hit you one time. When I was a baby. I heard you tell Willie Mae about it."

"That was one time, it was a long time ago, and he was under a lot of stress."

"Well, Marcus is under stress, too. He wants to apply to college."

"Yes, your father hit me, but I had a baby. I just had to make it work. And your father is not a violent man. Dana, you don't have chick nor child. Why stay with some boyfriend that can't keep his hands to himself?"

"You just don't want me to have my own life."

"You are not seeing this boy anymore. End

of discussion. I will go up to the school and tell the principal that he is harassing my daughter. James tells me he has faced charges already for statutory rape."

"Sixteen is the age of consent!"

"You have only been sixteen for a little while. I will have him put in jail, Dana. Don't make me do it."

"Mother," I said, "you're just siding with James. He just doesn't want us around his real family. Can't you see that this is all there is to it?"

My mother said, "I don't care what is in it for James. Your safety is what's in it for me. I am not going to let you ruin your life while you are living under my roof. So that's it. You are not seeing this boy again, ever. If I ever suspect you are, he's going to jail."

"Mother, don't do that."

"It's over. This relationship is over. It's not healthy."

I cried myself to sleep. What teenager hasn't? I woke up with a headache, and I remembered the lost jelly beans and cried some more. My mother tapped on my door at 10 a.m.

"Get up and get dressed. Let's go surveilling."

"No," I said, just for the satisfaction of denying her. "I never want to do that again."

9
No Quarrel

I am poor when it comes to grandparents. Flora, the wild woman, didn't have use for her own child, let alone a granddaughter. Although I saw my mother's father each spring, I spoke to him only once in my life. My mother believed in rituals, and on the first warm Saturday in April she took me to see him as he groomed the hedges in front of his house. We were accustomed to covert endeavors, but we were different when we surveilled my grandfather. When we shadowed Chaurisse and her mother, we were nervous and excited, like rookie cops. These adventures left us stimulated and hungry, like we'd been swimming. But our yearly visits to my grandfather made us nervous and unsure. On the day of our visit in 1986, my mother drove without the radio, wearing down her nails against the edges of her teeth. I picked at the skin on my lower lip until my smile was sore and raw.

Things between my mother and me had been tense since she and my father had forbidden me to see Marcus. Making matters worse, James initiated some sort of man-to-man conversation with Marcus's father and Marcus cut me off completely. I don't know what passed between our fathers, but I was pretty sure it wasn't the truth. I asked my mother if she found this all to be at least a little bit hypocritical. No, she said. She found it to be *ironic.* The conflict was between us, as tangible and opaque as drywall.

At my mother's request, I wore Flora's gold earrings because she hoped that my grandfather would look up from his weeding and pruning to see me there, looking like my mother and her mother. In her fantasy, he'd pause, look closer, and see the gold hoops, the proof that I was Gwendolyn's girl. She hoped the sight of me would inspire him to love me in his old age, to open his door. I would be the needle and my mother would be the thread looped through its eye.

Maybe I shared all my mother's fantasies. Her cravings were so straightforward, honest, and universal. Who doesn't want to be loved? Anyone who has been cast off knows the pain of it. Who doesn't know what it's like to just want to go home, to sleep in a bed that is your own, lying on a pillow that smells of your own hair?

And then there were the daydreams of my own. Maybe Grandfather would look up from the hydrangeas, fall in love with me, and not even think of my mother. My strict orders were not to identify myself. I was just to say "Good afternoon, sir" as I walked by. I could maybe compliment the flowers, but I couldn't give him any hint that I was his kin. We were not trying to force anything on anyone. We were merely providing an opportunity, nudging fate along.

My grandfather, Luster Lee Abernathy, was a narrow man, with white hair so fine his brown scalp showed through. Clipping the hedges with a manual clipper, his thin arms, ropy with muscles, flexed as he whacked the plants into spheres. I can't say what made this year different from the others, but when he saw me advancing in his direction, he stopped the busy shears and removed his cap as though giving me a chance to declare myself.

"Good afternoon, sir," I said.

"Afternoon," he said.

"Your yard is sure pretty."

"Thank you," he said, looking hard at my

face. "Where you walking to?"

"Oh, just taking a walk." I gestured in the direction of Boulevard Avenue. "Just stretching my legs."

"Be careful," he said. "It's not like it used to be. Don't walk too far in that direction. They all using that crack up there. Gone crazy."

"Oh," I said. "I didn't know."

The hedge between us was only half-groomed. One side was smooth and round, but the rest was wild with new growth and buds. My grandfather squinted at me. "How long you been walking?"

"A little while," I said. "Just looking around."

"You from around here?"

"No," I said. "I'm from North Carolina." The spontaneity of lies was always a mystery to me, as much a miracle as geysers or flash floods.

"You walked over here from the King Center?"

I nodded.

"You must be looking for MLK's childhood home. You need to go over a couple of blocks. You walked too far to the east. You could easily miss it. It looks just like all the other houses around here. But go see it. I hear they give a tour."

155

"You've never seen it?"

"Got no need to," he said.

"Thank you, sir."

"Please excuse my clothes and such," he said. "I was just doing yard work. I didn't figure on meeting you."

I put my hand to my cheek, and I could feel myself smiling. "You know who I am?"

"No, ma'am," he said. "I never seen you before."

"I'm Gwen's daughter."

"I don't know any Gwen," he said. "I did a long time ago, but it's too far gone. I don't even know what I would say to her. It's done."

"It's not," I said. "I could run and get her."

"No," he said. "Don't do that. You're a pretty girl. Seems like she did a good job of bringing you up. Don't throw your life away like your mama did."

"Do you want me to run and get her?"

"Naw," he said. "I got my life the way I want it. Hold still."

My grandfather turned and walked toward the front door of the bungalow. As the lock clunked in place behind him, I ran my hand over the trimmed half of the hedge, letting the fresh-cut stems prick the pads of my fingers. I imagined my mother sitting in the car looking at her watch. Maybe she would come looking for me.

Grandfather finally emerged from the house followed by a woman who carried a squirming baby. She was older than I was but younger than my mother. Her curls, held back with silver clips, were dinted where she had fastened the rollers.

"What is it, Luster?" she asked.

Grandfather said, "I want you to give this young lady directions to the King Center. She's lost, and you know that I am forgetful."

"Since when have you been forgetful?" she said in a tone that was half daughter and half something else. She shifted the squirming baby from one hip to the other. The baby, a boy, was chubby with a shiny face. He cooed at me.

"Look at him," his mother said. "Flirting already."

"Let me hold him," Grandfather said. "His name is Anthony."

I have thought back on this moment, as I have on many such moments of my life, and wondered why it is that I have been so careful with other people's secrets. My grandfather spoke to me for only a minute or so before deciding that I was the type of person to keep quiet and pretend to be a stranger before his new wife and son. At the time, I

157

was a little bit flattered to be the sentinel of information. My grandfather's wife, pointing the way to the King Center, thought she was happy. She thought she knew her husband, but I knew things that she didn't.

She was like my own mother, who thought she knew me but didn't know that I'd seen Marcus again, just for a couple hours, in Jamal Dixon's rec room. We drank peppermint schnapps this time, and I had to close my eyes against the same poster of Jayne Kennedy. She didn't know that Ronalda and I took pee-in-a-cup pregnancy tests every month, and she didn't know that I memorized James's unlisted home number and called sometimes just to hear Chaurisse's voice. I suppose Mother and I were almost even now. Before the day I poured jelly beans onto the carpet, I had thought that I knew my mother, too. But when she and James confronted me about Marcus, she acted like the girl half of a couple and treated me like a disposable friend.

After the woman finished talking and pointing, I thanked her and walked away.

"Good-bye, sir," I said to my grandfather, who had picked up his clippers again and was chopping hard at the bushes. He didn't say good-bye, but he gave a swift, efficient nod of his head. The flying twigs and leaves surrounded him like a swarm.

Back at the car, my mother was antsy, swiveling her head, biting her lips. She thought of herself as looking like her mother. Having never met my grandmother or seen a picture, I had to take her word for it. But in this agitated state, I could see that she took after her father as well. She had his same chin, a little weak but stubborn, and her shoulders carried the same slump of sadness. If I were to ask her, she would say that it's because they both lost Flora, but my guess is that it also comes from having lost each other.

"Did you talk to him?" she wanted to know.

"I said 'Good afternoon, sir,' same as last year."

She nodded, waiting for whatever was coming next.

"That's it," I said.

"Dana," my mother said. "Don't lie to me, okay?" She didn't say it as a threat, but just as an instruction. "You have to tell me the truth. I need information."

For a moment, I hesitated. It was as though telling my mother what I had seen would have negated the moment I shared with my grandfather. It excited me to think

159

of the minute or so I stood there sharing a secret that he couldn't share with his young wife, the mother of his wiggly baby. "Nothing happened."

"Something happened," my mother said, starting the car. "Don't lie to me. I can't have you lying to me." Her voice was different now; she was trying to reason with me. "Just tell me."

"We talked for a minute," I said.

"Did he recognize you?"

"I'm not sure."

"Listen. Think about this. If he recognized you, if he knew who you were, it wasn't that he knew you were yourself, Dana. If he knew you, he thought about you as my child."

"I don't know," I said.

"Tell me," my mother said. "Did he ask your name?"

"No, ma'am." I sighed. "He didn't."

"Exactly," my mother said. "Now tell me what happened."

"Nothing happened."

"It's good for us to share what we know," my mother said. "It's what makes us close."

"He didn't say anything."

"Then what took you so long?"

"I wasn't gone a long time."

My mother hit the steering wheel with the

160

heels of her hands. "Why are you doing this to me? Is it because I wouldn't let you see that boy?"

"What boy?" I shrugged and looked out of the window. This secret was mine, wrapped like a shiny present, lodged on a high shelf where Mother could see it but couldn't reach.

My paternal grandmother, Miss Bunny, died the very same year. James Lee Witherspoon loved his mother in the way that a son should. To my mother's understanding, a man who cared about his mother the way James cared for Miss Bunny would never willfully mistreat a woman.

"Understand this," my mother said. "James lost his daddy when he was a boy, leaving Miss Bunny to struggle. He saw that, and it made an impression on him. So he can't leave Laverne to suffer like that. It would be a slap in the face to his mother. And on the other side, he can't just leave us high and dry either. That would be an insult to Miss Bunny, too."

"But Miss Bunny doesn't even know we exist," I said.

"Of course not, it would break her heart."

"Well then, what you said before doesn't make sense."

"Yes it does," she said. "Love is a maze. Once you get in it, you're pretty much trapped. Maybe you manage to claw your way out, but then what have you accomplished?"

In 1986, Miss Bunny was dying as I was taking my AP exam in biology. The proctor tapped me on the shoulder.

"Your father is here," she said.

I looked toward the doorway, not believing. I looked back at my blue test book. "Where is he?"

"The principal's office," she said.

"Will I get a chance to take a makeup? My mother paid for the exam."

The teacher said, "Don't worry about the test."

I stood up, but I was worried about the exam. If I passed it, I would be able to take college classes over the summer for free. It would also look good on my application for Mount Holyoke. No one gets into an elite university without AP credits.

The proctor helped me gather my things, quietly so as not to disturb my classmates, whose responsibilities were less urgent than my own. Once we had shut the door to the classroom, she said, "I see where you get your pretty hair from." Then she touched the curls that spilled over onto my shoulder.

Raleigh, my father of record, was waiting for me in the lobby of the principal's office. He looked terrible; his pale skin, thin under the eyes, showed purple veins. He wore blue jeans and a shapeless maroon shirt with the nubby texture of long underwear.

"What's wrong?" I asked him. "Is my mother all right?"

"It's not Gwen." He covered his face with his hands.

"Is it James?" I said, believing myself to know the answer already. Raleigh loved no one like he loved my father.

"No," Raleigh said. "No."

I was stumped and a little annoyed with him. The AP exam was important. "Well, what is it?"

"It's Miss Bunny," he said. "She's dying."

"Who?"

"Miss Bunny," he said. "Your grand-mother."

"Oh," I said. "Miss Bunny. What's wrong with her?"

"Cancer," Raleigh said. "They say she's only got a few weeks, a month maybe."

I stood there in the lobby of the principal's office, not sure what I should do. I had never met my grandmother, a slight that bothered my mother more than me. Raleigh got up from his chair and picked up my backpack, my wool coat, and my lunch cooler. He made his way toward the door.

"Wait," I said.

Raleigh looked over his shoulder. "What?"

"I'm in the middle of taking my test."

Raleigh said, "Didn't you hear me? Miss Bunny is dying."

I stood dumb in the office. "I heard you. I'm sorry to hear it."

"So let's go," Raleigh said.

It took my legs a moment to get the message. "I'm going?"

"She can't go to glory without meeting you."

"Will Mother be there?"

Raleigh let his arms carrying all my things droop. "Just you."

"Does she even know?"

"James says he is going to call her."

When Raleigh drove, he let me sit up front beside him. James always insisted that I ride behind. *Black people need to become accustomed to luxury.* He taught me the protocol so if I am ever in a position to be chauffeured for real, I'll know what to do: Never touch the door handle, under any circumstances. Even if the goddamn sedan is on fire, wait to be let out. The same goes for being let in. His final rule was *never, ever*

164

scoot. If you enter the passenger door, stay there. If someone else is going to ride, the driver will escort her to her rightful side. For Raleigh, all that mattered was that I wore my seat belt. I climbed up front beside him and cranked down the window. "Do I look okay?"

"Miss Bunny won't care," Raleigh said. His voice cracked. "Miss Bunny won't care about that at all."

"Did she ask for me?" I wanted to know.

My father and Raleigh were known in Ackland as "Miss Bunny's Boys," though only James was her flesh-and-blood child. "These here are my sons," she would introduce them, daring anyone to make a distinction between James, dark-complected like his dead father, and Raleigh, white as a dinner plate. Miss Bunny herself was a medium brown color, as though she were the product of her boys.

Raleigh's real mother, Lula, was a red-bone girl from Richmond, Virginia. Why she would move from the relative metropolis of Richmond to a three-stop-sign town like Ackland was a mystery. When anyone asked her, Lula only said, "I couldn't get along with my daddy." She was fifteen when Miss Bunny met her. They worked together,

165

cleaning house for the same white folks. Miss Bunny arrived in the mornings and left in the evenings after the supper dishes were washed and walked herself home to prepare a meal for herself and her husband. Lula's job was to look after the children, so she stayed all night.

Miss Bunny and Lula found themselves pregnant at the same time, though Miss Bunny was pleased with her condition. She'd been married almost three years with no baby. Every married woman wanted a baby back then, whether she knew how she was going to feed it or not. Lula was miserable, and Miss Bunny couldn't blame her. It was 1942, but Lula said she felt like she was living on a plantation. Miss Bunny felt the same way sometimes, even though she had her little home to go to at night, and her own husband, and a thin gold-plated band to make it all clear.

James and Raleigh were born in the same month, but Miss Bunny hadn't seen Lula since she was seven months along and had run off with twenty-six dollars folded thin and stashed in the lining of her suitcase. She was trying to get to Chicago but only reached as far as North Carolina. She returned when Raleigh was six months old, sitting up by himself.

By then, Miss Bunny was keeping house for some new white folks. The hours were longer, but these employers were nicer, letting her bring home leftovers. Her husband didn't like eating cast-off food, but Miss Bunny said it was good food, she had fixed it herself. What difference did it make if she cooked it at home on her own stove or over at the white people's house? These new white people needed an overnight girl. Miss Bunny told Lula about the vacancy.

"What's the husband like?" Lula said. "I can't go through this all again."

"He's crippled," Miss Bunny said. "Polio."

They worked together several more years. Miss Bunny and Lula talked about everything except their sons. Miss Bunny was crazy about James Junior and Lula couldn't stand the sight of poor Raleigh. And it really was the *sight* of him that she couldn't stand. Who could object to Raleigh's mild personality and gentle smiles? It was his boss-man complexion and swamp green eyes that she couldn't bear. Miss Bunny tried to stay out of Lula's affairs. Raleigh was Lula's child; she worked hard every day to feed him and keep him in clean clothes. She could do what she thought was best. Yet every now and then, Miss Bunny would say, "Just try loving him, Lula. He's a sweet boy."

In 1949, when James Junior was almost eight, James Senior was killed in a mill accident. This I knew. James Senior died in the middle of the week, so Miss Bunny would get his pay up until Wednesday and that was all. She wanted to cry about it, and she did, but there was only so much time for lying in bed wailing. She had to eat. James Junior needed to eat. Miss Bunny knew she was going to have to find a live-in job.

Raleigh says he doesn't know whose idea it was. He doesn't know which woman — his mama or Miss Bunny — felt she walked away with the better deal. What he remembers is Lula packing all his things into a cardboard suitcase held together with a strap.

"You're going to live with Miss Bunny and James. She's going to look after you from here on out, okay? Don't look so sad. She's a better mother than I am by twice. When you grown up, you might hate me, but when you talk against me you can never say that I lied. You can curse my name if you want to, but you won't deny that this is the best thing that anyone ever did for you."

Raleigh was just a little boy, hungry sometimes, but lonely always. He cried, which was unusual for him. Having been underloved for all his short life, he'd learned not to attract his mother's attention in any negative way. When he came to understand that she was casting him off like an empty egg carton, he lost control of himself.

He has no recollection of throwing himself on the floor or the spasms ending with letting go of his bladder. He knows this happened only because Miss Bunny told him how Lula ran to her house and said, "You'll have to get him, Bunny. I can't face him. He's over there howling like a dog. I just can't take it."

Miss Bunny said, "Lula, he's just a little boy. What do you mean you can't face him?"

"You just go and get him, Bunny," Lula whispered. "If you want him, go and get him."

Miss Bunny told Raleigh she found him lying on the concrete porch. *Pissy* was one word she used. *Heartbroke* was the other.

"I'm going with you?" he said.

"Yes, son. You are."

She took his hand and they walked the half mile home. His wet pants scrubbed his thighs raw, but he was a child who had long before learned not to complain.

169

"I'm your boy now?"

"You are," Miss Bunny said.

"How come?"

"Because I love you."

Raleigh knows now that Miss Bunny could not have possibly loved him. He was a small stranger, piss-soaked and desperate. What Miss Bunny needed was a companion for James, whom she did love. She needed someone to sleep in the house with him while she cared for the white children at her job.

Miss Bunny was a kind woman, and generous. When she told Raleigh she loved him, it was like the music of laughter. He knew from the battered books at school what to say in return. "I love you, too."

Raleigh told me this story as we were riding in the limousine so I could, at last, meet Miss Bunny. He talked throughout the three-hour drive, but the rest of the story I'd already heard — how James and Raleigh lived alone in Miss Bunny's house six days a week. They ate cold sandwiches but also hot plates brought over by neighbors. He stopped the story when he and James were juniors in high school. Raleigh said he'd end the story there since I probably knew the rest. I didn't argue with him, because I knew that the real reason he ended the story where he did was because that was when Laverne entered their lives.

"Raleigh, what ever happened to Lula?" I wanted to know. "Do you ever want to find her?"

"I know where she is," he said. "I paid someone once to track her down. She lives in Mississippi. She got married, has a son named Lincoln." He gave a small smile that I didn't like. "I don't know if she named him for Abraham Lincoln, or maybe he was born in Nebraska. Could be she's got a thing for Town Cars."

"Did you go see her?"

"I started to," he said. "I drove the Cadillac down to Hattiesburg, burned up all that gas, but I wanted to take the best car. I parked in front of her house and sat there until she came out."

"Did you say anything to her?"

"No. I just stood there and she thought I was a white man. I could tell the way she looked nervous to see me there and the way she called me sir. I touched my hat at her and she turned around and went back in the house."

"Raleigh," I said. "Raleigh, I'll tell you a secret, okay?"

"All right," he said.

"Me and my mama do stuff like that. We do it all the time. We call it 'surveilling.' "

Raleigh patted my knee again. "Dana, baby. That's not a secret."

"What do you mean?" I could hear the fear in my voice.

"It's all right," he said. "I've seen you and Gwen a couple-three times in places you're not supposed to be."

"Did you tell James?"

Raleigh shook his head. "Why would I do something like that to Gwen? I would never do anything to hurt your mother."

"Does she know that you know?"

Raleigh shook his head. "It would just upset her. So let's just keep this whole conversation between us."

Then he smiled at me with something that I recognized as longing. I felt the rush of it. I breathed in panting breaths.

"Miss Bunny loves you," Raleigh says. "She doesn't know it yet, but she does."

Miss Bunny had been in the hospital for almost two weeks, but she wanted to come home to die. Home was the crooked-frame house in which she had raised her two boys and Laverne, too. The house was gray with a concrete porch. A vine grew up from a trellis on the north end. Raleigh pointed at it. "If it was later in the year, you wouldn't believe the roses. That's one thing that I remember from when Miss Bunny brought me home. Red roses with yellow insides."

"Is James already here?" I asked.

"He's been here two days. We've both been sitting with her, but James wanted me to go and get you and bring you here. We wanted you to see her while she is still herself."

I sat in the car and waited for Raleigh to open my door, then exited like my father had taught me, right foot flat on the ground and left hand extended to allow the driver to help me. I hoped that he was watching from the window.

"Careful," Raleigh said. "Watch out for the ditch."

The ditch, running where I would have expected curb, was half-full of brown water. I made a face.

"You are not a country girl, that's for sure," Raleigh said.

I didn't realize my father had come onto the porch until he spoke. "It's not the country. It's a small town." He held his arms out to me.

I ran into my father's hug with a little too much speed maybe, because he staggered back two steps. Since we were now the same height, he spoke directly into my ear.

"Oh, Dana," he said. "I am so gl-glad you made it."

I have since read in self-help books that people who are not accustomed to affection don't know how to receive it. I know for a fact that this is a myth. My father held me in his arms on my grandmother's front porch in full view of the world, and I enjoyed it. You don't need a dress rehearsal to know how to lay your head on your father's shoulder, to inhale his tobacco scent. It takes no practice to know how to be someone's daughter.

Raleigh said, "How is she?"

"No change," James said. "We've been talking most of the morning."

"Did you tell her?" Raleigh said, quietly.

James nodded.

"Does she want to meet me?" My voice was whispery, so I cleared my throat and tried again. "What did you tell her about me?"

"I told her that you are my daughter. I told her how smart you are."

"What did you tell her about my mama?"

"We didn't talk so much about Gwen," James said.

I didn't feel right. "Didn't she want to know where I came from?"

Raleigh said, "Dana, lower your voice. Miss Bunny is sick. She doesn't need to hear all this fighting. She's in a bad way. Just let her go in peace."

"Raleigh," I said, shrugging off his touch. He pulled back and for a moment I regretted hurting him. "I am not fighting with anyone. I am just trying to find out what all James told Miss Bunny. I want to know what he told her about my mama."

James said, "I t-t-told her about you. You are her kin and I want her to lay eyes on you before she goes."

"But what about my mama?" I said. "She's important, too."

Raleigh seemed on the verge of tears. "Please stop fighting. Let's just go inside."

"You didn't make my mother out to be a whore, did you?" I asked.

"No," Raleigh said. "James wouldn't say anything like that to Miss Bunny. Tell her, Jimmy. Tell her what you said."

"I told her your mother was dead," James said. "I told her you were raised by your grandmother."

"Did you at least tell her you loved my mother? That it wasn't just a quick thing?"

James nodded. "I told her that I love you, Dana. She knows if I love you, then your mama must be special."

I shook my head. That wasn't how it worked.

"Dana," Raleigh said, "don't waste Miss Bunny's time. She doesn't have much left."

My father took my hand and escorted me into Miss Bunny's bedroom, which was separated from the living room by a sheer curtain. Although I had been told how sick Miss Bunny was, I still expected her to be plump and lemon-scented like a second-grade teacher. I had no idea of what dying really looked like. The only people I had ever seen with serious illnesses were on hospital dramas, like *Trapper John, M.D.* Television patients wore lipstick and crisp cotton gowns. When they finally passed away, they were polite enough to close their eyes.

Miss Bunny was sixty-five years old, which seemed old to me at the time, but now that my own mother is nearing fifty, I understand how young my grandmother was when years of hard work, starchy foods, and bad genes caught up with her. She looked ancient, as old as anyone I had ever seen on television or in real life. Her skin was thick and stippled like the peel of an orange and her eyes were murky. The saddest thing was her hair. Someone, probably Laverne, had arranged it in a dozen pin curls, as though she were preparing to go to a party later that evening.

"Mama," said James, squeezing my hand. "This is my daughter, Dana Lynn."

"Come closer," Miss Bunny said with a voice that was strong and almost man-deep. "Come here, child." To James she said, "You and Raleigh go on to the Burger Inn or something. Go on. Don't worry. I'm not going to go to glory before you get back." She laughed, but no one else did. "Truly. You two get out of here. You wanted me to meet my granddaughter. How am I supposed to get to know her with you two breathing down my neck?"

Raleigh poked his head in between the pale curtains that served as Miss Bunny's bedroom door. "Jimmy?"

I could see how they must have been as children. Raleigh looking to James, not Miss Bunny, for direction. James looked into his mother's face.

"W-w-what d-d-do you need to talk to her about? Why c-c-can't we just visit together?" He went to the window and swiveled the wand to open the blinds.

"James, I want to talk to her about woman things. Now shoo, boy."

James backed toward the curtained doorway, as if he didn't want to turn his back on us. He bumped into Raleigh, and Miss Bunny laughed again. It wasn't a robust sort of laugh; she was too weak for all of that. But still, I knew that she found the situation amusing. She continued with the breathy laugh until James and Raleigh had left in the Lincoln.

When they were gone, the house was empty-feeling and more quiet than I was used to. Miss Bunny let her head fall back onto the eyelet pillow slip. She just lay there breathing for a while, and I didn't bother her.

"My left leg is gone," she said to me.

"Yes, ma'am," I said.

"They said taking the leg would save me. It wasn't a beautiful leg, but it was mine, and I had never figured on not lying whole in my casket. Life is full of things you never figured on."

I didn't say anything back. I knew I was a surprise to Miss Bunny, but nothing was a surprise to me.

"If I could get out of bed, I would hug your neck," she said. "I never turned anybody away from my door. Your daddy knows that. I took in Raleigh, and later Laverne. I have never turned anybody away. Never sent nobody back." She shut up and worked on her breathing some more. "I love you," she said to me, just as she had said to Raleigh so many years ago. I know that it was supposed to make me feel warm and welcome, but instead I wondered if she saw me the way she saw Raleigh — as an unfortunate bastard, unloved and pissy.

"Don't look at me like I am an orphan. My mother's not dead," I blurted. "She's a nurse and she takes good care of me. I was taking the AP exam in biology when Raleigh pulled me out of school to come up here. That test cost fifty dollars, and my mother paid for it."

"She takes good care of my James, too, I imagine." Miss Bunny sighed.

"She does," I said. "Her name is Gwendolyn Yarboro."

"And your name is?"

"Dana," I said.

"I know that. But what's your full name?"

"Dana Lynn Yarboro."

Miss Bunny touched her hand to her forehead. "Did James sign your birth certificate?"

"No, ma'am," I said. "But Raleigh did."

She shook her head. "Those boys. Brothers; I don't care what nobody says. If they are in it, they are in it together. Are you an only child, baby?"

I said carefully to Miss Bunny, "How

179

could I be an only child?"

Her face shifted, and she touched the space on the bed where her leg would have been. "I didn't mean anything by that. Lord. This is a mess. You ever seen Chaurisse?"

I shrugged. "Not really."

"She's a nice girl," Miss Bunny said. "I'm real proud of her. This is going to kill her. Her mama, too. But Laverne, she's from this town. She grew up hard; she'll bounce back. But Chaurisse was born and raised in Atlanta. She don't know nothing about suffering. This is going to tear her apart."

"That's not my fault," I said.

Miss Bunny patted the space on the bed again. "Sit down."

I moved to the place on the bed, crackling the plastic mattress cover. I didn't face my grandmother, keeping my eyes on the gauzy curtains of the doorway. She laid a hand on my back.

"You remind me of Laverne. When I first met her, she was about your age. Mad at the whole world, and with pretty good reason. Her quarrel was with her mother. Yours is with James, and you have a right to it. I'm not trying to take nothing away from you. You have a tough shell on you. Chaurisse, she doesn't have none of that."

"I don't feel sorry for her."

180

Miss Bunny said, "Dana, I wish James had seen fit to tell me about you earlier. I wish he had brought your mama up here today."

"She always wanted to meet you," I said.

Miss Bunny reclined in the hospital bed. "I really can't see a good way out of this."

We sat there a while longer, not saying anything to each other. I worked on my breathing, although the room smelled of camphor and just slightly of urine. Beside the bed was a bouquet of red roses that didn't give any scent at all.

"Take something of mine," Miss Bunny said. "Take anything you want out of this room."

I walked myself around the small bedroom. There wasn't much to choose from. On the dresser, where perfume bottles and figurines should have been, rested amber prescription bottles, a stack of rubber gloves, and a box of syringes. The only ornament was a porcelain ring holder in the shape of two fingers, displaying what looked like a man's wedding band. On the night table was a wooden jewelry box. Music tinkled out as I opened it. The only thing inside was a star-shaped brooch of faceted aquamarines.

"This?" I asked.

"Why did you pick that?"

I shrugged. "I just like it. It's pretty." I didn't know enough family history to know what mattered and what didn't. I chose the brooch the way I would choose something in a store.

"Good enough," she said. "I told Raleigh I wanted to wear that pin to my funeral."

I dropped it back into the music box. She had spoken the word *funeral* with a burst of air, like she had to force the word out. I twisted toward her, but she had turned her face toward the wall. "I can pick something else. Did somebody special give it to you?"

"No. I bought it with my own money. Years ago, when I was still interested in looking pretty. A couple of the stones have fell out, but it's still a nice piece."

"Yes, ma'am."

"I'll tell Raleigh to take it off my collar before they close the casket and put me in the ground."

"Ma'am," I said, "please don't say things like that."

My grandmother took my living hand in her dying one. "I never had no quarrel with the truth. I hope somebody says something like that at my wake."

10
UNCLE RALEIGH

In the summer 1978, my mother had come to a crossroads. I am neither religious nor superstitious, but there is something other-worldly about the space where two roads come together. The devil is said to set up shop there if you want to swap your soul for something more useful. If you believe that God can be bribed, it's also the hallowed ground to make sacrifices. In the literal sense, it's also a place to change direction, but once you've changed it, you're stuck until you come to another crossroads, and who knows how long that will be.

Although I was only nine, I was away from home two weeks that summer. My god-mother, Willie Mae, took me to Alabama to spend some time with her family out in the country. She thought I was too much of a city girl, that I needed to spend some time barefoot. Drawing my bath each night in the footed tub, Willie Mae looked more capable than she did in our living room drinking gin-and-tonics with my mother. Out in the country, she drew her hair back in two plaits and tucked the ends under; she stuck her feet in her shoes bare-legged.

I was accustomed to hot, muggy summers, but the heat in Opelika was more comprehensive. August was canning season, so the women were busy washing tomatoes, peaches, and beets. Willie Mae was saving her money to buy two window air conditioners; in the meantime we kept cool with window-box and funeral-home fans. The front door flapped behind what seemed an endless parade of Willie Mae's nieces, nephews, and cousins, who stole eggs from the icebox to see if they could actually fry them on the blacktop road. Across the street, a lady sold Styrofoam cups of frozen Kool-Aid for a dime, but my mother had told me not to eat from strange people's houses. I spent most of the time in the kitchen, up under Willie Mae, who would stumble over me from time to time. The atmosphere was thick with the sugary smell of boiling fruit. I would lick my forearm and taste salt.

At night, I shared a pull-out bed with Willie Mae, who dusted herself all over with talcum powder cut with cornstarch. I missed my own room, the noises of the city, and my beautiful mother. "Why didn't she call me today?"

Willie Mae arranged the sweat-damp sheet around me. "She can't call you every day. She loves you. I love you. Raleigh loves you. Everybody loves you. All you have to do is go to sleep and be patient."

I didn't know how to respond to this, so I settled myself down onto the oversoft pillow.

"She's coming for you, Dana. You can take that to the bank."

I learned things those two weeks in Alabama. I learned how to diaper a baby, how to hang clothes on the line so that the linens hide your ladythings. I learned how and when to kneel during a Catholic service and I learned that there are grown men who find little girls to be very pretty.

Willie Mae's uncle, Mr. Sanders, asked me to sit on his lap after church. I refused the gum he offered, but I climbed onto his lap because I didn't know that I could deny an adult any favor. I sat myself across his knees, but he tugged me toward him until the small of my back was flush against his abdomen and the top of my head fit in the nook beneath his chin. He was still wearing his green tie from mass as he bounced me on his thighs, breathing into my ear with breath that smelled of apple cores.

Willie Mae walked into the bedroom wearing only her slip, stained at the waist with sweat.

"Sanders," she said, "you put that girl down and stay the fuck away from her. Touch her again and I'll cut you, nigger. You know I will." She caught me under my arms and pulled me away.

Her uncle said, "I wasn't doing her nothing."

"You are a nasty dog, Sanders," Willie Mae said. "Get out of here."

The uncle ambled out and Willie Mae hugged me hard. "You okay? You all right, Dana? What happened?"

"Nothing," I said.

"You sat up on his lap and that was all? He didn't touch you anywhere?"

"No," I said.

"Lord have mercy."

"But —"

"But what?"

"But could he touch me and I wouldn't know it?"

Willie Mae hugged me again and gave a relieved little laugh. "Lord," she said. "Stay close to me till your mama comes for you."

"I want to go home."

"I know you do, but you just got a few days more. Gwen has some things to take care of."

That night, she placed a collect call to my mother. The very next day, I was sitting on the front porch with Willie Mae hulling peas when I saw the old Lincoln coming down the road.

Willie Mae squinted toward the car and the dust kicked up by its wheels. "Dana, your eyes are young. Tell me who's driving."

"It's the old Lincoln. That's Uncle Raleigh."

"Praise Jesus," said Willie Mae. "Praise him."

I wondered what my mother would say about the way I looked. I had ignored Willie Mae's mother's warning that I shouldn't play in the sun; my complexion, already dark, deepened into something richer. With my press and curl all sweated out, I scratched my dirty scalp as Raleigh helped my mother out of the car. She was dressed in a light blue suit and a hat to match. Even her shoes were the same swimming-pool shade.

"Did you do it?" Willie Mae asked.

"Not yet," Raleigh said.

"I didn't want to do it without Dana," my mother said.

"Do what?" I asked.

"Willie Mae," my mother said, "is there someplace I can talk to Dana in private?"

Willie Mae looked around us at all the kids playing in the yard. She looked toward the interior of her mother's house, which was certainly packed with women canning vegetables. "Sorry, Gwen. This place is all booked up."

Raleigh said, "Take my keys. You two can sit in the car. Make sure you turn on the air."

My mother took my hand and smiled. "You look like a wild animal."

Behind me, Raleigh took my seat beside Willie Mae and started snapping peas. She leaned over and whispered something to him that made him smile.

Raleigh wanted to marry my mother. That Wednesday over Tonk he put his cards on the table, in more ways than one. He said, "Gwen, you deserve something better than this. You deserve to be somebody's only wife."

She didn't take him seriously at first. She said, "Pick up your hand, I can see all your cards and that takes the fun out of it."

"I'm serious."

She laughed. "Well, do you have someone

in mind? Do you know somebody that wants to take me away from all of this?"

"I'm serious, Gwen," he said. "I have been thinking about this for a few years now, and I want to make a real commitment to you and to Dana."

My mother placed her cards on the table facedown, like she thought that they could pick up their game once this awkward conversation was through. "What are you saying, Raleigh? What are you saying to me exactly?"

"I am asking you to marry me. To be my wife. Legally. Respectfully."

My mother got up from the table and went to the couch and sat herself on the space where the cushion was split. Raleigh followed her. He was so long and lanky that he moved like something engineered to bend with the breeze.

Raleigh kept talking. "We can get our own house and live like ordinary people. I am already Dana's father on paper, so there is nothing complicated to figure out. And don't worry about James. He'll come around. He's got to see that it's not fair the way that he's been able to live for the past nine years. He'll have to see that it makes sense for you and me to be together. It will be better for Dana. James, he's got more

already than any one person can hope for."
He took my mother's hands and held them
to his mouth. "What do you say, Gwen?"

"You haven't said that you love me," my
mother said. "Why are you doing this? You
don't love me."

"Yes, I do," Raleigh said. "I love you
something terrible. I love you to my bones.
I love you, Gwendolyn Yarboro."

"No, you don't," my mother said.

"Yes. I've loved you since that first day I
met you hiding in your bed at that rooming
house. Please, Gwen. Let's do this."

My mother said, "I don't know."

"You don't know what?" Raleigh said.
"You don't know if I love you or if you love
me?"

"I know for sure that I don't love you,"
my mother said. "Not in that way. But I
don't know if you love me, either."

Raleigh leaned back on the couch. "You
don't love me? Not at all?"

"I love you some," Gwen said. "But you
are my husband's brother. There's a different way you love your brother-in-law."

"You are not my brother's wife," said
Raleigh. "He is not my brother and you are
not his wife."

"I don't know," Gwen said.

"You know, Gwen," Raleigh said. "You

know it." He got up from the couch and put Louis Armstrong on the record player. "Dance with me," he said, holding his arms out.

"This is not a movie," my mother said, suddenly angry. "Dancing with you won't make this right or wrong. You are asking me to give up my whole life for this."

"I am asking you to marry me."

"I don't know, Raleigh," my mother said.

Five days later, she was dressed in her blue suit sitting with me in the back of the old Lincoln.

"Dana," my mother said. "What would you say about Uncle Raleigh becoming your new daddy?"

"What do you mean?"

"I mean, how would you feel if we went to go live with Uncle Raleigh and he would be your daddy and I would still be your mother — I will always be your mother, there's no changing that ever — but it would be me, you, and Raleigh living together."

"You can do that?"

"People can do whatever they want."

I thought it over while scratching the mosquito bites on my legs. "What about James? I can't have two daddies, can I?"

"James will always be your father."

"So what about Uncle Raleigh?"

"Okay," my mother said. "It's like this. When you get older, you will say to people, 'My real father didn't raise me. My mother married my uncle and so I think of my uncle as my father.' You get it?"

"No."

"Dana," my mother said, "let's try this from another direction. If you could pick just one daddy, who would it be? Raleigh or James?"

"I don't know."

"It's up to you, Dana. Tell me what you want, because all I want is what's best for you."

"If we pick Raleigh to be my daddy, would James be mad at us?"

My mother said, "Yes."

"What about Uncle Raleigh? If you say he can't be my daddy, will he be mad at me?"

"His feelings will be hurt."

"Will he cry?"

My mother thought it over for a moment. "He might cry, but not when you are around. You won't have to look at him crying."

In the back of the Lincoln, I felt comfortable and cool for the first time in almost two weeks. I wished my mother and I could stay there forever, mulling over our options, being loved by my father and Raleigh at once.

"I don't want to hurt Uncle Raleigh's feelings."

"Me either, honey, but somebody's going to get hurt in this. There's no getting around it." She gathered me against her even though she was so clean and pretty and I was Alabama-dirty and sorghum-sticky. "I love you, Dana," she said. "I love you more than anyone." She pressed her face into my filthy hair. "You are my life."

I used to love her desperate love for me, her weighty kisses. Hers was an electric affection burning away everything it touched, leaving me only with the clean lines of a lightning rod.

"Mama," I said.

"Yes?"

"What about James? If we go off with Raleigh, he'll just live with his wife and his other girl?"

"Yes."

"That's not fair."

"Not fair to who, baby?"

"It's not fair that they get to just have James all by theirself."

"No," my mother said. "It's not fair."

"Why can't they be the ones to go be with

Raleigh?"

"It doesn't work like that," my mother said.

My mother sat beside me, leaving everything in my nine-year-old hands. I couldn't bear the idea of Chaurisse having my father all to herself, calling him Daddy and living her life like she was in a Beverly Cleary book. Even then, I understood Raleigh to be a good person, an excellent uncle, but an uncle wasn't the same thing as a daddy. There wasn't any such thing as a "new daddy." You got one father in the beginning, and that was it.

Through the tinted glass of the Lincoln, the scene on the front porch looked foreboding, as though a storm had come to town like a sinister carnival. Raleigh had his camera aimed at Willie Mae, who laughed and tossed a handful of pea hulls at him. He pressed the shutter again and again.

(In 1988, when we buried Willie Mae, I wanted to put one of those pictures on her funeral program, but my mother said she wouldn't have wanted to look so country. I have them still, in a silver box, beside my gold earrings.)

"Will we still get to see Uncle Raleigh if he's not my new daddy?"

My mother nodded. "Raleigh's like us. He

doesn't have anywhere else to go."

"Let's just keep it like it is," I said. "Can we do that?"

My mother and I got out of the car together. She held my hand as though I were a flower girl. As we approached the porch, Raleigh stood up, sending a shower of purple-tinted hulls to the floor, some landing on his just-shined shoes.

"We need to talk to you," my mother said.

"All right," Raleigh said.

"In private," my mother said.

Willie Mae took my arm with the same firm grip she'd used just the night before when snatching me away from her uncle. "Leave her here with me, Gwen. Don't get her all tangled up in grown folks' business."

My mother let me go; my free hand fell to my side.

"There's no privacy," Willie Mae said. "Except in the car."

Raleigh said, "I don't want to talk in the car. I don't want to get in that car." He was getting antsy, shifting his weight around, causing his camera to bounce on his chest against his pretty yellow tie.

"Go out in the back, then," Willie Mae said. "You'll have to go through the kitchen, but you can be alone out there."

They went into the house, saying "Excuse me" to the women and cousins clustered there. They would be confused until we had gone, and Willie Mae would explain that Raleigh wasn't really a white man, he just looked like one. At least one person would claim to have suspected it all along.

I sat back on the porch with Willie Mae and the pan of peas. She broke the seal of each pod with her fingernail and shoved the glossy peas out with her thumb.

"She's out there breaking his heart, huh?" Willie Mae said, without looking over at me.

"We are going to keep everything like it is," I said.

Willie Mae shrugged. "It's her life."

I struggled for a while with the peas, while Willie Mae's hands zipped through the task.

"She asked me who I wanted for my daddy."

"She did?"

"I told her I wanted to keep my same daddy."

"Gwen should know better than to put that weight on you."

"Is she going to tell Uncle Raleigh that I didn't want him for my daddy?"

Willie Mae put the pan of peas on the floor near her feet. "No, honey. Gwen would never sell you down the river like that.

Whatever you want to say about her when you get grown, you can never say that she betrayed you."

Raleigh and my mother had their conversation in the backyard among the laundry. The sheets provided wet curtains, sealing them in with the clean-soap sweetness and the unforgiving scent of bleach. They were standing where Willie Mae had taught me to hide the secret things, the clothes you didn't want visible from the street. I asked her to hang all my things there, not just my underwear, but my shorts, T-shirts, socks, even the towels I used. She laughed but did as I asked.

Willie Mae and I moved ourselves to the kitchen, where the women stirred pots and wiped sweat from their faces. We kept our eyes on the screen door, but we couldn't see anything but the sheets, still and impassive.

"Just keep your ears open," Willie Mae said. "You never know what a man will do when you try and quit him."

"Uncle Raleigh is not going to do nothing to my mama."

"This is not about your uncle, honey. It's just about being grown. Just listen for anything that doesn't sound right."

197

I listened, but all I heard was the sounds of canning. I couldn't make out their voices. I didn't hear the click of the camera shutter, but I know that Raleigh took pictures; I've seen them. Close-ups of Mother's face, eyes cast down. There is a photo of just her feet, the slender heels of her satin pumps sinking into the Alabama dirt. There is one of the palm of her hand covering the lens. The last in the series are six or seven of his own stricken face, his arms extended to hold the camera. These he must have taken once my mother had left him out there with the laundry, running to the kitchen and Willie Mae's waiting arms.

"I told him," she said.

"What did you say?" Willie Mae wanted to know.

"I told him that I couldn't do it to Dana. That she needed her real father. He started saying, 'Do you love me, Gwen? Do you love me, Gwen?' I told him that this wasn't the point, that it wasn't a game."

"Are you okay?" Willie Mae said.

"Yes," my mother said. "It could have been worse. It could have been so much worse."

I stood at the screen door staring out at the sheets. We had hung them out early in the morning, but here is was after noon and they were still sopping wet. Under the house, puppies whined, waiting for Willie Mae's mother to set out yesterday's table scraps. The puppies were fluffy and pretty, but I wasn't allowed to touch them, because they hadn't had any shots.

I pushed open the screen door.

My mother said, "What are you doing?"

"I'm just looking at the puppies," I said. "I won't touch them."

"Okay," my mother said.

I opened the door and eased outside. As the screen door slammed against the frame, I ran to the clothesline. A wet sheet hit against my face as I pushed by it. I found Uncle Raleigh standing, staring up at the sky.

"Hey, Uncle Raleigh," I said.

He didn't answer.

"Are you mad at me?"

"Naw, Dana," he said. "I could never be mad at you. You are a sweet girl."

"Do you want to take my picture?"

He shook his head. "I am tired of taking pictures for now. I'll take your picture next time." He sat down on the earth, which was wet with the drippings from the clothes. "Dana, I've had a very hard life," he said, holding his arms out. "Come sit with me for a while."

I remembered Willie Mae's uncle, who had said the same thing. I shook my head. "I'm not allowed."

"That's fine," he said, and I pushed through the wet curtain of sheet. "Tell her I'll be there in a minute," he said. "Tell her I'm getting myself together."

The drive from Opelika to Atlanta is about two hours if you take I-85 straight down. Raleigh opted to take the surface streets, saying that he wanted to see the countryside. My mother argued at first, saying that she didn't want to be three black people in a nice car roaming around the back streets of Dixie. Raleigh said any redneck passing by wouldn't see three black people, they would see a white man, a black woman, and a little girl. When we passed the sign to get on the interstate highway, he didn't put on his turn signal and instead kept driving along the two-lane road. He slowed a bit at every intersection, giving my mother the chance to ask him to change course.

11
THE PRIZEWINNER

As my junior year came to a close, and I started thinking about college applications, James assured me many times that Chaurisse was going to Spelman College, right here in Atlanta. "She's a stay-at-home girl," he said. "Takes after her mama, just like you take after yours." He spoke with conviction, without even a flutter of a stammer, but how could I trust his report? I, better than anyone, understood the limits of my father's ability to predict the desires, actions, and motivations of a teenage girl. Besides, James had not been right since his mother died.

After Miss Bunny's funeral, James spoke softly, ate less. He lost track of himself, leaving his hat on after he'd entered the house, calling my mother and me by the names of our rivals. How could we bring ourselves to be angry with him, pitiful as he was? The stubble growing on his chin was stiff and spiked with white. When he took off his jacket, I could see that he ironed only the collar of his white shirt, leaving the rest rough-dried. He had repaired his glasses with an unfolded paper clip.

My worried mother asked me to catch the school bus, so I would be at home within an hour of the final bell, so that someone would be at the apartment if my father were to drop by. She had beat me home one May afternoon and found him waiting on the back porch, cracking his knuckles until they were swollen and sore. When he stood up, the grime from the rusty chair left a butterfly across the seat of his good wool trousers.

"James needs us right now," my mother said.

He didn't show up very often, so I spent many afternoons alone in the apartment, reordering the keepsakes atop my chest of drawers, leafing through college brochures, and longing for Ronalda's basement hideaway. When we passed each other between classes one Thursday, she pressed a skinny joint into my hand, folded over in a discarded sandwich bag. At home, I turned on the bathroom fan and pulled open the thin paper, touching my tongue to the crease, but getting high without Ronalda only made me paranoid and depressed.

When my father did come over on those early afternoons, he quizzed me about my only conversation with Miss Bunny.

"What did she say to you?"

"I already told you."

"You didn't tell me word for word."

"I don't remember word for word. Do you want me to get you an ashtray? Do you need a gin-and-tonic?"

"Would you get one for me?"

I set his gin-and-tonic on a coaster in front of him while he tamped his cigarette pack against his knee.

"How's school?"

"Good."

"Are you working on your college applications?"

"I'm just sending off to Mount Holyoke. That's the only place I want to go. Okay?"

"I told you that you don't have to worry about it. Mount Holyoke is expensive, but I am going to pay for it. Did you tell that to Miss Bunny?"

"How do you know Chaurisse isn't applying to Mount Holyoke?"

"She's not applying."

"But how do you know?"

He took a swig of his drink. "She doesn't like cold weather. Now answer my question

203

about your grandmother. Did you tell her that I was going to pay for you to go to college?"

"She didn't ask me."

"You should have found a way to work it into conversation. What all did you say to her? I know I asked you before, but just run it all by me one last time."

He worried so much about it that my mother started worrying, too, although I had given her the details as soon as I came home that evening. I had told her everything, after describing the shiny blue brooch that was to be my only inheritance. When I reported that James had told Miss Bunny that my mother was dead, she gasped as though she had been poked in a delicate place, and then she let go only a couple of tears before gathering herself together. It was not the first time that I had seen my mother cry, but the experience troubled me in the pit of myself.

"I ask for so little," she said.

"I know, Mother."

When she came to me three months later, inquiring again about the details of my conversation with Miss Bunny, I said, "I told you everything that there is to tell. You don't want to go through it all again?"

She said, "When you told me before, I was

distracted by the shock of it. I just want to know, now, for the sake of information. Your father is tied up in knots and I am just trying to understand why."

"I don't know what he wants me to say. He asks me every time, and I don't know what I am supposed to say."

Mother sat down and took off her nursing shoes. "This is so peculiar." In the kitchen, she filled a basin with warm water, adding a scoop of Epsom salts and a squirt of soap before putting it down in front of the couch, letting the sudsy water slosh onto the carpet. She slid her feet into the basin. "My guess, Dana, is that she said something to him. People say all sorts of things on their deathbeds. At the very end, they just disappear inside themselves, but a couple of days before, they speak from the heart. She must have said something about us." My mother smiled and touched my shoulder. "Whatever you did, you must have represented us well." She wiggled her feet in the basin, soaking the carpet again. "Keep your fingers crossed. Sometimes change is good."

Ronalda wasn't worried about college applications. She had already made the decision to go to Southern University in Baton Rouge. She had long admired the school's marching band and hoped to be chosen as a Dancing Doll. I showed her the brochures from Mount Holyoke and the computer-generated letter that urged me to apply.

"Look how nice it is," I said.

"Are you sure you want to live up there with all those white people?" Ronalda asked.

"It's a good school," I said.

"Yeah," she said. "But living here, you don't know anything about white people. Where I'm from, everything is mixed. In Atlanta, at least out here where we stay at, everything is so black that y'all don't know what it feels like to be black."

"That doesn't make sense," I said.

"You'll see," she said. "You get out to Holyoke with those white people and you will see exactly what I mean."

"All I'm worried about," I told her, "is that Chaurisse will pop up and say she is going to Mount Holyoke. It will be the same as Six Flags, but worse."

"I still can't believe that," Ronalda clucked.

"I can't believe it either," I said. "You would think I would be used to his shit."

But I wasn't. Six Flags Over Georgia provided the most attractive summer employment for a teenager in Atlanta. Ronalda and I had planned to apply together, but she ended up making better money taking care of her little brother. After three interviews, I was offered the chance to spin cotton candy onto paper cones for a nickel over minimum wage. My first choice would have been patrolling the park, posing families for photos. Still, I was happy enough with the cotton-candy position; it would good practice in meeting people, and the money would come in handy, too. To fit in at Mount Holyoke, I would need Ivy League clothes, skirts and blazers. My mother liked the idea of me working, saying, "If you are going to try and get a hardship scholarship, you need some proof that you have held down a job before or else they will think you are just looking for a handout."

I hadn't even reported to HR to get my red-and-blue uniform and pin-on name tag when James arrived at Continental Colony bearing gifts. "I brought you a little something," he said, and I knew the news wasn't good.

He explained that Chaurisse, too, had applied for work at Six Flags. She would be strapping guests into a parachute ride called the Great Gasp.

I looked at my mother, who was busy filling two glasses with ice. Her face didn't flicker with anger, she just looked tired. I bit down hard on my lip. How could I not have anticipated this? Of course Chaurisse wanted to work at Six Flags. Everyone did. And of course she would get the job. She got everything.

"I'm sorry, Dana. I didn't know until now." James extended an orange paper sack in my direction, but I didn't reach for it.

"Take it," he said, pulling an album from the bag. Michael Jackson was wearing a white suit and cuddling a pair of tiger cubs. "I got it at Turtles. Don't you collect stamps from there?" James nudged me with the corner of the cardboard album jacket.

I crossed my arms over my chest. "I don't listen to albums. I like cassettes."

"It's n-n-new," he said.

"I got the job first," I said. "I've even been fitted for a uniform."

"Things happen," James said. "Things happen. What do you want me to do?"

I knew what I wanted him to do, but I also knew it could never happen.

My mother breezed in from the kitchen and handed James his gin-and-tonic. She handed me a glass of orange juice.

"So how will Dana spend the summer? I prefer something educational. Maybe you could come up with a small stipend for her. She was counting on having pocket change this summer." My mother was calm. This must be how she talks to patients who refuse to take their medicine. She lets them know they don't have a choice by speaking very quickly and pronouncing all her consonants.

By the time my father left, it was determined that I would be given twenty-five dollars a week, fifteen of which would go into my savings account and the rest into my pocket. I would also be given a summer membership to a correspondence course to help students score high on the SAT. My mother was satisfied; my father thought he had gotten off cheap; and I was still furious.

I passed the rest of June and most of July figuring out how to make educated guesses on multiple-choice questions when I had no idea what the answer was. This strategy was different from the one you were supposed to employ when you could at least rule out one of the options. It was not just a guessing game; it felt more like a kind of specialized lying. Raleigh came by on Thursdays to play cards with my mother, and he would quiz me on my vocabulary words. He photographed me memorizing a dictionary page. Years later, he sold that shot to the United Negro College Fund, along with a photo of Ronalda reading *The Color Purple* while balancing her little brother on her hip and at the same time flipping a grilled cheese.

It was not the best summer of my life, but it was manageable, until my mother was attacked at the mailboxes in the front of our apartment complex. The holdup man stole the mail and her handbag. Even worse, he pulled out a leather-handled knife and helped himself to a hank of her hair. The bald spot, just above her left ear, was about the size of a Kennedy fifty-cent piece. She easily covered it with all the shiny hair she had left, but her fingers worried the spot, making her seem nervous and old.

"The neighborhood is going down," she said. "Seventeen years ago, these were nice apartments. I was never worried about checking my mailbox. I used to walk around at two, three o'clock in the morning."

"I know, Mother."

"I hope you meet a good man when you go to Mount Holyoke. I am not saying that you need to find a Rockefeller or a football star. Just someone who will understand that you have obligations, who won't mind helping out a bit. I can't live here by myself."

When my mother's hair was stolen, I had been watching *The Cosby Show* while sipping from a can of grape soda. She opened the door calmly, locked it behind her, and walked to the couch, where I fanned myself with a magazine. She fell to her knees, took the magazine away, and guided my fingers through her hair.

"Can't James help us find another place?" I asked her.

"Your father has promised to sponsor your education," she said. "That's the best he can do. Bigamy is expensive."

I expected her to reward her own joke with a dry, angry laugh, but she just held her hand over my own, pressing my finger-tips onto the nubby patch.

"Don't forget me," she said as I rocked her on my lap, awash in a briny mix of guilt and gratitude.

But in the weeks following, I grew tired of her unhappiness, the impossible weight of it.

"It will grow back," I said. I grabbed a handful of my own hair, so much like hers, and said, "I would give you some of mine if I could."

"Don't try and act like you don't understand what's going on here," she said.

I spent as much time as I could away from the apartment. I was sick of my mother's compulsive tidiness, as though we were always expecting guests. I wanted to live in a house with walls painted in various shades of blue and green, instead of the eggshell hue that screamed renter. I used some of my summer stipend to buy a MARTA pass, so I could have unlimited access to the 66 Lynhurst. Marcus was home, but packing as he prepared to move to Chapel Hill. Ruth Nicole Elizabeth was still his girlfriend, but he and I spent time together in the mornings; by lunch we were done and I walked across the street to Ronalda's.

When I needed her to, she smoothed hickeys from my neck and chest. Calling Marcus "Count Chockula," she carefully pressed the blemish with the teeth of her comb, dispersing the blood gathered under my skin. When she'd done all she could, I covered the marks with foundation and said, "Want to play on the phone?"

I kept Laverne's business card in my purse, even though Ronalda and I had both memorized the number; the shiny finish had broken down with the oil of my dirty hands. The card was from the stack my mother hid in the kitchen, behind the flour canister. I liked the logo — a languid fox lazing across the letters. MRS. LAVERNE WITHERSPOON, PROPRIETRESS. "Playing on the phone" meant that we would call the Pink Fox pretending to be potential customers. Ronalda asked how much for a press-and-curl. Chaurisse, at least we thought it was her, said twenty-eight dollars with a cut. Ronalda said thank you and hung up. "Too rich for my blood," she said. I called once from school. "I want to know how much it is to get a Jheri curl?" This time, I was pretty sure I was talking to Laverne. "That depends. Would you like to come in for a consultation?"

Ronalda unplugged the telephone from her parents' room, took it down to the basement, and plugged it into the empty jack in her stepmother's study. We got in the habit of calling several times a week, disguising our voices and asking about elaborate services. "How much is it to just get a press without a curl?" "What is the cost of relaxer on virgin hair?" "What about finger waves?" "Do you take walk-ins?"

"That's what we should do," Ronalda said. "We should just walk in one day."

"No," I told her. "No way. If I were to get caught over there, that would be the end of my family."

Halfway through that miserable summer, Raleigh won a local contest for photography that earned him a four-hundred-dollar prize; the winning photo, taken in the days after Miss Bunny's death, was displayed in Greenbriar Mall for sixty days. The photo focused on Laverne as she was preparing herself to give Miss Bunny her very last hairdo. In the image, Laverne is slack-faced with sorrow while the straightening comb steams on the undertaker's hot plate. In the background is Chaurisse, wearing a plastic apron and looking over her shoulder to where Miss Bunny lies, out of the frame, lifeless and not yet adorned. My mother visited the prizewinning photo, standing close enough that her breath mottled the glass.

"There is something beautiful about that," she said. "Laverne is not my favorite person, but nobody can say that she didn't do her duty."

I also looked at the photograph, but my attention was on my sister. She was getting prettier as we grew older. Her features seemed to be settling into her face.

"What would happen to me if you were to die?" I asked my mother.

"You're almost eighteen. You don't need to worry about it."

"But what if you were to die tomorrow?"

"I won't die tomorrow."

My mother and I bought ice-cream cones from Baskin Robbins and ate them as we watched people take in the image. The caption read only GOING TO GLORY, so people didn't know what to make of it. "I can't believe they gave him four hundred dollars for that" was a common response. Some other people took a moment to just stare in silence and then went away disquieted.

"This is probably not the best idea," I said to my mother.

She smiled a very bright smile. "Are you reading my mind?"

I smiled back, pleased with our connection. I stood up to leave and she followed suit, dumping the rest of her ice cream into the trash can. She approached the prizewinner, hanging on the wall in between the eye doctor and the rent-to-own place. Because she stood so close, her reflection layered over the images in the frame.

"Mother," I said, "I thought we were leaving."

"These people are not better than us," my mother said, through clenched teeth. "We have everything that they have. I work hard every day. I have my associate's degree. She's only been to beauty school. And you are a better daughter. We are better people."

She was so near the photo now that her

lipstick marked the glass.

"Come on," I said, taking her by her arm. "Let's just go."

"You're fine, aren't you, Dana? You feel okay about your childhood, right?"

"Yeah," I said. "I'm okay."

"Because you know that a lot of black children never know their fathers."

"Chaurisse doesn't know her father," I said, trying to make her laugh.

My mother looked to the left and then to the right, like she was about to cross the street. Then she took the frame by its edges and lifted it upward until the wire on the back disconnected from the hanger. She tucked the portrait under her arm like she had paid for it.

"Let's go," she said.

"Mother, you have to put that back."

"I don't have to do anything," she said, striding for the door, looking determined and weirdly professional.

I jogged to catch up with her and reached for the frame, but she swept it from my reach. She made it through the double doors and into the back parking lot. She was running now, laughing like she had just stolen the *Mona Lisa*. Mother outpaced me, partly because my jellies, a half size too small, cut into my heels with every step, but partly because she was on fire with something I couldn't feel. The wind pulled her hair up as she ran, exposing the blank space.

"Mother," I called after her, "please slow down."

"I can't," she called over her shoulder. "I just can't."

■ ■ ■ ■

PART II
BUNNY CHAURISSE
WITHERSPOON

■ ■ ■ ■

12
A Peculiar Start

My family story starts in Ackland, Georgia, in 1958, when my mother, Laverne Witherspoon, was fourteen years old.

She had worn her Easter dress, lilac cotton with pressed pleats. At the time, this dress was her greatest achievement. Even in church, when the preacher led everyone in prayer, she found her attention pulled away by her beautiful sleeves and careful embroidery. Now it was to be her wedding gown. For a moment, Mama thought that maybe this was her punishment for thinking too much of herself, for spending too much money on the slick nylon lining. When Mama had twirled on Easter Sunday before church, her mother said, "You look like a bride."

Now, my Grandmamma Mattie pulled the used-to-be Easter dress from the chifforobe and tossed it on the bed where my mama lay, still as a cadaver. "Come on, Laverne,"

Mattie said. "The boy says he's going to marry you."

My mama still didn't move. Mattie pulled the covers back and found my mama naked except for her panties, ashy except for her tear-shiny face, and skinny except for her bulging-already stomach. Mattie made a couple of idle threats and even tried talking sweet, the way a mother is supposed to, but finally she set about dressing Mama the way you change the sheet out from under an invalid.

"You need to be out in the streets rejoicing, instead of making believe you're dead." Mattie jerked the bodice up over my mama's hips. Mama whimpered at the sound of the careful seams giving way, but she didn't help or resist as Mattie propped her into a sitting position. "What kind of mother are you going to be? You can't be stupid and be a decent mama."

My mama was so stunned, she couldn't speak. She didn't hardly even know my daddy yet. Like everybody else in town, she recognized him by his thick and square glasses, ugly as army issue. She knew his name and what church he and his mother went to. His father was long dead and his mama was a live-in for white people, so she left Daddy and Uncle Raleigh alone in the

222

house six days out of the week. This is what everybody knew about my daddy.

This mess came as a consequence of her cousin Diane falling in love with Uncle Raleigh. Love is what Diane called it, but Mama knew this to be a basic case of color-struckness. Daddy and Uncle Raleigh were just juniors in high school, but Diane was a senior and was starting to look for a husband, one that she could make some pretty babies with. Mama had gone in the first place only because Diane didn't want to go to the boys' famously unsupervised home by herself, leaving people plenty of room to speculate. So Mama went along with her cousin after school, and when her cousin disappeared with Uncle Raleigh, Mama was by herself with Daddy. This whole situation was just a matter of who was sitting next to who, when. Next thing Mama knew, there was a baby growing inside her and there was nothing that anyone could do about it. At fourteen, my mama couldn't believe that the events of one clumsy evening had led to this. She hadn't even known it was possible.

When Mama stopped being able to hold down her lunch, she was worried, but it was the burnt-penny taste in the back of her mouth that sent her to see Miss Sparks. From eight until noon, Miss Sparks served

223

in the capacity of school nurse, but Mama liked her best as the home ec teacher who praised her sewing. Miss Sparks was known for her high-pitched voice that sounded almost like opera when she scolded rowdy students with her trademark refrain: "Negro people! Remember your dignity." Miss Sparks's gentle reminder could break up a fistfight between boys or a squabble between girls. Once, when a silver bracelet had gone missing, a word from Miss Sparks had inspired the thief to return it, newly polished and wrapped in a sheet of tissue.

Mama told her mother everything Miss Sparks had said about her condition, but she didn't share the home ec teacher's parting words: "What a waste." This is what Mama was thinking of while Mattie dressed her; this was the memory that froze her in her place, aggravating Mattie so bad that she slapped my Mama's mouth for having the nerve to cry.

The morning after Miss Sparks told her she was wasted, and the day before her Easter dress turned into a wedding gown, Mama got up at 7 a.m. and ironed herself a blue blouse with a Peter Pan collar. She was boiling a pan of water for her bath when Mattie stumbled into the kitchen, sleepy-eyed and hungover.

"What you doing, Laverne?"

"Getting ready for school."

Mattie held my mama's arm. "They didn't tell you? You can't go to school no more."

"Oh," Mama said. "Oh," she said again, hanging the white-collared blouse in her closet and turning down the fire under the pan of bathwater.

Mama let her Murphy bed out, dressed it with heavy blankets despite the heat, and lay down. When her mother left to pick up the white people's laundry, Mama opened her eyes. "What a waste." She said it over and over.

The Henry County judge wouldn't do it, even though Mattie kept saying, "She's pregnant!" Mama cringed each time her mother pronounced the terrible word, which an emphasis on the first syllable. "She's *preg*nant!" The judge leaned over his disorderly desk and spoke to my mama.

"Are you pregnant?"

Mama looked to Daddy, who wore the clothes he wore to sing in the youth choir. Fresh white shirt and blue pants ironed with too much starch. Behind his glasses, Daddy looked, in turn, to Grandma Bunny. She was there, not in her Sunday best, but in a

good dress, the same green of unripe tomatoes. Mama let her eyes follow Daddy's and
waited for him to look back at her, but he
didn't. After searching his mother's face, he
turned to Uncle Raleigh, who just tugged
his shirtsleeves so that they would cover his
bony wrists.

"Young lady," the judge said.

"Sir," she said quietly.

"Are you pregnant?"

"Oh," Mama said.

Daddy spoke up. "I p-p-plan to own up to
m-m-my responsibilities, sir." He looked
again at Grandma Bunny, who gave him a
small but generous smile. Mama wondered
how it must feel for someone to be proud
of you like that.

"Son, nobody is addressing you. Young
lady . . ." he said again.

"I don't know," Mama said, hoping to
stop him before he said that awful word
again.

"You know," Mattie said.

The judge leaned over his desk a little
more. He had a reputation for being a
decent white man, much better than the
rest. Mattie's cousin kept house for his family for thirty-some years and nobody ever
laid a hand on her.

"You want to get married, gal? You want

226

to be a wife to this boy?"

"I don't know," Mama said again, looking now into the judge's face.

He settled back in his chair and fiddled with the tiny stone animals resting on his desk. He polished a quartz rabbit on his shirtfront before speaking. "I won't do it. I can't give you a license."

Mattie said, "What do you mean you can't? I'm her mother. There's his mother. We give our permission."

The judge shook his head. "The girl is not giving consent."

"But she's pregnant," Mattie Lee said. "What would you do for your own child?"

"I can't do it," the judge said.

"We'll just go to Cobb County, then," Mattie Lee said.

"You'll just have to." The judge looked up at the wall clock. "You can do it tomorrow. Today is done with."

On the second attempt, only Daddy dressed up. Mama wore the blouse she'd ironed on the day she found out she couldn't go back to school. Grandma Bunny was absent, as she couldn't get a second day off from her job, but the white folks did lend the car, a Packard, which Daddy drove the twenty miles to Cobb County. They left early, as

Marietta, Georgia, was not a good place to be colored after sundown; it was so racist that they had even lynched Jewish people.

Mattie sat up front with Daddy, with one hand on the dashboard to hold herself steady. In the backseat, Mama leaned herself against the door and Uncle Raleigh stretched his long pale arm over to touch her sleeve.

The second judge sold them the license without asking any questions of Mama or Daddy. He did look crooked at Uncle Raleigh. "You colored, son?"

"Yes, sir," Uncle Raleigh said.

"Just checking," the judge said, turning his face back toward the marriage license and signing his name in wet ink. Having done that, he held the document out in Daddy's direction, but Mattie plucked it out of his hands and snapped it into her A-frame pocketbook, clenched tight in the crook of her arm.

Taking my mama by the sleeve of the school blouse, she steered her toward the door. "Let's go, let's go, let's go."

Mama stumbled after her, while Daddy and Uncle Raleigh followed behind, close as brothers and separate from the urgency of women.

The boys lived like wild animals. This is what people said. Grandma Bunny was raising James by herself since his father got himself killed in a paper-mill accident. About that same time, Grandma Bunny took in Uncle Raleigh after his real mama, a redbone girl, ran off to have a better life for herself. Although she was light herself, she couldn't stand the look of him, that's what people said.

Grandma Bunny was a kindhearted woman, generous to orphans, mangy kittens, and other strays. Generations of cats lived under her house, fed on table scraps. Years later, when Grandma Bunny didn't have anyone to look after but herself, she bought kibble to mix in with the leftover oatmeal.

After the wedding, if you could call it that, although Mama didn't — she will go to her grave feeling that she had spent almost her whole life as a wife, without ever having been a bride — she went to her new home. Mama was alone in the house, while Daddy and Uncle Raleigh returned the white people's car. She peeked into the kitchen and found it to be much like the one in her mother's house, porcelain sink showing black where it was chipped, gas stove with two eyes, ice box. The bathroom looked about the same, too. Mama turned the knob on the left side of the sink and smiled when warm water gushed over her hand. At least there would be no heating up water just for a bath. Then she stopped grinning. She had never been naked in any home other than her own. Not even on the night that everything happened had she removed all her clothes. Lord, she wondered. What had she done? What had she gotten herself into?

Leaving the bathroom, she tiptoed into a bedroom that smelled of talcum powder. She figured that room for Grandma Bunny's. A large white Bible with gold-edged pages sat on a small night table. In a framed photograph, a man leaned up against an old car. Mama didn't linger over it, as her mother had a similar photo in her own bedroom; that one was a photo of Mama's father, and Mama assumed that this was James Senior. She envied his pose, leaning against the fender, head cocked, slanted smile. To Mama, this was the stance of a somebody who was never coming back.

Lastly, she entered the room that was to be James's and her own. The bed was so large that it embarrassed her. The bedspread was too narrow, not covering the sides of the mattresses. This was where she was to sleep at night, in her nightgown, just that thin covering of cotton. Here she would sleep next to James Witherspoon, a boy she hardly knew who was now her husband. What a word, *husband*. It didn't sound like it should have anything to do with her. Inspecting the bed more closely, she saw that this one large bed, the marriage bed, was actually a pair of singles pressed together. Looking around she figured out that this was the room that the boys shared. She had been so distracted by the bed, its sheer size, and insinuation, that she didn't see the clues that this was not a space a girl was meant to enter. It smelled faintly of boy: sweat, fried chicken, and fresh-cut grass. Mama went to the dint in the center of the bed and pushed until there was a gap between the mattresses. There was only one blanket, and she smoothed it over the bed that she decided would be Daddy's.

The boys. This is how she thought of them. She still calls them that, to this day. In the years that came after, she could think of Daddy as a man, and Uncle Raleigh as well, but she would always see the two of them as the boys they were when they returned from the long walk home after returning the car.

Daddy and Uncle Raleigh — "Salt and Pepper," some people called them, because of their coloring — were both hot and filthy. The crisp shirts they had worn to see the judge were damp now and musty. They fidgeted on their own front porch and rang the bell.

Mama opened the door for them. "Come on in," she said, like this was her house and not theirs, as though she were the lady of this house, as though she were a lady at all. "Y'all want some water?"

Daddy said, "Yeah." And Uncle Raleigh said, "Yes'm." This was funny somehow, and the three of them laughed.

"Y'all hungry?"

"Yeah," Daddy said. "Can you cook?"

Mama shrugged. "Depends on what you want to eat."

"I'm not hungry," Uncle Raleigh said.

"Y'all had something to eat over the white people's place?"

Daddy said, "No, we didn't eat n-n-nothing over there. M-m-mama sent us back here and said we needed to eat at home. She said we needed to get into a routine, with us coming home at a certain time, and you learning how to get the food ready and everything."

"Oh," Mama said.

Daddy went on, "And she said that I am supposed to show you where she keeps the starch and everything for the washing."

"I know how to do laundry already," Mama said.

"You don't have to wash none of my clothes," Uncle Raleigh said. "Miss Bunny says she'll keep doing my things same as always. You just have to take care of James because you're his wife now." Uncle Raleigh said this last part in a quiet voice that sounded almost ashamed.

Mama looked up at Daddy, who shrugged. "It's going to be okay. Once everybody gets used to everything. There's chicken in the icebox. Mama cut it up already. You just have to fry it. It'll be easy. And she said to tell you that you are welcome here."

"Y'all two are going to keep going to school?"

They looked at each other, confused-seeming. "Yeah."

"I can't go no more," Mama said quietly.

"Because you're married?" Uncle Raleigh said.

"No," James said. "Because she's p-p-p . . ."

The word seemed to stick in his mouth.

Mama had braced herself for it, but it was taking too long to be born.

"Pregnant," she said, finishing his sentence before spinning herself around and walking toward the kitchen.

This house seemed unsteady to her; the little blue cups in the china cabinet tinkled with her steps. She felt the eyes of the boys on her back as she made her way. It reminded her of the last time she had been here, when she came with her cousin Diane, who was not pregnant, who didn't even like Uncle Raleigh anymore. The house seemed different now, brighter. The days had been much shorter then; by 6 p.m. it was dark out and she could hardly see Daddy's face. He didn't stammer at all when asking her if she had ever kissed a boy. She said yes, although she hadn't. He asked her if she had done "anything else," and she nodded. And now she wondered why she had bobbed her head in that lie. He had seemed older then than he did now, three months later. Then he hadn't been parroting what all his mother had told him to do, what she had planned for him to eat. On that earlier day, it had seemed like he and Uncle Raleigh were the men of this house, that they lived here by themselves.

Mama recalled the black hairs sprouting

from Uncle Raleigh's Adam's apple as he had stirred liquor into the concoction in Grandma Bunny's punch bowl. The little glass cups hooked around the sides of the crystal bowl tapped against each other with a noise like holiday bells. It was a dignified object, this punch bowl, the sort of thing that Miss Sparks liked to talk about when she was teaching table manners. According to Miss Sparks, this was how you could tell the difference between crystal and regular glass. Mama had insisted on drinking her punch in the proper dainty-handled cup, laughed, and asked for more. The punch was somehow sweet and hot at the same time.

As he refilled her cup, she decided that she would have liked Raleigh, had her cousin not already claimed him for herself. She liked the way he always asked everybody how they were doing.

"How are you feeling?" he said to Laverne for no reason at all.

By this time, Daddy was sitting close to her and fondling her hair. She enjoyed the feel of his breath on her neck and even the sweet liquory smell. He placed a tingly kiss on the very spot under her hair that he'd been warming with his breath. "Is that fine?" he asked her.

She nodded, feeling wonderful and wanting more punch. She held out her cup, but Daddy took it away from her and put it on a cherry wood end table. "Don't drink too much," he said. "You don't want to get sick."

"Okay," she said, obedient as a child.

"Do you want to see my room?" Daddy asked her.

"Okay," she said again as he took her hand and pulled her to her feet.

Her cousin Diane, leaning against Uncle Raleigh's shoulder, said, "Don't do anything I wouldn't do."

The idea of this made Mama's head whirl. Diane was three years older and the possibilities seemed endless. She laughed again.

"James," Diane said, "take it easy with her. She's just fourteen and she's not used to drinking."

"Fifteen," Mama said, remembering the lie she'd told earlier in the afternoon. "Fifteen, remember?"

Uncle Raleigh said, "James knows how to act. Don't worry."

Diane put her hands on Uncle Raleigh's head. "You know you got some good hair," she said.

Mama pulled on Daddy's arm and he led her to the bedroom. "Let's give the lovebirds

236

some privacy."

It was a setup, a plan between the boys. They hadn't meant to change her life forever, to make a baby and provoke a premature marriage. It was just about the boys hoping to "get a little trim." These were Daddy's words to her, later that night after they'd eaten the dinner she'd ruined, chicken burnt at the skin, bloody at the bone. Daddy told her this that night, as they lay in the single beds, each on the other side of the gap. Mama slept in the clothes she'd gotten married in, her school blouse and skirt. She removed her shoes, but not her socks, and climbed into the bed. Daddy, she assumed was in his shorts and shirtless, but she didn't know for sure because she had turned her face away when he emerged from the bathroom. She didn't face him until he was under the covers, less than a foot away from her. His body smelled of strong soap and his breath carried the odor of baking soda.

"When is Miss Bunny coming back home?" Mama wanted to know. She was unsure what to think about this woman, Miss Bunny, whose instructions had led to the fiasco that was dinner and had caused her to spend what was left of the evening washing James's school shirts with lye soap and cranking the water out before hanging them on the line in her backyard while stray cats brushed against her legs. Her hands were still tender and she rubbed them together, concentrating on the throbbing.

"It's natural if you don't want to sleep in the bed with me right away," Daddy said. God bless Miss Bunny for words to her son, letting him know not to expect too much from his young wife. Her own mother had urged her not to be shy. "You don't want him to change his mind. Then where will you be?" Mattie Lee had said. "I'm not raising a baby for you, Laverne. I'm too old to start over."

"James," Mama said, "did you know that this is what was going to happen?"

He didn't say anything. He only breathed deeply with his eyes closed. Mama studied his face, which was softer-looking without his glasses. She observed the dip in his upper lip and the heat rash that stretched across his forehead. "Did you know?"

"Let me cut off the light," he said.

Daddy threw the covers off himself and knelt in the center of his bed, reaching upward for the frayed string connected to the yolk of light suspended from the ceiling. He was shirtless and under his arms grew patches of nappy hair; his chest was smooth as a crystal ball. He jerked the cord, killed the light. She could make out the shape of him as he settled himself back into bed.

"It wasn't supposed to be you. Your cousin Diane, she met R-r-raleigh at the picture show a day, maybe two days, before . . . you know, what all happened. She said she liked him and he asked her to come over to the house. She said that she didn't want to come by herself and Uncle Raleigh said that was just fine because he wanted her to bring a friend for me to meet. And Diane said she had a cousin here who was sixteen, same age as her. She didn't say your name. If she had said your name I w-would have said no way because you were too young to be sp-sp-spending time with us in that way."

Mama said, "But when I showed up, you knew it was me."

Daddy said, "I didn't mean for nothing to happen. We were all having a good time and you didn't seem scared or anything and everybody was just having a good time. You re-m-m-member, you were having a good time, weren't you?"

Mama remembered that day and she did have a good time. She couldn't forget the tinkle of the crystal cups against the crystal punch bowl and the sweet hot taste of the liquor. It had been fun. She could admit that much to herself, but not to Daddy. She knew that something wrong had been done unto her, that she was more sinned against than sinning and she wouldn't say that she had enjoyed herself, because that was all part of the trick, wasn't it? "I was too scared," she said.

"You didn't seem scared. You were asking me for more punch, remember? And I didn't let you have it because I didn't want you to get sick. I was trying to look out for you."

Mama whispered her next statement. She said it quietly, as it was a word more shameful than the one everyone kept saying, *pregnant*. This was a worse word than that, but she had to say it because it was a word that had been squirming in her throat since she found out that she couldn't go back to school. "James, was I raped?"

It took him some time to find the words. She could hear him making the tortured noises, not exactly grunts, as he tried to make his mouth, lungs, and voice box coordinate so he could speak. Mama who had been struck dumb herself several times in the past few days, pitied Daddy at that moment.

She asked him the question again, grateful in a strange way to be able to speak any words at all. "James, did you rape me?"

From his bed, there was a spasm of movement.

"No, m-ma'am," he said. "That is something I did not do. My mama asked me the same thing, she made me put my hand on top of her good Bible and tell her the truth. No. I have never forced myself on any girl. Can't nobody say that about me. And why you asking? You was there. You know that you laid yourself down on this very bed. Nobody pushed you."

And Mama did recall herself reclining, and no one had pushed her.

Daddy spoke slowly, letting each word out one at a time. "And I kept asking you if I was hurting you. I said, 'You okay?' and you didn't say nothing different. And you didn't cry. When it was all over you just put all your things back on and said good-bye to me. You said it real polite. You said, 'Good-bye, James.' And then you and your cousin left. I was on the front porch waving and you didn't even look back."

"But I didn't know," Mama said.

"You didn't know what? You didn't know you could get pregnant?"

In the dark of the bedroom in her pulled-apart marriage bed, Mama turned her face into the pillow. She had known she could get pregnant. Her mother had told her that when she first got her cycle, but she hadn't known exactly how it happened and that it could involve something as lovely as a cut-crystal punch set. She hadn't known it could happen so quickly, with so little pain and no blood at all. She hadn't known that there would be no proof for nearly two months, no sign whatsoever that anything was amiss. She hadn't known that the events of an afternoon could get her kicked out of school and thrown out of her mother's house. She missed her Murphy bed in the living room and the boiled bathwater. When she had withdrawn from school, they had taken her school books away from her. They were raggedy volumes, castoffs from the white-children's school, with their handwriting on the pages, giving away the answers before a person could figure them out for herself. Mama had gone through all her books with a rubber eraser, rubbing out all the marks that she could, and she covered each of them with book covers she fashioned herself from butcher paper and tape. If she couldn't have her books back, she wished now that she had been allowed to take those covers off. They were hers. She had made them herself.

After a while, Daddy said, "My mama also

says that a lot of good marriages get off to peculiar starts. People get together just like us, because of circumstances, and they are still together, so this doesn't mean nothing bad. And the only thing that matters, really, isn't how come two people happen to get married, but that the folks are married before the baby gets here. Nobody wants to say that their child is a bastard. That's the thing that's important." Then he lowered his voice. "Look at Raleigh. He's a bastard."

"My daddy never married my mama," Mama said. "I never seen the man."

"But that's okay. All you can think about is the future. That's what my mama says."

Mama lay in the dark. She had been wearing her girdle too long and her feet were starting to tingle. She longed for her mother. She had never slept anywhere but her own home. She pressed her hands to her abdomen. She knew that sometimes women died while having babies, and she thought that if she were lucky, this is what would happen to her.

After several minutes had passed, Daddy spoke again. "My mama also says that I shouldn't worry too much about you crying yourself to sleep. She says it is only natural, but that nobody should worry too much, because you'll cry yourself out in a couple days."

Mama was getting sleepy, but she had another question. "How's the baby going to get out of me?"

Daddy was stammering so hard, she thought that he was going to strangle. "T-t-talk to my mama. She'll explain everything to you."

"And she did," my mother told me, that day in the funeral home as we prepared Miss Bunny for her grave.

Mama kept saying, "Miss Bunny was good to me all my life, and we are going to do right by her. We are going to fix her up perfect." There wasn't much for me to do. I handed Mama what she needed and tried not to look at Grandma Bunny's frozen face. When I did peek, I had to admit that Mama did a fine job. Once Grandma Bunny was dressed, rouged, and finger-waved, there was no trace of the great sadness that weighed her down at the end. Mama held on strong until it was time to pin on the aquamarine brooch that Grandma Bunny had loved so much she wanted to be buried in it.

My father entered the room while Mama was fumbling with the brooch. She stuck herself with the pin and left a faint streak of red on Miss Bunny's collar. "D-d-don't worry about it," he said, slipping the brooch into his pocket. I turned away, staring into the hot plate, where the straightening comb steamed. Behind me, I heard the hiss of film advancing as Uncle Raleigh snapped our picture. As I was blinking from the flash he took three or four more.

"Don't worry, Raleigh," Mama told him. "We got Miss Bunny looking real nice. It was the least I could do."

Uncle Raleigh said, "I miss her already."

"Me, too," Mama said. "When my son was born, with the cord around his neck, just as dead as anybody, as still as Miss Bunny here on this table, she took care of me. She washed me, put me in bed, changed my linens."

By the time she delivered, Mama had gotten used to being married, used to living with Daddy and Raleigh. It was too late to go back to school; she wouldn't be allowed. After they buried that baby boy in the churchyard, she had said to Grandma Bunny, "You going to send me back?"

"Not unless you want to go," said Grandma Bunny.

"She did right by me, righter than rain, and

righter than my own mama," my mother said.

"I miss her," Uncle Raleigh said again. He turned away from where she lay on that metal table. My mama took the straightening comb from the hot plate and set it on a wet towel. While it sizzled, she turned toward Uncle Raleigh and laid her hands on his back and pressed her wet face to his clean shirt.

My father and I stood there, left out of their embrace. Miss Bunny was our blood relative; we weren't her took-ins, but we loved her, too. "C-c-come here," he said to me, spreading his arms. I sank into his hug, which smelled strong with tobacco, and maybe a trace of gin. He clapped me on the back like I was a baby with colic. I believe he kissed my hair. Against my cheek, I felt Grandma Bunny's brooch stashed in his lapel pocket. I pushed against it harder, hoping to emboss my face with the jeweled star pattern.

13
ONE HUNDRED PERCENT DRIVEN SNOW

"You never know," my mother said to me. "You never know what means what."

"True," I said. I was just nine years old, give or take, but I had learned not to interrupt my mother when she was on a roll, especially not when she was talking to me in the deep voice she used with the women in the beauty shop. She didn't talk this way to all of them, of course; different people got different treatment, just as some people had to pay for every clip of the shears and other people got their bangs straightened for free. On that day, in the car, she talked the way she did with the longtime customers, the ones who got their lips waxed on the house, the ones who called me "Miss Lady" and called my mother "Girl."

"George Burns cheated on Gracie," Mama said. "Can you believe that?"

I didn't believe or not believe it, as I wasn't absolutely sure who George Burns was. "The man who plays God in that movie?"

"Yes," she said. "Him. He hasn't always been old, you know. He was young and handsome and he was married to Gracie."

"Oh," I said. "I remember." This was the key. If I talked too much, asking her to clarify, she would remember I was a kid and then she wouldn't talk to me like this.

This was a long time ago, way back when Jimmy Carter made a fool of himself by telling *Playboy* magazine that he had committed adultery in his heart just by looking at pretty women and thinking the wrong kind of thoughts. My mama thought it was touching how devoted the president was to his wife, but my father got all discombobulated watching Johnny Carson crack jokes about it on TV. Daddy said, "He came home every night to Rosalynn, right? I tell you me, white folks look for things to worry about."

"I don't know," my mama said. "I like the last part of what he said, about people not judging each other."

When she said this, Daddy scooted closer to her on the couch, touching her cheek with his glass of gin-and-tonic. "You got something you don't want to be judged for, girl?"

Mama laughed and pushed the glass away. "James, you are so crazy."

"I'm just getting started," he said.

Maybe it was because I spent half my life in my mother's beauty shop, but it seemed that I knew quite a bit about marriage, even when I was just a little girl. It was probably a bad sign when I touched my kindergarten teacher on the knee when she looked unhappy and said, "Marriage is complicated."

This was my mother's favorite refrain. She said it at least daily to some woman dripping wet in the shampoo bowl. A shift in pitch flipped the meaning entirely, but the words were always the same. In the car that day on the way to the beauty-supply store, talking about George and Gracie, she didn't say "Marriage is complicated" in a between-the-lines way, like she did when she tried to talk over my head. This time she said it like she needed a word from another language, but she just had to settle for "complicated."

I nodded, enjoying the sound of her voice. It was like I was her best friend. And maybe I was. For sure, she was mine. Even before puberty changed the stakes, I never had much truck with girls. Spending so much time with grown women had ruined my timing and dated my speech, making me poor company for my peers. As much as I tried, I never could get any traction. Not that I was an outcast. I got invited to slumber parties and I went, as eager as anyone, but I was no one's best friend, and the best friend is the only friend that matters.

"So where was I?" Mama said.

"You were talking about God."

"No I wasn't," she said. "I was talking about how irritated I am to be spending my Saturday driving way out here to return this dryer. When I bought it, I asked her, 'Is it quiet?' She said it was quiet as rain, and then I turn it on and it sounds worse than a lawn mower." She lowered her voice and winked. "One of the customers said it sounds like a cheap vibrator."

I nodded, although I didn't know what she meant.

She adjusted the *I Dream of Jeannie* ponytail clipped so high up on her head that it grazed the roof of the car. My mother collected hairpieces, wigs, and falls like other women collected Lladró, Swarovski, or souvenir thimbles. She displayed the full wigs on Styrofoam heads jutting from the walls of her bedroom like the trophy heads of deer. The half caps and smaller pieces lived in her dresser drawer. Because she didn't approve of girls dressing up like grown women, she never let me wear them, only allowing me to stroke the stiff curls before laying them back down in their nests of scented tissue paper.

From time to time I asked anyway, if I could just try on one of the ponytails — I was most interested in Tempest Tousled, a long spiral curl. Other girls I knew made do with towels around their heads as stand-ins for long flowing hair. A boy I knew from church arranged a sour mop on his head just to see what he would look like if he were a white girl. I didn't want any of these homemade costumes when I knew my mother had a dresser drawer stocked with the real McCoy, but she refused to let me hold the hair next to my face, even if I promised not to try and actually attach it. "You need to get a handle of what you really look like before you start playing pretend."

If nine years wasn't long enough for me to figure out what I looked like, I didn't know how long it was going to take. I had been in kindergarten when I figured out that I wasn't pretty. That is the worst thing about being a little kid; nobody is shy about letting you know these things. The fireman who teaches you to stop, drop, and roll if you happen to catch on fire — he picks the cutest girl to sit on his knee and wear his cap. At Christmastime, the ten prettiest girls get to be in the angel choir. Plain girls twirl in the candy-cane dance. Ugly girls pass programs. I never handed out playbills, but I never for a minute thought I would be in the angel choir.

My parents are not good-looking people, either. My dad is medium everything — medium height, medium age for a father, medium brown, medium afro. His glasses are thick as the bulletproof window at the liquor store. Thank God that didn't get passed down to me. It's bad enough living with his hair, fine as spun cotton; even a soft natural-bristle brush pulls it right off my head. My mother, when she isn't wearing her falls, could be anyone's mother — as medium as my father, but a bit on the plump side. If you saw them walking down the street, if you noticed them at all, you would think the two of them might produce invisible children.

"So, like I was saying. George Burns cheated on Gracie." My mother chuckled and used the hand that wasn't on the steering wheel to adjust her *I Dream of Jeannie.* "Back before you were born, he had a wife named Gracie and he loved her to pieces. I mean, he was crazy about her. It's the kind of love that most people never experience. L-o-v-e."

I nodded. "Love."

"But he strayed. He cheated on her with some tramp. One time and one time only. I think he had been drinking."

I nodded.

"So here's the good part of the story. He had betrayed his One True Love. What if she left him? He *loved* her! So he bought her a tennis bracelet."

"A tennis bracelet?"

"Diamonds, Chaurisse. Major jewelry. And he never stepped out on her again. Cheating on her made him get his priorities straight. He almost lost her and it tore him up. So every time he saw that bracelet on her wrist, he remembered how much he cherished her. Don't you love that?"

I said, "I don't know."

"And there's more. This is the important part. Listen to me, Chaurisse. This will serve you well the rest of your life."

"Okay," I said.

"Years and years later, Gracie was sipping gin martinis with some country club ladies, when George heard Gracie say, 'I was always hoping that George would have another affair. I want a bracelet for my other arm!" At this, my mother laughed her thick laugh. She knocked her hand against the steering wheel a couple of times. "You get it?"

I shook my head. "Your blinker is on."

"But do you get it?"

"Sort of," I said.

"The point is that Gracie knew the whole time. She just didn't act all ignorant about it. Two things to learn from that story: (a) you know in your gut who loves you."

"So how come he did it?"

My mother smiled at me. "Sometimes I forget how young you are. I love you so much, do you know that?"

I turned my face toward the car window. I liked it when she turned her light on me like that, but it embarrassed me, too. "Yes'm."

"But here's the thing to remember, and then we'll drop it."

"Okay."

"Men do things all the time that they don't mean," she explained. "The only thing that matters is that he loves you. George loved Gracie. He loved her so much, that when he dies, he is going to make sure that he is buried underneath her, so she will always have top billing."

"But why did he mess around with some other lady?"

"Chaurisse, you are not getting it. This is the point: If you are a wife, behave like a wife. There is nothing to be gained from acting a fool, calling up the other woman at her house, cutting her tires, or whatever. My own mother was like that, always fighting in the streets over some nigger."

"But how come he did it? Why did that God guy cheat on Gracie?"

My mother switched on the turn signal and sighed. "All I am saying is that if you are a wife, act like a wife and not a two-dollar whore."

This, of course, was before I got a reputation for being a fast-tail girl, without even being one. When I was fourteen, I bruised my reputation and lost my virginity. In that order, mind you. Life is crazy like that. The start of it was basically a misunderstanding, a misunderstanding that happened at church — and there is no worse place for a misunderstanding that makes you seem like a tramp. I was standing in the choir closet with Jamal Dixon, the preacher's son. We were talking. He was talking, really, I was just listening. At that point, I was one hundred percent driven snow. Jamal was sharing some heavy stuff, about his mother. Apparently, she drank all the time. Every day. She hid bottles in the laundry room behind the hot-water heater. She drank out of a wineglass; she drank out of her toothbrush cup. She crashed the reverend's Coupe de Ville at three in the afternoon in the parking lot of Kroger. It was getting to be a problem. "Can you tell?" he asked me.

I shrugged. "I wouldn't put anything past anybody."

I didn't mean it, about putting what past who, but it was something I often heard my mother say. It was the perfect response to a woman getting her hair done complaining about their husband. This way, you could agree without talking bad about him. So when the couple reconciled, the wife would still be comfortable getting her hair done in your chair. If you want to be a hairdresser, you have to understand the way people are wired.

I felt sorry for Jamal. With his blinking eyes and twitching lips, he looked like he was about to cry right there, and I knew enough of men to know that he didn't want me to see it happen. I turned my face to the robes, keeping my hands busy making sure all the hangers were turned the right way. Jamal kept on about his mother and how she gets carried away with the peppermint schnapps and how his father won't do anything about it but pray. The family would be together in the living room on their knees, holding hands and breathing in the boozy-minty smell that beamed out from her lips and even from her skin. He swore that even the butter she scraped on his toast in the mornings tasted of peppermint. I didn't tell him about my own mother, who could be, on occasion, a little bit boozy-peachy. She never crashed any cars or did anything to hurt anyone, but she swilled Fuzzy Navels on Monday afternoons, dabbing her eyes at her soap operas.

Jamal told me that he wasn't sure he believed that God is looking in on each and every one of us. He said he had some questions about the whole dynamic with the sparrow. He agreed that God made the world; the universe had to come from somewhere, but after that, who knows who's in charge? I was thinking that the human mind and the power of suggestion are really something, because I could sort of smell something like Doublemint on the rocks. He kept going and I pressed my lips together, imagining what peppermint schnapps must taste like.

The robes parted on the rod, Red Sea–style, and who was there but Mrs. Reverend Schnapps herself, tall and steep as though she had been designed by an architect. I had to hand it to her; Jamal's mother's asymmetric junior-miss flip had been cut by someone who really knew what she was doing.

"Jamal," she said. "That's enough, son."

"We weren't doing anything," he said. "Just talking."

"Is that what you call it?" said Mrs. Reverend.

As I waited on the curb for my mother to pick me up, Mrs. Reverend told everybody how worried she was about me. The women on the usher board and some of the deaconesses were told to pray for me. Even while Mrs. Reverend's words were telling them to pray, her tone was telling them to remember Salome. Even before my mother confirmed this to me in a whispered-but-urgent conversation in her bedroom, under the watchful eyes of the wig-heads, I knew the women at church were aiming their sharpened prayers at me.

I was a quiet girl back then. Not that I was shy, I just didn't have anything to say.

"I haven't told your father," my mother said.

"Told him what?"

"About Jamal Dixon."

"There's nothing to tell."

"I know, baby," she said.

I was still defending myself a week later, as we drove to Decatur for my appointment with her ob-gyn. The last time he saw me, I was being born. I told him the same thing: "I'm not doing anything."

"It's just to regulate your cycle," he said.

Heading home on I-20, we hit a traffic jam, and I tried again. "I'm not doing anything."

"Do you know how lucky you are that these pills exist? Do you know how lucky you are that I am taking you to the doctor?"

"But I'm not doing anything," I said again.

"Take them for me, baby," Mama said. "Just to be on the safe side."

Jamal Dixon was the first one. We arranged to meet at Marcus McCready's house one afternoon after school. While I stared at a Jayne Kennedy swimsuit poster on the ceiling, he apologized for his mother's behavior. He didn't mean to get me involved. He knew I was a nice girl and he felt bad that everybody was talking about me like that.

"I don't care if people talk about me."

"I'm sorry," he said. "She was never like this before."

"I understand," I said.

He looked at me and turned his head.

"What grade are you in?"

"Ninth," I said.

"I'm a junior," he said.

I didn't tell him to stop or to come hither. I was curious, really, to see what would happen. Jamal looked like a younger, thinner version of his father, whom I'd often admired standing in the pulpit with his arms outstretched in his beautiful robes. He preached in a thunder-deep voice, but he sang sometimes in a sweet Al Green tenor.

"You're a nice girl," Jamal said in the tone you might use to soothe a dog that may or may not bite.

"Pretty?" I said.

He nodded. "You have nice lips."

I was a little afraid, but I knew I was now on the safe side.

"Don't touch my hair," I said. "Don't mess it up."

He said he was sorry. He said it twice.

Then I was different, although I looked exactly the same.

The Pill was a secret between my mother and me. My father was not to know about the peach dial pack, the white pills tasteless but potent and those seven green sugar pills that allowed the blood to come. This was women's business. Besides, my father loved

me best when I was his baby girl, his Buttercup. Fathers are that way. All they want
is that you be clean, entertaining, and ador-
ing. When he came home from work, I
fetched Daddy a gin-and-tonic, kissed the
top of his head, and petted his tired
shoulders.

Although fathers are simple, husbands are
not. Marriages are tricky, but children bring
love into even the most complicated situation. They are gifts from God. I was my
mother's miracle child, a replacement for
the baby boy who died. It was a close call,
my entry into the world, four weeks early.
They almost lost me, too. I spent more than
a week in an incubator. My mother couldn't
commit to loving me until it was clear I was
going to live, but my daddy was all in from
the start, balling his hands into fists, mut-
tering, "Come on, champ. Come on."

If we were real Africans, my daddy would
have held me up to the sky like Kunta
Kinte's daddy did. Instead, he took me to
Olan Mills and bought portraits, even paying extra to have the images printed on
stretched canvas, etched with brushstrokes.
He made a large donation to the church and
gave up smoking. Of course, the habit got
the better of him after a week and some

change, but he never smoked in my nursery. The walls of our house have to be repainted every year to cover the yellow smoke-tinge on the walls, but my bedroom remained the same hopeful pink of my birth announcement for six years. My father loved me. My birth changed him. Everyone says so.

14
A SILVER GIRL

The summer before my last year in high
school was a hard one for our family.
Grandma Bunny dying nearly killed all
three of my parents. I can't say which one
of them got hit the hardest, because all of
them fell apart in their own ways. For Uncle
Raleigh there was no comfort except in crying. We would be eating dinner and he
would put a spoonful of potatoes in his
mouth and his lips would start shaking and
he had to excuse himself from the table.
His eyes streamed when he was driving, but
luckily the passengers didn't see anything
but the back of his head. My daddy drank
and basically let himself go. The bitter
scratch of his unshaven good-night kiss will
always, for me, be the sensation of grief.
My mama didn't change herself in any way
that you could easily put your finger on.
She still opened the shop at seven thirty,
taking care of the old ladies who got up at

five, and she closed down at eight thirty, having taken care of the women who worked in offices. Everything was almost the same with her, but she went about her business in a way that put me in the mind of an old matchbook. You can scratch the head against the strip in the same way you always have, but you are not going to get any kind of spark.

I was as devastated as anyone, but I didn't have much to take my mind off my grief. There was Jamal, but every time we were together, he made me kneel on the floor with him and beg Jesus to forgive us. After Grandma Bunny passed, I didn't feel like asking Jesus for much of anything. I guess I should have practiced my flute — that was the whole point of going to the performing-arts magnet — but I wasn't exactly a virtuoso and who can take comfort in doing something that you're bad at? That left only the mall.

Greenbriar wasn't the best place to shop. It wasn't straight-up ghetto like West End, but it wasn't swanky like Phipps Plaza, either. Still it was close enough to my house that I could go there without planning to. Sometimes I would start at 10 a.m. when the mall opened and systematically work my way through every shop, even the rent-to-own furniture place. I could spend an hour in Pearle Vision staring in the mirror through empty eyeglasses. I would do anything to keep from being alone with my thoughts of Grandma Bunny. Her leg had been amputated eighteen months before she died. The night before the surgery, she called my mama collect after midnight. I picked up the phone at the very beginning of the ring — teenager's instinct. I accepted the charges and yelled for my mama. She picked up the extension with a voice dry from sleep.

"Hello?"

"Laverne," she said. "It's Miss Bunny."

"Miss Bunny," Mama said, "what you doing up? Where's James and Raleigh?"

"They in the back room, sleep."

"Miss Bunny, what's wrong? If you need something, wake them up. That's why they down there."

"Laverne," said Miss Bunny. "Listen to me, child. I changed my mind. I don't want this operation. Don't let them take my leg. What man is ever going to have eyes for me if I don't even have legs to stand on?"

"Miss Bunny," Mama said. "Don't worry about that. Go wake up Raleigh. Miss Bunny, you don't sound like yourself. Is somebody helping you with your medica-

265

tion?" Then my mama paused, pitching her voice through the air and not through the telephone. "Chaurisse Witherspoon. Please tell me you are not on this telephone."

I eased the phone back onto the cradle and pretended to be asleep. I lay in the bed, kept up all night by the weight of my grandmother begging to keep her legs, still hoping to be pretty to someone.

My last stop at the mall was the drugstore. There are two kinds of pretty, my mama always said. Natural Beauty, which is whatever your mama gave you. Everybody can't be that lucky, so for us, there is Pretty in a Jar. This was for people average or worse, who could use time and cosmetology to put ourselves together. Sometimes she called it "bootstrap beauty."

In the cosmetic aisle of SupeRx, I laid my hand on an eye-shadow crayon. Drawn to the color, I turned it over in my palm, trying to remember where I had seen this particular shade of green before. The gold letters pressed into the side said BURIED TREASURE, but that didn't ring any bells. Above the display was a little mirror so you could hold products up to your face and imagine what you would look like with the color rimming your eyes.

It took me a second to register that the

girl in the tiny mirror was actually me. My mother, exhausted by grief and worn down by my pleading, had given in and finally allowed me to augment my hair. That's the term we used when we talked about it to customers. You never used the word *fake. False,* though kinder, was on the forbidden list, too. What my mother stitched on to my head was sixteen inches of synthetic fibers, dark and shiny like motor oil. I moved the eye crayon from my cheek to my hair. Leaning my neck forward, I let the hair swing forward before snapping it back. I smiled at my reflection and repeated the motion. It was beautiful, that hair.

I was just about to go for another toss when I heard a weird noise over my left shoulder. I wasn't sure what it was. Maybe it was a stifled sneeze, a little shriek, or a gasp. Embarrassed to be caught admiring myself in public, I turned to see a silver girl dropping a tube of cuticle remover into her bag.

"Silver" is what I called girls who were natural beauties but who also smoothed on a layer of pretty from a jar. It wasn't just how they looked, it was how they *were.* The name came from a song my mother sang sometimes when she was getting dressed to go out somewhere special. She sang along with Arethra Franklin at the end: "Sail on, silver girl . . . Your time has come to shine. All your dreams are on their way."

I never had much luck with the silver population. They were never all-out mean to me, unless you count the one that hemmed me up in the girls' room at National Six at a matinee showing of *Purple Rain*. For the most part, silver girls were polite, especially if their parents knew mine, and especially if my mama did their hair, but none of them ever took me in, told me their secrets. Take somebody like Ruth Nicole Elizabeth Grant. I'd shampooed her hair once every two weeks for almost three years, but I didn't know that she was going with Marcus McCready until she strung his class ring on her add-a-bead chain, and even then I had to ask whose ring it was. She answered me in an offhand way that let me know that this was as far from a secret as you could imagine.

Silver girls liked to be friends with each other, keeping all their shine, which, in my opinion, was a little bit selfish. Silverness was catching, but it could only be shared girl to girl, and this could only happen if both parties tried really hard. Sharing a boyfriend with a silver girl wouldn't make you silver; that would just make you a slut.

But let's say in the past you'd never had much truck with girls your own age because you had been cooped up in either a limousine or a beauty shop all your life. If that person was you, and you could make friends with a silver girl, she could teach you how to shine.

Quiet as it's kept, augmented hair makes you brave, like sweet wedding champagne that goes straight to your head, turning you into a bolder, prettier version of yourself. Knowing the silver girl was watching, I dropped the eye crayon in my purse, feeling like a good girl gone bad. "Hey."

The silver girl licked her lips but didn't speak. She looked so scared that I checked behind me to make sure that the manager wasn't standing there. "What?" I said once I saw that no one was behind us but an old man selecting a pumice stone. She kept staring in my direction, eyebrows up, and taking shallow breaths through her mouth. I turned, looking all around until I saw what she saw: a small video camera mounted above the emery boards. "Oh," I said.

The silver girl still didn't move. She stood there like Diana Ross in *Mahogany,* holding a pose for that crazy photographer guy. Even though this was a bona fide emergency, I couldn't help noticing that this silver girl was especially gorgeous. I wanted to kiss her, just on the cheek, where she had smeared fuchsia-colored rouge. I know a lot of people get into redbone girls, but what I love to see is a dark brown girl with a pretty face and lots of hair. This girl had a good twenty inches of the real thing, thick and heavy. A Barbie doll dipped in chocolate, she was the silverest girl I had ever seen.

"Empty out your bag," I said. "Just put everything back."

She didn't move, but I did. I groped down in my flea-market Gucci and pulled out the eye crayon. For good measure, I also dropped the box of Dexatrim that I was planning to pay for at the front desk like a regular person. The silver girl stood motionless, still posing for that invisible photographer. I reached for her purse, sliding my hand inside her LV (a nice fake) and found a foil chain of Trojans, pink nail polish, and a package of bath salts that looked like something you would give as a gift to your teacher.

"What's wrong with you?" I said. Finally, she did something, even though it was something stupid — zipped up her bag just as the manager stormed toward us, almost tipping a display of Sea Breeze.

270

"Come with me." The manager was probably my mother's age, with marcelled waves and a slick coat of foundation. Its creamy smoothness ended just under her chin.

"We don't have to go with you," the silver girl said with a flip of her hair. "We haven't done anything wrong." Another toss of her tresses — that's the word that came to mind. This was storybook hair. So pretty it made both my hands itch.

"Open your bag," the SupeRx lady said to the silver girl.

"She doesn't have to do anything," I offered. "She has civil rights."

"Both of us do," said the silver girl.

I smiled at the word *both.* "I will call my parents," I said. I was grandstanding now. Maybe I was still under the influence of my new hair, but something about the moment didn't feel quite real. It was like we were in a movie, a comedy starring the two of us, where she and I were equally beautiful, equally charming.

The manager ignored me and rummaged through my purse anyway. When she was done with my belongings, she moved on to the silver girl, but you could tell she had lost her hope of punishing us.

"You owe her an apology," I called out as the manager went back to the counter after

271

telling us to get the fuck out.

As though we were square dancers, I linked my arm through the silver girl's. This close, I smelled her perfume. Anaïs Anaïs, the same as mine. Her beautiful hair stank of cigarettes. "You smoke?" I asked. On the busy sidewalk in front of the mall, teenage girls walked by in intense clusters. The silver ones talked only to each other, but the regular girls looked at everyone they passed, hoping to see something that would change them. On the street, boys drove large American cars outfitted with louvers and bras. They blew their horns, activating my smile reflex. The silver girl smiled as well, waving even, although she nervously fiddled with her add-a-beads.

"You okay?" I pulled her out of the thoroughfare so she could lean against the wall. I held her by her wrists. "Say something."

She took a belly breath and closed her eyes as she blew it out. She did it again, as girls walking toward us cut their eyes and raised their eyebrows.

"Are you having a seizure?"

Finally she opened her eyes, coughing out a whisper. "Is it a wig?"

I took a little step back and touched my nose with the tips of my fingers. My face burned and although I wasn't light-bright like Uncle Raleigh, I knew the silver girl could see it. Tilting my shoulders, I hid my face in case my eyes started to cry or something like that.

"I didn't mean anything by it," she said.

"You can tell, can't you? It looks fake."

"Not really," she said. "It looks really natural."

"You're just trying to make me feel better. It was the first thing out of your mouth."

"Well," she said, "the first thing you did was to tell me that my hair smells like smoke."

"No," I said. "I didn't mean it like that. My hair probably smells smoky, too. My dad smokes two packs a day."

"Mine, too," she said.

On the backside of Greenbriar were painted concrete structures that looked like giant corn muffins. I could never figure what they were for. Despite the little tags that said "Keep off," young people sat on top of them while they waited on their rides and ate frozen yogurt.

"Let's sit down," the silver girl said, walking to one of the muffins. With her strong arms, she hoisted herself up. I knew how to get up there, too, but I had never mastered the smooth silvery motion, so I just stood beside her. My eyes were about on the same level as her bustline. This close, I could see that her polo shirt wasn't a real Izod, after all.

It was hot out, but that was to be expected in July. Her baby hair curled at her hairline, and I could feel the water gathering under my arms. We were both wearing stretchy jeans, which were all but fused with our skin by now.

"You have a job this summer?" she wanted to know.

I shook my head. "I was supposed to work at Six Flags, but just four days in my supervisor started getting funny with me, so I had to quit."

"What happened?"

"It didn't get out of hand, but he was making reasons to touch me all the time."

"You tell anybody?"

"Told my uncle, who told my mama, who told my dad." I tried to laugh. "Living in my house is like playing telephone."

"So what did he do?"

"Who?"

"Your father."

"He was so mad he couldn't get the words out. He has a stammer and it gets really bad when he's riled up. I thought he was going to kill somebody. He jumps in the limo . . ."
I paused, waiting for her to say, *Wait a*

minute! A limo?

She said, "Then what happened?"

"I wasn't there, but my mother told me that he raised so much cane that they had to call security." I smiled a little bit, because I liked that part of the story.

She pulled her fingers through her hair. I did the same, but augmented hair is for looking at, not for touching. The strands were unbending against my fingers.

"Be real with me," I said. "Does it look bad?"

"No," she said. "It looks nice." There was a little bit of a downward slant in her voice, like she was talking to a little kid.

"Okay," I said. "Be real with me again."

"Okay."

"Is that your real hair?"

"Yes." She said it like I had asked her whether or not she believed in God.

"You sure?" I said. "I thought we were being honest with each other."

"It's my real hair," she said, bending double from her perch on the concrete muffin. The crown of her head was in line with my face, the add-a-beads swung to her nose. The cigarette odor was as insistent as love.

Human hair gives when you push it. I pressed a few strands between my fingers. "It's real all right."

275

"I told you," she said, unfolding herself. She extended her hand toward my head. "Can I?"

My hand made its way to my face again. It smelled like her hair, sweet with oil sheen. I looked up at her hand, which hovered right above my head like I was a dog she wasn't sure she should pet.

"Yes," I said, softly. "You can touch it."

The silver girl pushed her fingers into my scalp, exploring with her fingernails. "What's that? Feels like a ridge."

"That's where my mama sewed in the weft. She's a cosmetologist."

I started overexplaining, telling her that this new process was technically called "hair integration," but for short, people called it a weave, and that my mother was one of only twenty hairdressers in the city who knew how to do it. I bragged that it was the next big thing. I jabbered on as her careful hands explored my whole head. Passersby, even the other silver girls, noticed and turned toward each other to talk about us. Old people gave a quick look and swept their eyes away the way they do when they catch people kissing on the MARTA train. It was excruciating, really, imagining the feel of my synthetic hair to her real hands. It's the way you feel when you go too far with a boy you don't know so well. It stops feeling good, but you've done too much to tell him to stop.

Finally, she pulled her hands away. "Sorry," she said.

I laughed to try and sound casual. "So what's your name?"

She reached again for her add-a-beads.

"You shouldn't do that. You're going to break the chain."

"I know," she said. "I had to have it soldered twice already."

"So what's your name?" When she didn't answer I spoke up. "I'm Chaurisse."

She nodded.

"My real name is Bunny — don't ask — but I go by Chaurisse." She didn't laugh like most people did. Entire homerooms had broken into guffaws during roll call, but this silver girl winced.

"I was named after my grandmother." Grandma Bunny's memory rushed at me, blinding me like a camera flash. My throat tightened and the beginning of a headache made a knot behind my eyes. "I miss her."

Twisting her finger in her necklace, she said, "My name is Dana."

"Dana," I repeated.

"Dana."

"Let me give you a card," I said. "My

277

mama has a beauty shop. Call me and I'll do you a wash-and-set. On the house. Or maybe we could hang out again?" She took the card from me and zipped it into her handbag. I took out another card. "You can write your number on the back." I rummaged around for a pen, but all I could come up with was a navy blue eyeliner. "I guess you have to write with this."

She looked at the brand. "This is expensive."

"It's my mom's, she won't miss it. You want it?"

She turned the eye pencil over in her hands. "For real?"

"No," I said. "For play-play."

She looked confused and maybe even a little hurt.

"No," I said. "You can have it."

She put it in her purse and gave a firm little nod.

"But write your number down."

"I can't give my number out. We're unlisted and my mom doesn't like for people to call the house."

"Oh," I said, not sure whether to believe her. I had only known two people who weren't allowed to share their phone numbers. One was Maria Simpson; her deal was that her parents were very old. The other person was Angelique Fontnot, and it made sense because her father was a city councilman or something.

"I'll call you," she said. "I swear to God."

"Okay."

"I have to go," said the silver girl. "I've been here too long already."

"Don't run off," I said. "Wait with me until my ride comes. You ever rode in a limousine before?"

"No," she said. "I can't do that."

Then, like Cinderella, she was gone.

15
GIRLS ARE TOO MESSY

Beauty parlors, in general, are confessional spaces. A place like the Pink Fox is even more intimate than your average salon because it's a business that's also part of our home. If a client needs to go to the toilet, she uses the same bathroom where I take my shower in the morning. If she has an emergency, she might lift a panty liner from underneath the sink. Not to mention that there are customers who have been coming to my mother since before I was born.

The Pink Fox, with its two pump chairs, shampoo bowl, and three hooded dryers represented a generation's worth of progress from the days when my mama sat hollering on the front steps rounding up customers for her own mama. "Miss Mattie is pressing hair today. Two dollars!" By 1967, my mama was making decent money renting a chair at a salon on Ashby Street, and Witherspoon

Sedans was turning a good profit. There was money enough for my parents to put a down payment on a house, and Uncle Raleigh figured it was time to try living on his own. The Peyton Wall was long gone, Mayor Allen had said he was sorry, and black folks were moving in while white people were hightailing it to the suburbs.

Mama and Daddy had their pick of several houses, as the market was flooded. They drove the Lincoln slowly up and down Cascade Heights like they were browsing the kennels at the pound, looking for the perfect puppy. Daddy was leaning toward a new house because he didn't want something that had been "ate off." Mama didn't care about new, she just wanted central air. Our house, 739 Lynhurst, a three-bedroom ranch in the middle of a busy block, near the bus stop, was reduced even further in price because the garage had been converted into a two-station beauty salon. A wooden sign staked in the yard read CHAURISSE'S PINK FOX.

Nine years married, with no high-school diploma and no baby to show for her efforts, my mama was not a lucky person. Blessings were rare enough that they caught her attention when they showed themselves, and she had good sense enough to snag a good thing before it could get away.

"Do you take walk-ins?"

The real answer to this question was "sometimes." The Pink Fox was a small operation. I served as shampoo girl. In a pinch I could give a wash-and-set and a few other nonchemical procedures while my mother kept her hands busy with the women who book their appointments as much as three weeks ahead of time.

It was early in November and we were slammed like it was New Year's Eve. Between the Sigma Gamma Rho debutante ball, Clark College homecoming, and the encore of *The Wiz,* we had customers stacked up to the ceiling. Although my dad would have a fit if he knew, I took the day off from school to help my mother with the crunch. It didn't matter; I was a senior. The clock over the no. 2 chair said three forty-five. Mama was doing a blow-dry in the best chair. I was leaning over the shampoo bowl, giving relief to a pregnant girl who had scratched her head the night before, even though she had known she was getting a touch-up; the force of the water on the chemical burns made her screw her eyes shut.

"I'm almost done," I said, looking up at

the would-be walk-in, and who did I see but Dana, my silver Cinderella.

"Hi," I said. "I can't believe you came to see me!"

My mama said, "No walk-ins today, baby."

"But maybe you can come in tomorrow?" I said. "I'll be here."

"It's okay," Dana said. "It's not a big deal. I am thinking about cutting it all off. I guess I can just go to a barbershop."

You would have thought that she had just promised to stick her head in the oven. All conversation in the shop shut down. The pregnant girl in the sink raised up to get a look at Dana. The old lady in chair no. 1 frowned so hard it was like her face was folding. Only my mama kept it together. "Now why would you want to do that, baby?"

Dana said, "I just want to cut it off. Long hair is a hassle. I'm tired of living like this."

My mama looked hard at Dana. I think she was trying to figure out if Dana really was thinking about cutting off all that gorgeous hair. Even caught up in a high ponytail, you could see that it was waterfall hair, wild, tumbling, slick, and beautiful. Lord knows it isn't fair how nature parcels out the goodies.

My mother said, "How old are you?"

"Seventeen. Seventeen and a half. This is my half birthday."

"You are too young to mutilate yourself. Come back in six months if you want to follow through with that foolishness."

"Can I sit down?" Dana said. "I won't stay long."

"Chaurisse, when you get through rinsing her, put on a protein pack and then take this young lady upstairs and pour her a Coca-Cola."

"Yes, ma'am."

Keep in mind that this was midway through the first term of my senior year of high school. People at my school were going places and couldn't stop talking about it. My school, Northside High School, was a performing-arts magnet, like in the movie *Fame.* Back in ninth grade, when I was accepted, I thought I could flute and piccolo my way into something remarkable, as if that were possible, even for people *with* talent. Three and a half years in, no one had suggested that I apply to college to study music. My counselor encouraged me to apply to the women's colleges, saying it would be good for my self-esteem. She had gone to Smith and said maybe they were trying to diversify. With her help, I put in applications for the Seven Sisters, plus Spelman

College. "The stepsister," she said with a wicked grin.

My mother had her heart set on my attending Spelman, because it had been her dream to study there. Her home ec teacher all those years ago, the one who reminded teenagers to "remember your dignity," was a Spelman lady, dazzling my mother with snapshots of black girls with hard-pressed hair wearing chrysanthemum corsages.

I pretended to be bored with the idea of a girls' school, and a little bit above it all. "I don't like to hang out with girls." I also made a big deal out of sending in an application to FAMU in Tallahassee. But the truth was that I was terrified and also thrilled at the idea of attending Spelman College. When I explained why I wasn't interested in having friends, I complained that "girls are too messy," but it was a lie. The messiness was what I craved. I wanted to tell someone everything I knew. I wanted to name names and tell the whole story.

When I met Dana that time at SupeRx, I didn't know yet if she could be that girl, if she would understand my place in the world, because girls with looks and hair move in different circles than ones like me. Just having the thought, I could hear my guidance counselor in my ear talking about

Smith and self-esteem, but I wasn't crazy. I have eyes. I know what I know.

Dana was the same shaky-scared she'd been at the mall as I led her up the concrete staircase that connected the rest of our house to the Pink Fox. Mama and Uncle Raleigh constructed those stairs themselves, when I was about ten years old. They worked on Mondays for the whole summer, drinking tiny cans of beer and mixing cement in a wheelbarrow. Dana paused at the top of the steps. She pressed her hand to the base of her throat and then touched her own forehead, as if checking for fever.

"That door is open. You can just walk in."

She hesitated and wiped her hands on her jeans. "You sure?"

"Yeah," I said. "Just open the door."

She pushed the door open and walked into the kitchen carefully, as though she was walking on a just-mopped floor.

"You okay?" I asked her.

"Is this where you eat dinner? In the kitchen? Or do you have a dining room?"

"You don't have to whisper," I said. "We eat in the kitchen."

"Where do you sit? How come you have four places set? Who eats with you?" She ran her hands over a chair and picked up a checkered place mat.

"Are you okay?" I said again.

"Where does your father sit?"

I pointed to the chair nearest the window. "Right there."

She sat herself in that seat and set her hands on either side of the place mat. She nodded, in a satisfied-seeming way.

"Are you sure you're okay? Do you want a Coke?"

"Yes," she said. "Can you pour it in a glass?"

I poured the Coke over a handful of ice cubes and handed it to her. "So what's the deal?"

I talked to her like we were old friends, another trick I'd learned from boys. Talk familiar and you'll get familiar. This was different from what I felt even for Jamal. This thing I felt for Dana originated under my scalp and stretched itself behind my ears, snaking down the back of my neck and down my spine. Girls like us, the ones who have been found out, our nerves are on edge like broken teeth.

"You told me to come," she said. "You gave me your card."

"You don't want to have short hair, trust me," I told her.

"I thought I might like to have an Anita

Baker cut. Low on the sides and fluffy up top."

I shook my head. "Short cuts are for people who can't grow hair."

"Where's your father?"

"My dad?" I shrugged. "Working the line at the airport. What difference does it make?"

"Doesn't make a difference."

"Okay, so what's up?"

I wanted her to admit that she was curious about me. I know how people act when they have an interest. When boys do it, my dad calls it "sniffing around." I heard him say to Raleigh, "I never thought it would bother me so much, all these hard legs sniffing around my daughter." It's a good way to say it, capturing that animalness of people. But it's not just boys. Girls do it, too, when they want to know more about you.

She didn't say anything, she just looked around our kitchen like she had never seen one before. She stood up and opened the drawers, picked up a spoon and frowned at her reflection. "Can I open the fridge?"

I shrugged and she pulled open the door, taking a long look, like she was counting my mother's cans of Fresca lined up on the door racks. She shut it and opened the freezer side. "No ice maker?"

I shrugged, but I felt embarrassed. "Ice trays make good ice."

"Y'all have all new appliances? Electric range?"

"I don't care," I said. "My mama is the only one that cooks."

"She cooks every day?"

"We go out to dinner sometimes. All of us. Red Lobster. Piccadilly."

"Did he ever take her to the Mansion?"

"Maybe, on their anniversary. Now sit back down. Stop trying to get me off track. Tell me why you came over here." This was a trick I used with Jamal. I made him say exactly what he wanted.

"You don't want to know," she said, returning to my father's chair. She sniffed the air like a rabbit. "I smell cigarettes."

"My dad smokes like it's going out of style."

Dana whipped her head toward me. "You mother lets him smoke in the house?"

"There's no *letting* him do anything."

Underneath us, I knew my mother was wondering where I was. On busy days, my job was to get the clients into the shampoo bowl as soon as possible. A woman with a dry head can walk out if the wait becomes unbearable, but if she's dripping wet, she won't go anywhere. I wanted to get Dana back downstairs. Get her in the shampoo bowl and make her my hostage.

"Are you going to let me give you a wash-and-set?"

"I haven't decided. I have a lot on my mind. I've been trying to tell you that."

I looked at her carefully and turned my head to the side. "Are you pregnant?" I whispered.

She laughed. "Why do people think that is the only problem a girl can have?"

"Are you?"

"I thought I was one time."

"Me, too."

"It was stupid because I'm on the Pill."

"Me, too!"

"But nothing is foolproof."

The coincidences were making me loopy. "I know!"

She smiled and moved her hand like she was going to touch me, but she didn't.

"I have too many things on my mind. I'm applying to Mount Holyoke," she said. "Early decision. Where are you going to college?"

"Don't know yet."

"Where are you applying?"

I shrugged. "A lot of places."

"Mount Holyoke?"

"If it's one of the sisters, I did, but Spelman is the only one I care about."

"If you got in, would you go?"

"I guess," I said. "But don't change the subject. Tell me how come you're here."

She raised her eyebrows and pulled her hand through her high ponytail. "Maybe I just wanted to be friends."

I hated how she talked to me. *I just want to be friends.* People who really wanted to be your friend didn't say things like that. If they really wanted to be your friend, they just did it. They just took your hand, listened to you talk.

"Don't turn your face away from me," she said. "I really came over here to thank you for saving me in the store that time." She gave a wobbly smile. "You can fix my hair for me if you want to."

There was a knock on the floor. My mother, in the shop, was jabbing the ceiling with a broomstick.

"I got to get back downstairs," I said. "I'm on the clock."

"She pays you to work in the store?"

"Five dollars an hour."

"Are you close to your dad?"

I said, "More when I was little. It's different now that I'm growing up."

"Me, too," she said with a bit of a sigh.

She waved her hand to indicate her face and chest. "He can't deal with it."

I nodded. "I know what you mean. He can't deal, and he doesn't even know the half of it."

"Exactly," said Dana.

"I gotta get back downstairs," I said. "You want a wash-and-set or not?"

"I want to see your room," she said.

"Next time."

She turned around the kitchen, pivoting on her left foot. "Your kitchen isn't anything special."

"Who said it was?"

When we were leaving, I heard her brass bangles rattle as she slipped my father's napkin into her fake Louis Vuitton.

We entered the shop through the back door. My mother was blow-drying the client I had shampooed. According to the big clock with shears as hands, we had only been gone fifteen minutes.

"Everybody come back to their senses?" Mama said.

"Yes, ma'am," Dana said.

"Good," Mama said to her with a kind smile. "Come back another day and we'll do you something pretty."

"Tomorrow?" Dana asked.

"Not tomorrow," my mama said. "I got

plans." She batted her eyes and all the customers laughed. "My husband is taking me to dinner, so I will be trying to do something with my own hair." Then she said to Dana, "Now don't go cutting in your head before we see you again."

"No, ma'am," Dana said. She was like a different person now. At first I thought she was trying not to laugh, but now it seemed like she was trying not to cry.

"Show yourself out," Mama said. "Chaurisse has work to do."

I nodded and wrenched the top off of a large jar of basting oil. Dana stood at the doorway with her hand on the push bar, looking at us like she was about to go off to war. "Good-bye," she said.

She couldn't have been at the end of the driveway before everybody started talking about her.

"Something feels sad about that girl," my mama said.

"I was about to say the same thing," said the lady with the lap baby. "I wonder what kind of home she's going back to."

"There was a girl like that at my high school," my mama said. "Had a baby for her daddy. She had that same beat-down way about her."

"But such a pretty girl," the old lady said.

"And all that hair."

"Pretty ain't everything," I said, surprising myself by speaking up.

"You jealous, Chaurisse?" my mama said.

"No. I'm just saying there could be more to her than just that. And she might have a good home. She could just be lonely. It's a lot of people walking around that's lonely."

Since it was a Wednesday night, Mama and I sat down to dinner by ourselves. My mother stood at the counter tossing a large salad. She was always watching what she ate. My mother was on a diet on the day I was born. On the bottom of my foot, there is a birthmark, several small brown splotches arranged like a little constellation. These are orange seeds, I am told. There was a rumor that pregnant ladies who consumed lots of vitamin C would lose their baby weight faster. It didn't work. My mother grew two dress sizes after I was born, firmly lodging her at a size 18, which made her eligible to shop at the fat ladies' store.

I went into the fridge and pulled out two cans of Coke, diet for mama, regular for me.

"You want a glass, Mama?"

She said, "Can is all right for me."

We sat at the table, across from each

other, she at the nine, and me at the three. The twelve and the six are for Daddy and Uncle Raleigh, even if they aren't here.

Mama squeezed a lemon over her salad while I layered mine with Green Goddess.

"There's no point in eating salad if you're going to do that."

"I know," I said.

She shook her head at me. "That girl this afternoon, she looks familiar. What was going on with her?"

"I don't know."

Mama said, "She nervouses me."

"She's all right," I said. "I kind of like her.'

"She tell you what her problem is? She pregnant?"

"She was worried about going to college. That's what she was talking about."

"It's good for her to be concerned about her education. I didn't finger her for the type."

"Can't judge a book by its cover," I said.

"What are you thinking about college?"

"What do you think about Mount Holyoke? That's where Dana said she was going."

"Never heard of it, but it can't be any better than Spelman College. That's where I would have gone if things had turned out different."

My mother finished her salad and looked into the bowl with a sort of empty dissatisfaction. She reached for a saltine cracker and ate it slowly. She rubbed her eyes with the heels of her hands.

"Your daddy'll be home after while. What do you think he wants for dinner?" She got up and opened the freezer, and found four chicken legs. She set them in a bowl of warm water to thaw. "I should make enough for Raleigh, too."

"Yeah," I said. "Might as well."

16
THE REST, LIKE THEY SAY, IS HISTORY

When I was just three months old, sick as a dog with colic, only Daddy could calm me down. I would wake up crying that high-pitched miserable cry and Daddy would get out of bed, go to my room, wrap me up in a couple blankets, and we might spend the rest of the night touring the back roads of DeKalb County in the Lincoln. It wasn't just the fresh air that soothed me, though I still like to drive with the windows open, even in winter. It was the going that I liked. Around that same time, Raleigh bought me a baby swing from Sears, Roebuck. He assembled the pink and yellow contraption with a flathead screwdriver and an Allen wrench. Once it was upright and sturdy, Uncle Raleigh and Mama waited for me to start crying. Being as I was a preemie, born almost dead, I cried all the time. At the first whimper, Mama and Raleigh scooped me up, strapped me in, and started the swing to rocking. When the whimper switched over into something more in the category of a howl, Daddy was the one who rescued me, told them to give it up.

While he and I were cruising all over southwest Atlanta, down by Niskey Lake, even winding through the beautiful paths at West View Cemetery, Mama and Raleigh were taking the baby swing apart and fitting it back in the cardboard box. All that back-and-forth did nothing for me. I needed forward motion and the quiet hum of a well-tuned engine.

We kept up our motor excursions even after I stopped crying in the night. It's illegal now to drive a car with a three-year-old in your lap, her little palms on the wheel, but this still remains one of my fondest memories. I can still remember stretching my hands to grip the steering wheel, Daddy saying, "There you go, Buttercup. There you go." When I was twelve, it was time to take things to the next level.

Although the state wouldn't allow it until I was sixteen, I was ready to drive. Daddy took me for my first lessons at the Ford factory off I-75. We went on Sundays, when the almost three thousand union workers were home sleeping in, leaving the massive parking lot almost empty.

"You know what?" he said to me on our way to my first lesson. "Driving is the most important thing you can know how to do. When I was a boy, I used to drive for white people, the same white people that my mama cleaned for. At first, when I was fifteen, sixteen, I used to wish I was the one riding in the backseat. I could picture myself walking out of the school building and there being a man in a hat, waiting to take me somewhere."

"Where did you want to go?" I asked him.

"I didn't even know for sure. I guess I imagined I would have the car carry me to Atlanta. Or just to a nice restaurant where I could sit down and eat something good, like steak and a glass of sweet tea. Maybe a baked potato. A country boy like me, that was all the finery I could imagine. Sour cream on the potato. I had never even tasted it before, but I always heard white folks asking for it or saying they didn't want it." He shrugged and smiled over at me. "You didn't know your daddy could be so silly, did you?"

I smiled back at him and tried to imagine him as a boy. I had seen a couple of his old school portraits, the black-and-white tone blurring into something gray and indistinct. JIMMY WITHERSPOON was written right below the collar of his white shirt. When I stayed with Grandma Bunny for a month each summer, that picture was the first thing I saw when I opened my eyes, but I could never get my brain to accept that this Jimmy Witherspoon with the lazy eye and confident smile was my father.

"So the idea I had — to have my own driver one day — led me to thinking what kind of job I would need in order to have somebody to drive me. My mama's white people, they got their money because they owned the paper mill, and I knew I didn't want to have nothing to do with the paper mill. Just the smell alone was enough to run you away, no matter what the money was like. So I couldn't think of nothing else, and it started making me depressed. Crazy as it was, I wanted to have a white man driving me around, to let him see what it feels like." Daddy laughed. "My imagination was in overdrive. A black man having a chauffeur was crazy enough, but hiring a white man to drive? Absolutely insane. But this was my dream, and I didn't tell nobody about it except Raleigh."

"What did Uncle Raleigh say?"

Daddy said, "You know how Raleigh is. He don't like to argue. He just asked me if I was going to let my white driver use the front door or the back door when he showed up for work. I said I would go on and let him walk in the front. Then Raleigh asked me if maybe I could just use a real light-skinned black man to do the driving, that way it would look like I had a white driver, but I wouldn't have to deal with all the problems that might come along with trying to boss a real white man. I laughed and told him that the only person in the world more uppity than an actual white man was a light-skinned nigger. I think that hurt his feelings, but I wasn't talking about Raleigh. Your uncle is a special case, you know."

I said I knew what he was talking about.

"Truth of the matter is that it was Raleigh who gave me the idea of starting my own business, but I don't want to get ahead of myself. This here is a good story and I want to tell it properly.

"I used to drive these white people around all the time. Me and Raleigh used to take turns with the job, but the white people didn't like Raleigh all that much. So I took on the driving full time, and Raleigh had to go over to the mill. He stank so bad coming back home, but me and Laverne never said anything to him about it. Didn't need to, I guess. He got a nose. We waited on him to wash up before we ate dinner, but you could still smell the mill on him.

"One day, I was driving the white lady somewhere. She was all dressed up, hat, gloves, pink lipstick drawn where lips would have been if she had any. I just let her in, closed the door behind her and set off. No radio, no nothing, me and her just riding along listening to each other breathing. Anyway, I was driving and I saw a sign up on the left for the highway. I seen that sign a hundred times, but this time I really saw it, and it occurred to me that I could just twist my arms a little bit, turn the steering wheel and go wherever I wanted to. That lady in the backseat wouldn't have no choice but to come along for the ride. I started laughing then, laughing hard. I liked to choke on so much laughing. I could see the lady in the backseat looking scared, like she was trapped in the car with a crazy nigger. All I had to do was like this here" — he rotated the steering wheel to the left, changing lanes — "and me and her would have been on the highway headed toward Hilton Head. You get it, don't you, Chaurisse?

"It takes a lot of trust to let somebody drive you around. People don't think about it — you should see them just hopping into taxicabs downtown, not knowing who they got behind the wheel. That's why I don't get in no airplanes, neither. I was having all these thoughts while I was driving the car and laughing like a loon. The white lady looked like she was going to throw up. Then I stopped laughing and try to seem like I had some sense. All the time my mind was just working.

"I couldn't wait to tell it to Raleigh. He had just come home from the mill. I usually gave him his space when he got home, and not just because of how he was smelling but because he didn't like to be around people until he got his constitution together. But I just had to tell him. He was walking up the steps to the front of the house and he didn't even get the doorknob turned good before I busted out with it.

"I said, 'I don't ever want nobody driving me around. Whoever is doing the driving is really the one in control.'

"Raleigh looked at me like, 'You just now figuring that out?' Your uncle is a very intelligent man. He's like Albert Einstein and George Washington Carver rolled up into one. Then he said, 'Can we talk about this after I got my bath?'

"I said 'Okay.' Your mama was in the kitchen frying some fish. We had been married about two years, maybe three, and she was just finally at last learning how to cook.

She almost killed me and Raleigh both with food poisoning. Did I ever tell you that story? It's funny now, but it wasn't funny at the time.

"I was just burning up with my new way of thinking. Raleigh was taking his sweet time washing up. He's not like that now, but he used to be a pretty nigger when we was younger, rubbing baby oil on his arms to make the hair lie down. Stuff like that. So by the time he got his pretty self ready, I had already told it to your mama and she didn't seem to be moved by what I had to say.

"Finally we sat down at the table to eat. Your mama was still into religion back then, so we said grace and 'Jesus Wept.' Raleigh reached for a piece of fish, and I couldn't hold back any longer.

" 'You didn't tell me what you think of my idea.'

"Raleigh said, 'What idea?'

" 'My idea that when you are driving the car, you are always the boss. Did you ever think of that?'

" 'The boss is the one that pays you,' Raleigh said.

" 'But every time they get in the car with me, they are putting their life in my hands.'

" 'That's true,' your mama said."

Daddy laughed and hit his hand on steering wheel. "When we were young, your mama was 'Yes, baby' this, 'Yes, baby' that." He laughed again. "Those were some good days. We struggled, but those sure was some good days.

"Raleigh said, 'The boss is the one who owns the car.'

"And just like that, it clicked: I needed to own myself a car and let people hire me to drive them around.

"I can't say those other two were ready to hop on board. I mean, we all knew we wanted something else out of life. Your mama was doing white people's laundry, didn't have her high-school diploma. Me and Raleigh had our diplomas, but neither one of us had the kind of job you could be proud of. It was, what? 'Sixty? 'Sixty-two? Something like that. We were young and ready to break out into the world. Raleigh had his eye on going to college. He didn't know how he was going to get there, but he wanted it so bad, he was thinking about the army. I said, 'Man, are you crazy?' He lucky he didn't get drafted. So I saved up some money, and Miss Bunny gave me what she had. Raleigh and Laverne gave me their pennies, too. They both had other plans for their money, but I knew this was going to be the ticket. If things went the way I needed them to go, there would be money later for beauty school and college. I bought the first car. That Plymouth. It wasn't nice like this here Lincoln, but I kept it clean and even crammed a little flavored pillow under the seat. Your mama stuffed it with cinnamon sticks and other nice-smelling things; she even sewed some embroidery on it.

"I started driving colored people around, not the well-off folks, because who would pay money to hire a car that wasn't as good as the one you have in your driveway? People hired me especially on occasions like funerals, weddings, things like that. After a couple years, I gave your mama and Miss Bunny their money back. I told Raleigh I was prepared to return his investment — I had it for him in a brown envelope, looked all official and everything. I said, 'Raleigh, here you go, every penny back, with interest. I got it for you right here, or we can make a deal, a partnership, save up for another car and go into business together. Fifty-fifty.'

"The rest, like they say, is history."

17
TIME AND A HALF

In the eighties, you could still smoke in restaurants but only in the smoking section. I don't smoke, will never smoke. I even refuse to date smokers because their ashtray kisses remind me too much of my father. Still, I feel a little pang of sympathy when I see a NO SMOKING sign. The diagonal slash seems heartless, cruel even. My daddy took the ban personally, said it reminded him too much of Mississippi, but he laughed it off with the same sad joke. "Just when they took down all the signs that said 'No Coloreds,' they had to come up with a new way to keep me out. Ain't that right, Raleigh?" Then Uncle Raleigh would say, "If it ain't one thing, it's another."

"I know that's right," I would chime in, thinking not of the smoking bans but of the slew of Sweet Sixteen parties that year. My mother, who had been doing hair for more than fifteen years, had never seen anything like it. Daddy thought it had something to do with Ronald Reagan. Although no self-respecting black person would cast a vote for that joker, Daddy had to admit that the man had a way about him that was infectious. "Carter was a good man, but he didn't exactly make you want to go out and hire a limousine for your kid's birthday party. What do you think, Buttercup?"

"I think it's *Dynasty*. Everybody wants to be Alexis."

"Even black folks?" said Uncle Raleigh.

"Everybody," I said. "Even Diahann Carroll herself."

"What about Bill Cosby? You don't think people want to be high on the hog like the Cosbys?"

"Bill Cosby makes you want to buy a hundred-dollar sweater," I said.

"Well," said Uncle Raleigh. "I'll admit that I enjoy a nice cardigan, but in general, I am a simple man with simple taste." He waved his arm to take in our environment, his cigarette making a ghostly trail.

We were at IHOP on North Avenue, killing time while Ruth Nicole Elizabeth Grant was having her Sweet Sixteen at the Hilton downtown. Her parents went all out, requesting the limo, the Town Car, and an attendant — which was me. All I had to do

308

was be on hand in case somebody needed a tissue or breath mints on the ride. Tucked in my canvas pack was a handy bottle of club soda in case someone spilled something on their clothes and a barrel brush in case there was a Shirley Temple back there that needed twirling. I never had to dab a stain from a dress, although curls always could use a little tending to. For the most part, I was getting paid six dollars an hour just to ride around. We were even on the clock sitting up in IHOP eating pigs in a blanket.

Uncle Raleigh and Daddy both wore their dress uniforms, but they left the jackets in the car. They horsed around like boys as they sucked down cup after cup of thin coffee, loosened up with cream and sugar. Sitting on opposite sides of the booth, they often looked up at one another and grinned. I always alternated my seat when I went out with the two of them. I don't know that they ever noticed, but it wasn't right that Uncle Raleigh should have to be alone all the time.

Women at the Pink Fox wondered aloud why Uncle Raleigh was still available, and I knew at least three ladies who would be more than happy to do something about it. Uncle Raleigh didn't come around the salon much, and neither did my daddy. (My mama says it's just that they don't want to see where pretty comes from.) Uncle Raleigh kept his visits short and sweet. When he entered the shop, delivering a package or something, the ladies who were already curled and looking pretty flirted outrageously while the ones who were wet and still nappy hid behind their *Ebony* magazines, taking interested peeks over the tops of the glossy pages. Uncle Raleigh, knowing his role, complimented everyone, including Mama and me, before leaving with a tip of his hat.

Once he was gone, the speculation began in earnest. They ran through the respectable options first. Had he been hurt by a woman so now he was gun-shy? Was he married to the limo company? Lord have mercy, had he been to Vietnam? (At this point, the conversation could get pretty intense depending on the age of the women getting their hair done. It was always a brother-in-law that they talked about having been driven crazy by that war. It was never a husband or, thankyoujesus, a son.) The romantics wondered if maybe Uncle Raleigh had a woman but for some reason — like maybe she was the mayor's wife — he had to keep it secret.

Mama denied all these theories. "He's set in his ways," she'd say, or "He's just waiting to meet the right person." Sometimes one woman would be brave enough to ask the question that was on everyone's mind. The asker was either the oldest or youngest person in the shop. "He's not funny, is he, Verne?"

Mama said no, that wasn't it at all.

The truth was that Uncle Raleigh wasn't really a bachelor. He had us.

Mama told me once, on a Monday, while she was working in my relaxer, that she had seen Uncle Raleigh with a woman before. The woman was dark-skinned, really dark, like Cicely Tyson, but with hair for days. I had seen the woman, too, but I couldn't say anything. It was just before Jamal graduated, before I figured out that you can be safe and sorry at the same time. Jamal and I were at Adams Park, in the middle of a school day. We didn't have anywhere else to go — my mama operated a business out of my house and his mother (as she told anybody that would sit still and listen) "didn't have to work," so she was home all day. So we were stuck with public places. He was eager to get back to the car, which he had parked in a discreet spot near a bank of pine trees. I said that I wanted to play on the swings for a while. It was a lie, I didn't care anything about the swings, but I wanted him to coax me back to the car, for him to say how much he had missed me all day in school, for him to thrill me by pressing my hand to the front of his jeans, for him to say that he worried that he was going to bust the zipper just by loving me so much. I was going to ride the swing, flashing him when the air flipped my skirt until he had to say, "Chaurisse, I am crazy about you."

I had just settled my hips on the swing and used my tiptoes to push back a few paces when I saw my uncle and his lady friend. Uncle Raleigh and I looked right into each other's faces. My hand floated up to my nose, the way it did when I was afraid. Uncle Raleigh cocked his head like dogs do when they're confused. Jamal turned to see what I was looking at and Uncle Raleigh's lady friend did the same. We were, all four of us, caught up in something, but at the time, I couldn't say exactly what. Then Uncle Raleigh put his finger to his lips like a watchful librarian.

He never brought his girlfriend around to the house and I never asked. It was simple courtesy, really, one of the rules of our house. We were a polite family back then. For example, on this Saturday night, no one asked me why I wasn't invited to Ruth Nicole Elizabeth's Sweet Sixteen, although we lived in the same neighborhood, had belonged to the same Brownie troop, and our mothers took the same dance class at the YWCA. Not only that, but I'd been to Ruth Nicole Elizabeth's parties in the past, and my mother always made sure I gave her a good gift. Just last year, I presented her with three fluted add-a-beads — fourteen karat. The previous parties had all been held in her big backyard or in their nice finished basement. Her Sweet Sixteen was to be an elaborate catered situation, which was different. Her parents had to pay a specific amount for each guest. If you were going, you had to RSVP, and rumor had it there was a wait list.

Uncle Raleigh struck a match and lit the cigarette dangling from his thin lips. "You want some of this, Jim-Bo?" he said, offering the burning stick to my dad, who leaned his cigarette into the flame.

I asked the waitress for a refill on my Diet Coke.

"Get a regular Coke," Daddy said, looping his arm around my shoulder.

"Too many calories," I said.

"Why you and your mama are so hung up on this weight thing? Don't nobody but a dog want a bone."

"And even he wants some meat on it,"

313

Uncle Raleigh said.

They laughed and kept eating.

"What time is it?" I asked, with a flip of my hair.

My dad frowned. He didn't care for my augmented look. He said it was because I didn't need it.

"It's only ten thirty. The event is scheduled to go until midnight," Uncle Raleigh said.

"It's a big deal, this party," I said. "Mama did the hair. Ruth Nicole Elizabeth, her mama, her best friend. We worked on them all day."

We did, and it had been a pretty miserable afternoon. To her credit, Ruth Nicole Elizabeth never said the word *party* while I basted her head. She didn't even complain when I tugged too hard at a tangle behind her ears, removing the soft strands at the root. We finally got them out of the shop at 4:30 p.m. They went home to slip into their "after-five attire" and I went upstairs to put on my blue-and-white so I could go work with Daddy and Uncle Raleigh. For the record, I did own an after-five dress. It was lavender, with asymmetric tiers and a sweetheart neck, junior size 13. My daddy brought it home late one night; he won it in a poker game.

Even though we were flush straight

through spring, my mama was never in a good mood getting people ready for formals. You wouldn't know it from watching her, but that's called being a professional. She would be all smiles six weeks later when the girls gave her wallet-sized photos of themselves dressed in *Gone with the Wind* hoopskirts; above the shampoo bowl hung a corkboard just for these displays. But when we finally closed down the shop, she flopped in her chair with a tiredness that was more than just one day's exhaustion. "The money is good, but I don't envy Raleigh and James. Driving those girls around and calling them ma'am! Sixteen years old. Help me, Jesus. It will be prom season before you know it."

"Your mama is looking at things all the wrong way," Daddy said, slicing into his sausages. "Twenty years ago, none of this would be possible. Your mama can't see good news when it is staring her right in the face."

"How much you think a party like that would cost?" Uncle Raleigh asked.

"I don't know," I said.

"Four thousand? Five?" Daddy said. "But I am just talking out the side of my neck. I don't know nothing about this kind of thing. You ever want a party like this, Buttercup?"

"It's too late for me to have a Sweet Sixteen, Daddy. I'm seventeen already."

"You could have a Sweet Eighteen."

"Doesn't exist," I said.

"Graduation party?" Daddy suggested.

"Not my speed."

Uncle Raleigh said, "I was thinking about for Laverne."

"I don't know," I said. "This kind of stuff gets on her nerves. She turned so many spiral curls last week that she had to wear a brace on her wrist."

"It's different," Daddy said. "It's different being the guest of honor."

"I don't know," I said. "She isn't really like that."

"Maybe she is," Uncle Raleigh said.

"She's not," I said. "I'm sure of it."

"We've been knowing Laverne a lot longer than you," Daddy added, and together they chuckled.

"She hates fancy parties," I said. "I'm with her all the time. I know how much she hates them."

Uncle Raleigh said, "By my calculation, it's coming up on the twentieth anniversary of the Pink Fox."

"There you go," Daddy said.

They smiled at each other and turned

their faces to me. There was no challenging them.

"We'll tell her it's your idea," said Raleigh "I thought it was supposed to be a surprise party," I said.

"She won't like that," Daddy said.

"Verne does not like surprises."

"That's the truth," Daddy said.

And there was no arguing. They had been knowing Laverne a lot longer than me. And with the matter settled, they went on to other topics. To Uncle Raleigh, Daddy said, "We could probably make some good money if we could bring back the photography angle to the business."

Uncle Raleigh poured a little puddle of raspberry syrup on his plate and dunked the tines of his fork. "Nope, Jim-Bo. No. No. No."

"How come?" I said. "You like taking pictures. Teenage girls like having their picture taken. Their parents like spending money. Seems like a good deal all around."

"I don't want to take prom pictures," Uncle Raleigh said. "I want to be evocative."

Daddy said, "Evock in your spare time. Think about it, man. People are going to college next year."

By *people*, he meant me.

"Where do you want to go to school?" Uncle Raleigh asked.

"I'm thinking about Mount Holyoke," I said.

My father and my uncle looked at each other. "You d-d-don't say," said Daddy.

"It's still early," Uncle Raleigh said, more to my father than to me. "It's still early."

After we paid the check, we headed back to the Hilton. Daddy sent me in at eleven thirty to see if things were winding down. On the ride up to the twenty-third floor, I straightened my collar and smoothed the accordion wrinkles from my skirt. The bullet-shaped elevator was glass, allowing me a full view of Atlanta. The door opened and I looked around for the Magnolia Room. It took a couple trips up and down the carpeted hallway before I ran into Mr. Grant, Ruth Nicole Elizabeth's dad. Tiny comb tracks made roadways in his Billy Dee waves.

"Witherspoon!" he said, after patting down the pockets of his brain, trying to remember my first name. "I almost didn't recognize you with your hair down."

"Hello, Mr. Grant. I just came up to see how things are coming along."

"It's a beautiful night," he said. "Go on in

and fix yourself a plate."

"Oh no, sir," I said, tugging at my hem. "I'm working tonight."

"Don't be silly," he said, putting his arm around my shoulders. Mr. Grant smelled nice, like good cologne and cognac. I knew that I smelled like fried food and cigarettes.

"You are such a pretty girl. Such a young lady." He kissed me on the top of my head and gave me a little squeeze around the tops of my arms. "Go on in. Enjoy yourself."

He opened the door of the Magnolia Room, leaving me no choice but to step inside. For a moment, I was queasy with a wave of déjà vu, as this was the setting of one of my nightmares. In the dream, I walk into a fancy party. Everyone else is dressed for prom, but I am fat and wearing a two-piece bathing suit. My stomach sags over the leopard-print bikini and I am afraid to raise my arms because everyone will see that I haven't shaved. When I have this dream lately, I know that I'm dreaming, but this understanding isn't enough to wake me up. When I'm finally able to open my eyes, grateful for my familiar bedsheets, my body is damp and cold.

In the Magnolia Room, the partygoers were all silver as tea sets, and no one noticed me at all.

The DJ was playing a slow song, "Against All Odds." In the center of the dance floor was Ruth Nicole Elizabeth, swaying with her boyfriend, Marcus McCready, home from college. His hands rested respectfully at the small of her back, just above the satin sash. Ruth Nicole Elizabeth's dress, like her skin, was the color of sand. Her hair, glistening from a cellophane rinse, reminded me of an oily lunch sack. Over the top of her head, Marcus met my eyes and kind of winked. I turned away and rushed toward the food.

The lady serving the cake, old as Grandma Bunny, was dressed almost the same as I was.

"Is it good?" I asked.

"It's pretty," she said, sliding a piece of cake onto my plate.

"Thank you." I headed toward the door even though the plate probably wasn't supposed to leave the Magnolia Room. On the twenty-three-story trip down, I tore into the lemon layer cake with my dirty hands.

In the lobby, I set the plate on a shiny-topped coffee table. I was tempted to follow the signs to the washroom so I could clean my hands, but I couldn't bear the idea of mirrors. Instead, I set myself on the couch and sucked my fingers like a barbarian.

"Psst," someone said from the direction of the bathroom. My mother had told me that a man who doesn't talk to you with actual words isn't worth your time, but still I looked around. When I didn't see anyone, I turned my attention to my hands. Pale yellow icing rimmed my cuticles so I stuck my thumb in my mouth, wondering if everything on the twenty-third floor had been engineered to match Ruth Nicole Elizabeth's magnolia-cream complexion. I had busted out of the party before I had a chance to check out the hot-food buffet. I amused myself imagining a pale spread — cauliflower, baked fish, mashed potatoes. Enjoying these petty, jealous fantasies, I took my thumb out of my mouth and rearranged my hair.

"Ooh," said a voice. "You got spit in your fake hair."

"Dana!" I hated the hopeful lilt in my voice.

"Hey, girlie," she said, strolling toward me. "Have you seen a security guard around here?"

I shook my head.

"You sure?" she said. "He's cute, like a DeBarge, but he was hassling us." Dana looked behind her. At the wave of her hand, another girl appeared. This girl was even less silver than me. Her haircut had a kind of homemade look, like she had trimmed it with paper scissors; her ears were scabbed from amateur attempts with the curling iron. Like Dana, she wore a purple keyhole top and stretch Gloria Vanderbilts. They even wore the same shoes — purple dyed-to-match pumps, the kind other girls wear with prom dresses.

"This is Ronalda," Dana said.

"We're best friends," Ronalda said, as if I didn't catch the matching outfits.

"Nice to meet you." I sighed.

Dana and Ronalda sat together on a leather love seat across from me. Ronalda dug into her bag and produced a tube of lotion. She squeezed a little on the tips of her fingers and dabbed the teardrop of skin inside the keyhole of her shirt.

"You so crazy," Dana said, taking the lotion and doing the same thing. "You want some?"

"No," I said. "I'm okay."

"So," Dana said to me. "Where does your mother think you are?" She nudged Ronalda with her shoulder. "We are supposed to be in a lock-in at my church."

Dana put her hand in her hair and then stopped. She felt her ear. "I lost my earring," she said.

Ronalda said, "Nobody move," like she was looking for a lost contact. Dana's voice climbed in pitch. "I hope I didn't lose it on the MARTA. They're my mother's and her mother gave them to her. Oh my God."

Ronalda was on her hands and knees, looking under the love seat. Dana muttered and walked herself in little shaky circles. I got up and ran my hand in the crevices of the sofa. "We'll find it." I took the cushion off the love seat, even though the ladies working the front desk were looking at us cross-eyed.

"I don't see it," Ronalda said, standing up.

"Hold on," I said to Dana. I stepped toward her, lifting her hair from her neck. There, snagged at her neckline, was the hoop earring. I twisted it free and handed it to her. It was antique-looking, like something Grandma Bunny used to wear. The gold was etched with a careful pattern of leaves.

"Oh my God," she said. "Thank you. Thank you so much." She threaded it through the hole in her ear while Ronalda put the furniture back together.

I sat back on the little couch, and this time Dana sat by me. "You saved my life," she said.

I was pleased enough to break into song, but I waved it away. "I didn't do anything."

"So how come you're here?" Ronalda said.

"How come y'all are?" I shot back.

"We tried to get into the party upstairs," Dana said. "But we got turned away."

"Just because we weren't invited," Ronalda snorted.

"I went inside. It wasn't all that great."

"Who was there?"

"I don't know. People. Ruth Nicole Elizabeth, her boyfriend Marcus."

Ronalda sucked her teeth and Dana tapped her fingers against her cheek.

Dana said, "So you and Ruth Nicole Elizabeth are friends?"

"No," I said quickly. "I been knowing her since kindergarten and she didn't even invite me."

"She lives down the street from me," Ronalda said.

"She sits next to me in calculus," Dana said.

"So," Ronalda said. "If you're not here for the party, then how come you're here?"

"I'm working," I said. "My dad has a limo company. We're handling transport for Ruth Nicole Elizabeth and her family."

"You can drive a limousine?" Ronalda asked.

"I *can,* but I'm not. I'm an attendant." I spoke to her slowly, like she didn't speak English.

"Your dad is here?" This was from Dana.

"Yeah," I said. "You two want to go outside and see the cars?"

Ronalda spoke up. "No, we are not into all of that." She stood and held out her hand. Dana took it and pulled herself up from the sofa. "We got to go."

"Wait," I said, scrambling up. "Dana, you never did make your appointment for your wash-and-set. You want to come in on Tuesday?"

"No," she said, doing a quick look-around to make sure she wasn't leaving anything. "I can only come on a Wednesday."

"Bye," I called as Ronalda pulled my silver girl away. It was like a Shakespeare play; they just sort of vanished into the wings, with Dana watching me over her shoulder.

I got back in the elevator and rode down to the parking garage. Uncle Raleigh and Daddy were leaning against the hood of the Town Car, passing a single cigarette back and forth like a joint.

"Is that party almost done with? Me and Raleigh are running out of smokes."

"They'll be out soon," I said.

Something in my voice made my daddy

turn his attention from the shared cigarette to me. "What's the matter, Buttercup?"

"Nothing," I said.

"Oh, it's something," Uncle Raleigh said.

"I just don't have any friends," I said. "I know people or whatever, but who's my best friend? Who's going to invite me to their Sweet Sixteen and let me ride in the limo with them?" I covered my face with my cake-sticky hands. My father and Uncle Raleigh looked at one another. It would have been funny to an onlooker. Their confusion had a sitcom quality, like two men who are forced to see to a woman that's going into labor.

"F-f-forget about them," my daddy said. "Our party is going to be ten times bigger than this. And we won't invite Ruth, Nicole, or Elizabeth."

"And we are going to charge them time and a half for all this extra time they got us sitting out here," Uncle Raleigh said.

Daddy said, "Goddamn right."

18
LOVE AND HAPPINESS

On October 18, 1974, when a really pissed-off black woman flung a pot of hot grits on Al Green, her hair was freshly pressed and curled by none other than my mama. As a result of our little brush with Negro history, nobody made Al Green jokes in our house, or even in the Pink Fox, where you can imagine a lot of women fantasized about taking revenge on a lying man. I think the women liked the story not just because of the drama of it, but because grits were the weapon of choice. The boiling cereal reminded them of being stuck in a hot kitchen, poor and barefoot in the days before they had even heard of waffles or hollandaise sauce. That girl, whatever her name was, took the entire state of Mississippi and used it to kick somebody's ass. All you had to do was say "Al Green" and "grits" in the same conversation and the titter of laughing started, but my mama cut it off with a quiet

"That's not funny." You couldn't hear it in her voice, but if you looked at her face, at the way she closed her eyes and tucked her head down like she was in prayer, you knew that she was serious.

The woman who did it was named Mary. The *Atlanta Journal* said her family name was Sanford while *Jet* magazine called her Woodson. She told my mother she was visiting Atlanta for a few days in order to attend an AME Usher Board convention. Even before she noticed Mary's cross pendant — simple, the jewelry equivalent of two sticks tied together — Mama knew that the woman was saved. Even after what happened next, Mama said she never doubted that Mary had come to Jesus. The truly saved don't have to go around talking about it. They just have this quietness about them like they know exactly where they're going.

Mary walked in on a Tuesday evening, opening the door at seven thirty, after Mama had finished her last customer of the night. As a matter of fact, Mama was untying her apron and switching off the gas under the irons when Mary crossed the threshold, looking like a kindergarten teacher at the end of a long day. She wore a pink pantsuit, stylish, but the topstitching on the pockets gave away that it was homemade. Mama said she will never forget that face, smooth as a brown egg, no lines or crinkles, like she had never laughed or cried in her whole entire life.

This was not a good night for a late customer. My mama wasn't all that steady on her feet, as this was her first full week of work after her gallbladder operation. These days they can do the whole thing with lasers and make only a little hole in your belly button, but in 1974 the doctors had to cut you open, straight down the middle, gut you like a fish. Mama was laid up for two weeks, and during that time Grandma Bunny came down to see about her. When Mary came into the shop, Grandma Bunny was only two days gone back to Ackland. To make matters worse, I had come down with a cold and a touch of fever. In the corner of the shop, I dozed fitfully on a pallet, coughing and whimpering in my sleep. Besides, it was time for Mama to change the bandage on her wound.

"Do you take walk-ins?" Mary asked. "I know you are likely closing up, but maybe you can find it in your heart to help me?"

Although it was only a couple weeks into October, something put my mother in the mind of Christmas. Maybe it was just as simple as the name Mary, but Mama felt that God would want her to take this stranger in. "I'm not well, but I might could help you," my mother said. "Depending on what you need."

"I'll tip you good," Mary said, sitting in the chair like my mother had already said yes. She pulled half a dozen bobby pins out of her scrawny bun and unwrapped a red rubber band that came away clotted with hair. "Thank you. And God bless you."

Mama got Mary into the shampoo bowl, and half her hair lay down straight and docile under the faucet. That's what happens when you have been getting hard presses for more than twenty years. Some of the kink just gets lost.

"Can I talk to you?" Mary asked my mother.

"Of course," Mama said. "Nobody in here but us."

"I'm leaving my husband," she said. "We're not equally yoked." Mary, like my mother, had married young. Mama didn't say anything one way or another. She just combed through Mary's half-nappy hair, sectioning it off and plaiting it up to dry.

"The Bible says your mate got to be your equal. Y'all have to both love the Lord in the same way." Mary's voice was calm and steady.

It was warm for October, so Mama had the door propped open to let the breeze in. She could smell burning leaves. "You have children?"

Mary said she had three, but they would be all right with their father. The Lord, she said, had called her to another man. They were going to the minister together. This new man was going to take some working on, some praying over, but the Lord was inside him. She could feel it burning through his skin. This boyfriend, Mary said, was chosen. "You ever touch the hand of a preacher that is truly righteous? That has healing in his hands? You know how it's like he empties out your body and just fills you up with spirit?"

Mama nodded her head, because she had met a preacher like that years ago, when she was still a girl in Ackland. This was just after the baby boy died and she was wandering around looking for somewhere to go. This preacher that touched my mother was a child, a little girl, black as a cast-iron skillet, with a nurse's cap pinned over her short hair. My mother was walking by, struggling with a basket of laundry, when this girl preacher grabbed her by the arm; Mama felt herself hollowed out and filled with light. The little-girl preacher held a white leather Bible in her dark hand. "Will you pray with me, sister?" My mama said she didn't have time, although she was warm from the child's touch. "Are white people's dirty drawers more important than your soul, sister? Come to me," the little girl said. "Get on your knees with me." My mother looked over her shoulder. They were standing in front of the colored high school, where Raleigh and James were in class. Mama could imagine the home ec teacher looking at her out of the window and seeing her kneeling in the street with this pickaninny preacher and the basket of laundry beside her. "I can't," Mama said. "I just can't." The little girl said, "That's pride. Give me your hand, sister. Your vanity is your burden. Lay it down. Let me touch your soul." My mama extended her hand, greedy for another dose of that touch. The child squeezed my mother's hand. "You don't have to get on your knees. He can touch your heart while you are on your own two feet." My mama says her legs just gave out under her and she was on her knees in the road and that little girl stroked Mama's face and talked to Jesus while my mama sobbed. "Ask the Lord to take care of my baby," Mama begged the girl. "He'll take care of you, too," the girl said, and with every caress of her tiny hands my mother felt her spirit mend.

"Yes," my mama told Mary. "I have been touched by an anointed preacher. Just one time."

"This man I got," Mary said. "He sings. No matter what he's singing, he's got God in him. People come to hear him and start crying. They think he is crooning about love between a man and a woman, worldly love, but what he's doing is making them feel the Jesus. He's a miracle. We are going to build a ministry together."

On my pallet, I woke up sweating and confused. I sat up and called for my mother. I called for her with a sound like a frightened question, as though it was the middle of the night and I was all alone.

"I'm here, baby," Mama said to me. "Lie back down, okay." To Mary she explained. "She woke up with a fever this morning. I've been giving her aspirin."

"Ginger ale is good, too," Mary said. "If you have some fresh ginger, grate some of that in the glass. She won't like it, but it'll help."

I called for my mother with a voice full of

tears. She set the hot comb down and walked over to me, but didn't bend down to hold me. I stood up and grabbed her around the legs.

"Mary," Mama said. "Can you help me? I've been operated on. I can't lift her."

"Where's your husband?" Mary asked, walking over to me.

"If she won't let you hold her, don't be hurt," Mama said. "Sometimes she doesn't cotton to new people."

"I love children," Mary said. "I have three. Two girls, a boy. I miss them. But you got to do what the Lord calls you to do." She reached for me and I released my mother's knees and held out my arms. I was big for my age, but she lifted me easily. "She's got a little bit of a temperature," Mary said to my mother. The story is that she held me in her lap like I was a little baby although I was nearly five years old. I just rested my head on her breast, sweating a dark spot onto her pink lapel.

After Mama finished pressing Mary's hair, she smoothed it with a boar-bristle brush. Mary's fine hair crackled with static; ghost strands stood up on their own and danced.

"It's not just lust when we're together." Mary twisted in the chair and searched my mother's face.

Mama said, "I know."

Mary didn't want the curls combed out, since she was going to have to ride the bus eight hours to Memphis and she needed her hair to be fresh when she got there. She took Mama's address, writing the street number on a folded index card pulled from the bottom of her purse. "I am going to write to you when I get everything set up. You'll have to come to meet him. You need to feel that healing touch again. My man is true," she said. "True as the Word."

When she was done, Mama didn't even want to take her money, so Mary tucked the twenty-dollar bill in the little pocket of my dress. Mama didn't notice because of all the commotion I caused when Mary tried to leave. She set me down and headed toward the door and I threw a fit. "Don't go," I said over and over, grabbing for Mary's legs. Mama was so embarrassed that she forgot her condition and bent to pull me away. The pain caught her by surprise and she staggered a little bit. Mary picked me up again and kissed my feverish little face. "Jesus loves you," she said. "And you, too, Laverne. You just have to trust and believe." Mary rubbed my back in easy circles while I watched my mother from over her shoulder, holding on so hard that Mama felt a little jealous.

Just then, Daddy came into the shop, with Uncle Raleigh close behind carrying a bucket of chicken.

"W-what's going on here," he said, reaching for me. He had to pull me away because I refused to unhook my arms. "L-let her go." He yanked so hard that I started to cry.

Mama was embarrassed. "There's nothing wrong," she said. "She was just helping me out because my stitches are hurting me."

"Good-bye, Laverne," Mary said. "Don't let this trouble you none. I'll be seeing you again."

When the door clapped shut behind her, my daddy leaned to kiss my face, but pulled back as a shock hurt his lip.

They fought over it, my parents did. Mama complained at the dinner table, trying to eat the chicken Daddy and Uncle Raleigh had brought. "You just don't want me to have a friend," Mama said. "Why did you treat her like that?"

"You didn't see her face," Daddy said. "There was something wild in her face."

Mama wiped her eyes with the cheap paper napkin from the chicken place. "I need to take a pill. I don't feel well."

Uncle Raleigh got up to find her a glass of water. Daddy said, "You can't take codeine on an empty stomach. Eat your dinner."

"The doctor said no fried foods. I told you that."

"I'm sorry, Verne," Daddy said. "Do you want me to fix you a sandwich?"

"I just hate the way you treated her," Mama said. "How often do I get to have a friend?"

About three weeks later, Daddy came home early on a Wednesday. He walked into the shop while my mama was trying to do three heads at once. Somebody was holding me, but Daddy didn't pay it any mind.

"Laverne, can I talk to you for a second?" he said.

My mama wasn't in the middle of any chemical procedures, so she went outside and sat with Daddy on the porch. "What is it? Is Miss Bunny okay? Raleigh?"

"Nothing like that," he said. "I was just wondering. That woman that came in late that night, the one in the pink?"

"Mary," Mama said. "Mary was her name."

"I saw her picture in *Jet*," Daddy said, handing my mother the folded-back page.

"She was the one that threw hot grits on Al Green. I told you she was crazy."

Mama looked at the article, tracing the words, moving her lips as she read what happened in Memphis just one night after Mary left our shop.

"What did he do to her?" Mama said.

"What did he do to her? She threw a pot of hot grits on the man when he was getting out of the bathtub and you want to know what *he* did to her?"

"Oh, Mary," Mama said.

"Black women," Daddy said. "Y'all know y'all is crazy when you don't get your way."

"Oh, Mary," Mama said again. "Oh, girl."

This is not a story my mama tells often. To her, it's not just gossip, it's something closer to gospel. One late night Mama was fixing up a girl who was half bald on the left side from snatching at her own head. She opened her mouth to show Mama where she clamped her jaw so tight that she busted one of her molars. While Mama rubbed Magical Grow in the bald places until her naked scalp shone like it was wet, she shared the story of Mary.

"You listening, baby?" Mama said. "When you love a man that much, it's time to let him go."

19
UP A NOTCH

After Ruth Nicole Elizabeth's Sweet Sixteen, my father and Raleigh became obsessed with the idea of a party for my mama. Speaking across the radio waves, Lincoln to Lincoln, they used words like *soiree* and *salon*. On Saturday morning they got themselves all gussied up in their three-piece suits and headed to the Hilton to find out how much it would cost to rent the Magnolia Room for the evening of June 17. After they'd gone my mother asked me, "Where are those two headed looking like a couple of undertakers?" They told the events manager at the Hilton that they wanted whatever Harold Grant had ordered for his daughter, only "up a notch," which translated into premium catering — miniature crab cakes, a roast-beef station, and four hours of open bar. Waiting at the airport for fares, my father flipped through bridal magazines, pulling out pages that he liked, tucking them into the inside pocket of his uniform coat.

The invitation, they decided, would say "semi-formal." Yes, "after-five attire" sounded classier, but they didn't want anyone to be confused. "And," Daddy said, "irregardless of what we tell other people to wear, me and Raleigh are going to have on tuxedos with morning coats."

I flipped through the sheaf of pictures he had culled from *Modern Bride.* The dresses were all part princess, part Renaissance hooker — deep necklines, pinched waists, and very dramatic skirts flaring over stiff crinolines.

I went through the stack twice, searching for something that looked like a dress somebody's mother could wear. I didn't even comment on the stock photo of Lady Diana Spencer. "You have to let her pick her own dress."

"You're right," Daddy said. "She's going to need to try it on, or what have you. We'll show her these photos as a suggestion, just to let her know the sky is the limit."

Dana came two Wednesdays after Ruth Nicole Elizabeth's party, ready at last for her wash-and-set. I lowered her into the shampoo bowl, careful to cushion her neck with a folded-over towel. This close, I could smell her perfume. Today she smelled like my mother, White Shoulders.

"Your father and your uncle are throwing a birthday party for the Pink Fox?" she said.

"No," I said. "For my mother. The anniversary is just the occasion."

"Why?"

"For all the hard work she does."

Dana sat up from the shampoo bowl and watched my mother as she eased ammonia onto a customer's roots.

"My mother works hard," Dana said, "but she never had a party or anything close to it. Do you know that?"

"Lean back if you want this shampoo," I said, smothering the urge to defend my father's crazy idea. "And keep your voice down; it's sort of a surprise." She leaned back and I turned the water on and squeezed the sprayer. "How does that feel?"

"Good," she said, but the cords of her neck were still stretched tight.

"Relax," I said. "I know what I'm doing."

I squirted shampoo into my palm and rubbed it into her thick hair, using my nails on her scalp until she moaned.

"Feel good?"

Relaxers are good for business, there's no doubt about that. Back when everybody got a press-and-curl, they would come to the shop only when they had money. Everybody had a hot comb tucked in the kitchen drawer, and in a pinch you could iron out your own naps. But the relaxer needed to be done by a professional to get the hair bone-straight without processing it right off your scalp. Even my mama was unable to handle the back of her own head. I worked it in for her, forcing the crinkles flat with my gloved fingers. Still, we both missed the days of the press-and-curl, just for the transformation factor. Used to be when you washed a woman's hair, it went back to its natural state, the way it was even before she was born. She sat up in your chair with plaits in her head, showing you the way she was when she was small and used to sit between her mother's knees. There was magic in taking them from where they were, to where they wanted to be. It was a miracle every time.

Now, you get them under the hose and the hair gets nothing but wet, and you have to content yourself with just a glimpse of the roots. You just reach your hands down under the processed stuff like a blind man trying to figure out if he's in love or not. Dana's roots under the pads of my fingers were kinky, strong like ground wire.

"I'm getting wet," she said.

I whispered. "When we have this party, you're invited."

Dana shook her head. "I don't think so."

"What if you could bring your friend Ronalda? The invitation says you can bring a guest."

She sighed. "You know I can't hardly get out of the house."

"Well, bring your mother." Dana's head jerked in my hands, so I made the water cooler. "Is that better?"

"Chaurisse," she said with a shaky voice. "I just can't come, okay?"

"Why?"

"For one thing, Ronalda will be gone by then."

"Gone where?" I helped Dana sit up and wrapped a clean towel around her cold, wet head.

"Gone back to Indiana," she said, and told everyone in the shop what had happened. Ronalda, it seemed, had taken Nkrumah on a quick errand and the little boy was hit by a car. Not bad enough for him to spend the night in the hospital, but bad enough for the kid to scream and holler so bad that you would have thought he was dying. Somebody called the police, and one thing led to another. Ronalda's father and her stepmother were having the biggest, most complicated fight ever. And the little boy wasn't even hurt. That's the thing Dana couldn't get over. But her stepmother was completely hysterical.

"Fairburn Townhouses can be a little shady," Dana admitted, "but only at night. And that's where Ronalda's boyfriend was staying, so that's where she had to go. You can't explain that to Ronalda's parents because they are really bourgie people, you know what I mean?"

My mother said she knew.

What was Ronalda supposed to do? Leave Nkrumah by himself in the house? So, Ronalda didn't have any choice but to carry him with her. "They used her like a maid, you know what I'm saying? You never saw her without that little boy on her hip."

Ronalda loved this boyfriend and was having some problems and she couldn't just ignore him. "He was in need!"

According to Dana, the parents claimed that they didn't like the boyfriend because he was twenty-four and in the army, saying that he was too old to be going out with a high-school girl, but the truth was that he didn't have enough education for them. And besides, the boyfriend was having serious, serious trouble and he needed a friend and fifty dollars. Nobody could accuse Ronalda of being fair-weather.

She went to Fairburn Townhouses to deliver the money — which she earned from watching that bad little boy and everything went fine until Ronalda went inside to say good-bye to her boyfriend's mother. While Ronalda was just trying to be polite, the little boy ran out into the parking lot and got hit by a car. *Tapped* by the car, really. But still. Police were there in five seconds. Asking Ronalda if Nkrumah was her child.

Her stepmother got there and started freaking out because Nkrumah had this tiny cut on his eyebrow. You would have thought he had been shot or something.

"You can understand that," my mama said.

Yes, Dana could understand her being upset, but there was no cause for her to act out how she did. Being talked to like that was worse than being spit on. And now Ronalda had to go back to Indiana.

My mama said, "That's a shame, for everybody. I'll pray for all of them."

"No," Dana said. "Pray for Ronalda. She's the one who needs it most."

My mother looked up from her work. "I got prayers enough for everybody."

Dana picked up the edge of her cape and

dabbed at her nose. "I am going to miss her so much. And it's not her fault. She can't help who her mother is."

My mother put four or five clips in the Jheri curl and joined me at chair no. 2 and took over the blow-drying. She murmured to Dana the way you would talk to a crying baby that needs help falling asleep. As my mother brushed her hair forward, Dana closed her eyes before it covered her face like a shroud.

I finished Dana's hair well before the five-thirty rush, but she stayed on, talking to my mother. Her mood had mysteriously brightened as she asked questions like she was a friendly reporter. What did my mother like to eat? Did she think it made so much of a difference where a person went to go to college? Could she give her some advice? My mother opened like a flower, laughing at Dana's jokes and swatting away her compliments. Only one question seemed to hit the wrong note. "Mrs. Witherspoon, would you say you're a happy person?"

Mama set the curling iron on a wet towel, frowning as it sizzled. She licked her finger and touched it to the hot metal, still frowning. "I don't know," she said.

"And whose fault do you think it is? Who do you blame?"

Mama looked a little dizzy. To her customer, she said, "Kids these days. They are more sophisticated than we were."

The customer said, "Nobody is truly happy."

"But could you be?" Dana said with her eyes on Mama.

"I'm happy," I offered.

"I'm not," said Dana. "I think I'm lonely."

"Oh, honey," Mama said, and invited her to stay for dinner.

We both looked a little melancholy when Dana said, "Thank you, but I have to go."

She also refused a ride, so I walked her down Lynhurst to the bus stop.

"Do you get lonely?" she said.

"Sometimes," I said.

"It's because you're special. It's hard for people to understand you."

I shrugged because I was as ordinary as scrambled eggs, but I appreciated the compliment. "Is being special how come you're lonely?"

"No," she said. "I'm lonely for all the regular reasons."

We got to the bus stop, which was marked by a concrete pole lumpy with several layers of white paint. "You don't have to wait with me," she said.

"I don't mind. Make sure you tie your hair

up at night. Sleeping directly on the pillowcase gives you split ends."

She said she would try to remember.
"What's the real reason your dad is giving
your mom this party?"

Her face was kind, but I felt a chill of fear
work its way from my hands up to my
elbow. "I guess because he loves her."

Maybe my face showed her something that
I didn't mean to display, because she
reached out and touched me on the arm.
"Everybody loves you the most, all your life,
and you probably don't even know it."

I gave a tense laugh. "I need more than
just my parents to love me."

She whispered, "I love you. Can't you
tell?"

I didn't say anything at first. It was as
though I was suddenly struck with my
father's stammer, but the words were
jammed up in my head, not in my throat.
Sometimes I wondered if Dana actually
liked me. She could be sarcastic and even a
little mean. Could there be other people out
there loving me who had just never mentioned it to me? I thought of Jamal, five
hundred miles away in Hampton, Virginia.
Did he love me as he studied for his exams,
as he pledged his fraternity, as he chased
doctors' daughters, taking them out to din-

ner, asking them to meet his parents? With the exception of my kindergarten teacher, no one outside of my family had ever claimed to love me. It was jarring, dumbfounding, and very exciting.

"See?" she said. "You couldn't even tell." She shook her head like she couldn't believe how blind I was. She twisted away at the sound of the approaching bus. "Don't you feel like we've been friends a long time?"

"Yes," I said, still reeling with all this talk of love, spinning with the possibility of secretly having been adored all my life.

As she boarded the bus, she looked over her shoulder sadly. "You didn't say it back."

"Say what?" I said as the doors closed. She made her way to a window seat, but she didn't look my way even though I stood on the corner waving like a child.

There was no dissuading my father when he got his mind wrapped around a Big Idea. When he wanted to start Witherspoon Sedans, nobody thought it was a good plan except Raleigh. Miss Bunny, God bless the dead, wanted him to get a job driving for white people. Even my mama was iffy about the plan. She thought that maybe he should go into the army, use the GI Bill to go to college and veteran's benefits to buy a house in Macon. He says he knew in his gut that he and Raleigh were meant to be their own bosses, and now he knew in his gut that my mother desperately wanted a formal party. "I know what I know, Buttercup."

"But I'm with her all the time," I said, as we left the stationery store. "When there is a big party coming up, she says, 'That don't make no kinda sense.' And she gets migraines during debutante season."

My father raised his eyebrows. "Is that so?"

"It's so," I said.

"You ever hear of sour grapes?" Daddy said.

He opened the glove compartment and fished out a monogrammed handkerchief. "You've got something on your chin."

I touched the cloth to my face. "She's not jealous."

"You got to learn how to listen sideways to what people are saying to get at what they really mean." He pulled up in front of the shop. "Don't fight me on this. We'll do something for you one day, too."

"I'm not having sour grapes, if that's what you're getting at."

Daddy lowered his window with a smooth electric motion. "I'm serious. You'll get your

350

party, too." He touched the brim of his hat, and I felt myself smile as the car eased down the driveway.

They decided to spring the news on her on a Monday afternoon as she was sitting on the couch having a Fuzzy Navel and watching her stories. I'd just come home from school when I heard my name in a stage whisper. I turned to find my dad and Raleigh hiding in the doorway of the guest room.

"She's in there watching soaps," Raleigh said. "She doesn't suspect a thing."

"I don't know," I said, which is the same thing I had been saying to them for the past three weeks. "At least clear the date with her," I had begged as they plunked down deposits with the caterers, florists, and stationers.

"It's a surprise, Chaurisse," they said.

"She doesn't like surprises."

"She wouldn't want a surprise party, but she won't mind being surprised *with* a party. Trust us. We've been knowing your mother a long time."

The idea was that I was to walk into the family room carrying the roses Raleigh handed to me, wrapped in a paper cone. Daddy would put on music, Stevie Wonder

singing "I Just Called to Say I Love You."
No, they assured me, it wasn't corny. "It's
s-s-sincere." Daddy wanted me to walk on
the beat "like a bridesmaid." Once I had
presented the flowers, Daddy would hand
me the invitation, I would hand it to Mama,
and Raleigh would snap a couple thousand
photos.

"You g-g-got it?" Daddy asked me.

I rolled my eyes. "I guess. But mark my
words, she is not going to like this."

Raleigh said, "She's going to love it."

Daddy said, "Can you change into a
dress?"

I did change into a dress, a red and white
polka-dot number I had bought with my
own money at Lerner Shops. I even slipped
on some patent-leather sling backs, but I
didn't bother with panty hose. You had to
draw the line somewhere. I looked in the
mirror and painted on some lipstick. I
looked a little longer and rubbed some
foundation on my cheeks to cover up the
acne scars. I couldn't get Dana out of my
head, her knowing looks. I was uneasy with
the way she talked to my mother. It was a
little woman-to-woman, a little daughter-to-
mother, a bit student-to-teacher, and maybe
even a splash of vice versa. It was like my
mother was a newspaper that everyone

could read except for me.

Under my feet, the family room carpet crackled. Silly as it seemed, I tried to walk in time with the music.

My mother was curled up on the couch in baggy clothes. She called these outfits her "prison sweats" to distinguish them from the embellished running suits she liked to wear to the mall. Mondays, in her book, were "grooming optional," and on this day she had opted to tie her head up in a greasy satin scarf. At her right side, beside the remote control, was a bowl of M&Ms, because diets were suspended on Mondays as well.

I once heard my father joke to a young man we were driving from the airport. He looked sort of nerdy, clutching a skimpy bouquet of Gerber daises to give to his fiancée. The young man told us that he was meeting his future in-laws for the first time. "Smart move," my dad joked with him. "You never want to marry a girl before you see the mama. You need to know what you're getting." My dad laughed and the young man in the backseat stared into the flowers, worried about what sort of magic mirror he was about to look into. I took in my mother sprawled exhausted on the couch and I wondered if this was what I was going to grow up to be. If that nervous young man in the back of the limo were to see my mother standing on the front porch waving him in, what would he think?

I goose-stepped toward her with the bouquet of roses and she looked alarmed. I glanced over my shoulder back at Daddy and Raleigh. Here we were trying to do something nice, and we scared her.

"Chaurisse," Mama said, "what you got there? Somebody sent you some flowers?"

I looked again at my dad, as we hadn't really prepared ourselves for dialogue. Raleigh waved his hand, so I forgot the medium tempo of the song and hustled toward her with the roses outstretched.

"They're for you."

The rest went almost as choreographed, although I forgot and set the flowers on the coffee table next to the remote, when I was supposed to hand them to her. Daddy looked a little bothered, but he handed me the envelope with the invitation and I forked it over. Mama opened the outer envelope and giggled upon finding the smaller one tucked inside.

"What is this?" she said, grinning as Raleigh snapped her photo.

When she made it to the tiny square of tissue paper that was packaged with the invitation she said, "Ooh, expensive," and not in the snide voice she used when opening the invitations that clients gave her, but with real appreciation. Then she read it and let out a little yelp.

Miss Bunny Chaurisse Witherspoon
Requests the honour of your presence
At a soiree to celebrate her mother,
Mrs. Laverne Vertena Johnson
Witherspoon,
On the Occasion of the Twentieth
Anniversary
of
The Pink Fox Salon
June 17, 1987, at 7:00 p.m.

She stood up from the couch and hugged me to her in a firm grip. Her body shook against me as she cried on my shoulder. I wasn't sure what was happening. I returned her hug, patting her back as she mewed like a newborn kitten. With the party invitation in her hands, she couldn't get enough of the feel of us. She let me go and then reached for Uncle Raleigh and cried a wet spot onto his white shirt. Then it was Daddy's turn, and she grabbed him like she had just won the Showcase Showdown on *The Price Is Right.* Then it was my turn again. "I

355

never had something nice like this before,"
she said. I didn't say anything back, struck
dumb by the energy of her startling embrace.

It's funny how you think you can know a
person.

20
BLOWOUT

Nineteen eighty-seven was the Year of the Party. First there was Ruth Nicole Elizabeth's Sweet Sixteen in February, which showed everyone how it was done, and then there were a couple others which were almost as swanky. It got to the point where a person didn't even feel right having a party if it wasn't going to be catered. Bucking the trend, Marcus McCready came home from Hampton in April and decided to throw a spring break jam, not formal but *Animal House*-style, except that just about everyone that was invited was in high school. The bash was going to take place on the shore of Lake Lanier, about an hour and a half north of Atlanta.

Dana was so excited about that she didn't go through her usual wishy-washy I can–I can't routine. She said yes when I mentioned it and on the day of, she was waiting for me at the back parking lot of Greenbriar, on time and bearing gifts — two identical tube tops that would show everyone that we were best friends. It's what she used to do with Ronalda, she said, as we changed in the backseat of the Lincoln, trusting the tinted windows to guard our privacy.

Ninety miles isn't so far on the odometer, but you know the old joke: "Be careful when you leave Atlanta, because you'll end up in Georgia." Marcus's family had bought the house on Lake Lanier after his father, a country boy from Mobile, remarried a woman from New York, who insisted that she needed a "country home." Egged on by a real-estate agent who insisted that Lake Lanier was going to be the Martha's Vineyard of the south, Marcus Senior made the purchase even though my daddy personally warned him against it. "Forsyth County ain't nothing but a clump of sundown towns."

Once I had cleared the city limits and the traffic cooled off, I pulled over to a gas station to fill up and get a look at the map.

"You always get full service?" Dana said.

"I'm putting it on my dad's card. He doesn't like me pumping my own gas."

She smirked.

"It's not up to me," I said, unfolding the

map while a thin white kid screwed off the gas cap.

"I know the way," she said. "I've been out there before."

I must have looked puzzled, because she came at me with a little bit of attitude. "You're not the only one who knows rich people."

"That's not what I was thinking," I said. "I was wondering how come you didn't tell me earlier. We're supposed to be friends."

"We are friends." Dana turned in her seat, getting on her knees, crumpling my map. "This car has a huge backseat. You ever use it for recreational purposes?" She smiled in a way that made it seem like she had spent a lot of time in parked cars.

I had only done it once, and truthfully, it wasn't all that comfortable. "Sex in a car is one of those things that only works in the movies," I said, hoping to sound worldly.

"I knew it," she said. "I knew that nice-girl thing was just a front."

I raised my eyebrows, trying again for sophisticated and mysterious, but Dana kept howling and hooting like she had won a bet. "I knew it!"

I felt my smile droop at the edges. "Not a lot of people. I mean, somebody, but nobody lately. Most of it was when I was in the tenth grade, and one time last summer."

"Don't get all sad," Dana said. "You just have a history, that's all. Who you got a history with? You don't have to give me a full roster. Highlights are plenty for me."

"Jamal," I said. "Jamal Dixon."

"Whoa," she said. "That big-time preacher's son?"

"Yeah," I said, not sure if I was bragging or confessing.

"He seems like a nice guy. Four corners, you know what I mean? I didn't think he did statutory."

"It wasn't like that," I said.

"Don't get all weird," she said, inspecting her own cleavage. "I understand where you're coming from. Believe you me."

"We went to the same church," I explained. "Jamal is a nice guy. He cares about me."

"I know," she said. "I met him before. Marcus, on the other hand, is not a nice guy."

"If you don't like Marcus," I asked her, "then why do you want to go to his party?"

"Because I hate him so much I can't stay away from him." She was still smiling, but there was a bit of wildness in her face. I'd seen it somewhere before. She smiled again, but it was just a flashing of teeth, and I knew where I had seen the fury that creased her face right between the eyes. Once when I was on a road trip with my mother on our way to visit Grandma Bunny, we passed a group of prisoners on the side of the highway. Most of them were black, some were old, and all of them were picking up trash. There was construction on the road, so we drove by slowly. One man in the group looked at me. I waved my hand at him. He gave me the same teeth-only smile, but the rest of his face and even the angle at which he held his body let me know that he wanted to kill someone.

"Let's hit the road," Dana said.

"No," I said. "I want to go back to what you said about hating Marcus. What are you going to do when we get there?"

"I was just playing," Dana said, but she still had that chain-gang tension in her jaw. "I won't make a scene. My feelings just got hurt a little bit, that's all." Her voice went powdery. "I know you know what I'm going through."

I nodded. I did know. I told her that while we still went to Mitchell Street Baptist Church, Jamal stopped talking to me in front of people. It wasn't like he was mad at me, it was more like he couldn't face me and his mama at the same time.

"Lean forward," she said.

I did and she tugged my tube top, straightening the rainbow stripes. Then she stroked my *I Dream of Jeannie*. "It looks really natural," she said, reaching behind my head to smooth out the nappy hair at my neck. "Let's go."

Evening turned into night quickly. We were only five miles or so up I-75 when I flipped on the headlights as Dana cranked up the music. "Can you dance?"

I shook my head. "My whole family is uncoordinated."

"Your mama, too? She seems like she could shake a tail feather."

"My mama is featherless," I said.

"You have a good sense of humor." Dana scrolled the dial, trying to find something else to listen to. By the time she realized that we were too far from Atlanta to pick up another R&B station, she couldn't even get the station she had in the first place. "While we're on the subject," she said, "any word on colleges?"

"I didn't get into Mount Holyoke, any of the sisters. Spelman put me on a wait list."

"Could be a blessing in disguise," Dana said. "You never know."

She had returned to the lost cause of the radio when we heard the bang. Dana ducked down in her seat as though it was a gunshot, but I knew it was a blowout.

It's hard for me to remember what happened; to this day, I keep replaying the reel in my head, zooming in on details, and in this telling I want so badly to say that I noticed the signs, that I felt something amiss. It's embarrassing that I had nothing but my five dim senses to guide me.

"Hold on, hold on," I said, keeping my elbows soft and steering into the swerve. I glanced at the speedometer and was grateful that we were going just fifty-five. The Lincoln was shaking like a washing machine. Strips of tire rubber flew around in my peripheral vision. Beside me, Dana whimpered like a stray puppy. I was breathing hard enough to bust out of my tube top, but I kept my wits, and handled it like my daddy had taught me. Finally, I was able to apply gentle pressure to the brakes until we came to a bumpy halt on the shoulder.

"What was that?" Dana said.

"Tire blew," I said.

She sat up and took a deep breath, and then another one. "I thought we were dead."

"The key," I said, "is not to panic." I turned on the hazard lights. The double arrows lit the car with regular bursts of yellow light. We were going to have to ride the rim to the next exit. As I pulled the car onto the roadway I told Dana, "It's just going to be bumpy."

She nodded and kept taking those belly breaths.

"If you keep breathing like that, you are supposed to use a paper bag. You can hyperventilate."

"Okay," she said. "That was terrible. I thought we were going to die."

"Wouldn't it be terrible to die while you're still in high school?"

"It would be just my luck to die before I get to go to Mount Holyoke."

I gave the car a little bit of gas and we clunked along a little faster. "You don't have to rub it in. I'll probably have to go to Georgia State." Maybe it was just the release of all the tension caused by the blowout, but I was suddenly very sad. I wanted to travel, to leave Atlanta. I had never thought about Massachusetts before, but now I wanted to go there more than anything. I had almost six thousand dollars saved — that was a lot of five-dollar hours — I wanted to spend it all on tweed blazers and lobster rolls. I wanted a future.

The exit had promised gas, food, and lodging, but the sign didn't tell us how far off the interstate we would have to travel to find these services. On the way back home, after everything, I would notice a sign letting me know that we were only a half mile from the freeway the whole time. But still, a half mile is a long way when night is falling on two black girls alone in the sticks. The sound of the damaged car on the almost empty stretch of road was obnoxious in the quiet evening, like the noise of high heels in an empty hallway.

"Don't cry, Chaurisse," Dana said. "You never know what's going to happen."

21
THE MEN ALL PAUSED

The gas station was small and out-of-date — not so old-fashioned as Andy Griffith but dated enough to let us know we weren't in Atlanta anymore. The pumps, boxy with flip-over numbers, did not display a sign saying you had to pay first. Just from the curb, you could tell that the convenience store didn't sell anything but chewing gum, Coca-Cola, and motor oil. I aimed the Lincoln at the corner of the lot, where a pay phone was mounted in a glass booth.

When we stopped the car, the lights on the small lot got a little brighter, like we were approaching a private home and somebody flipped on the floodlights. The clerk, a white lady about the age of my mother, stuck her head out the door and looked around. Her auburn updo, permed half to death, was proof that people should never be allowed to apply chemicals to their own hair.

Dana said, "She can't help us fix the tire."

"No," I said. "The rim is all bent up by now anyway. We're going to have to get a tow."

"Towed to where?" She said it so fast that it came out like one word.

"Back home," I said. "We're not going to make it to the party."

Her face took on that wild cast again. "It's just a tire. Somebody can get us on the road again."

"The rim is all bent out of shape. We drove on it for, like, two miles." I spoke slowly, like I was talking to a child.

She answered speaking even more slowly. "No, Chaurisse. We are going to the party. You invited me to a party." She picked at the hair around her temples. The gentle brown of her scalp gleamed through. "I'm going inside to ask for help. It's a gas station; somebody in there has to know how to change a tire." She hopped out of the car and jogged into the little store, leaving the car door open.

It wasn't warm enough for our matching tube tops; this much was clear as I walked over to the pay phone. The superman booth made the whole setting seem make-believe, like we were on a movie set. "Collect call from Chaurisse," I said to the operator.

367

"What is it, Buttercup? You okay?"

"I'm okay, Daddy. But the Lincoln's not."

"You had a wreck?"

"No, Daddy," I said. "A blowout."

I heard him say to my mother, "She's all right."

"I kept control of the car," I told him. "I steered with the swerve."

Daddy said, "That's my girl. Where are you?"

"Up I-75," I said. "We got off at exit twelve. You'll see a Chevron."

"You by yourself?"

"No, I'm with one of my girlfriends."

"Well," he said. "Me and Raleigh are headed out right now. You and your friend get back in the car and lock up. You do not want to fool with those peckerwoods out there."

"Okay, Daddy," I said, watching Dana prance out of the store with a skinny white guy. He wasn't fully adult, but he was plenty old enough to buy booze.

Dana said, "This is Mike. He's going to change the tire for us."

Mike grinned, surprising me with pretty teeth. "For a negotiable fee, of course."

"It's okay," Dana said to me. "I can pay for it."

Mike looked like the dream boys they

write about in Sweet Valley High romances. His hair was darker even than Dana's and his eyes were the same blue as the stripe on her tennis shoes.

"Anybody ever tell you that you look like Robin Givens?" This was for Dana.

"Sometimes," she said. "Now come around here and look at our tire."

But Mike was busy now, looking at me. I reached up and straightened my *I Dream of Jeannie.* It's funny how it is that a man looking at you can make you feel chopped into pieces. Self-conscious about everything — from the bulge where my shoulder met my torso to the acne scars slicked over with Fashion Fair — I reached up again and pressed the pins holding my hair in place.

"I'm trying to figure if you look like anybody famous."

"I don't," I said.

"No," he said, sadly. "I reckon not."

"Mike," Dana called, so he went over to the ruined tire and whistled through his shiny teeth. "I'm surprised you didn't run off the road."

"I didn't steer against the swerve," I said, but he didn't look up at me.

"Can you fix it?" Dana squatted down beside him. He put his hand on the small of her back, touching the bare skin above her jeans where the tube top rode up.

"Not sure," he said, stroking the fender with the hand that wasn't stroking Dana. "This is a nice car. I always vote for Lincolns over Caddies. Whose car is this?"

"My dad's," I said.

"He's a chauffeur," Dana explained, shooting me a look. "It doesn't belong to him or anything."

"I figured," said Mike.

"So can you fix it?" Dana said.

"Maybe. If you got a jack."

"Chaurisse? Do we have a jack?" she said in a sweet voice, batting her eyes at me like I was some stupid boy.

"We bent the rim, I keep telling you. My father is coming to get us."

"What?" Dana said.

"My dad is coming to get us."

"No," Dana said. "Why did you call him? I told you I was getting help. Why couldn't you give me ten minutes?"

Beating her hands on her thighs in the gas-station light, she didn't look silver, she looked crazy.

Mike stood up with a crackle of knees. "Well, since you got this all took care of . . ."

"Wait," Dana said following him. "Please fix our car. I can pay." She stood on her tiptoes, lengthening her body so she could

370

slide her fingers into the front pocket of her tight Gloria Vanderbilts. She moved her fingers like tweezers until she produced a bill folded into a paper football. She unfolded it and waved the crinkled money at him. "Don't you want twenty dollars?"

Mike looked at the money and looked at Dana. The light bounced off her makeup, making her face look like a jack-o'-lantern, lit from the inside. "Twenty bucks," she said.

"I can't do nothing if your sister won't give me the jack."

"She's not my sister," Dana said.

"Look," said Mike. "I'm not trying to get involved in nothing. I'm just going by what you told me."

"Dana, calm down," I called to her. "Let's just wait in the car."

"I can't," she said. She spun toward Mike. "For twenty dollars, will you drive me to Atlanta?"

"To Atlanta?"

"Yeah," she said. "I have the money right here."

"Oh no, darlin'," he said. "I am not going to Atlanta at night. I ain't a coward, but my life is worth more than twenty bucks."

He walked away in the direction of the store. Mike was *Seventeen* magazine in the face, but watching him walk away in his

Levi's, I kept thinking "Jack and Diane."

Dana hurried over to the phone booth and closed herself in. She covered her mouth while she spoke, like she was worried that maybe I could read her lips through the glass. Although it was impossible, I thought I heard my name and thought she said "Raleigh." I know for sure that she said "hurry up," because she screamed it. Then she placed the phone back on its cradle, gentle, like it was made out of spun sugar, before taking a couple of chest-expanding breaths. She smiled at me, but her face was all chain-gang.

"I want to go to the party," she said. "So I asked my mom to come and get me and take me there."

"I thought you said she doesn't have a car."

"My aunt Willie Mae does. They're coming together."

"Anyway," I said, "let's just wait in the Lincoln."

The clock on the dashboard shone nine fifteen. If we hadn't had the blowout, we would be walking into the party by now, in our matching tube tops, looking like two girls who went to parties all the time, two girls with beautiful hair. Marcus would be mixing some purple punch, offering it to all the girls except Ruth Nicole Elizabeth; she would sip on a Cherry Coke the whole time. It would be the very same scene as at his Christmas party last year but without the blinking blue lights. Jamal would be sitting in the corner like he didn't want to be there, drinking from a plastic tumbler like it was a cup of coffee. He would say hello to me, tip the tumbler in my direction, and tell somebody that I was like a little sister to him. Right now I should be smiling a patient smile at him, saying "No thank you" to the punch, waiting while he drank, studying his face, and watching for his eyes to droop just a little.

At Christmas, Ruth Nicole Elizabeth's father sat outside in his Volvo for exactly forty-five minutes before blowing his horn in three foreign-car toots. Marcus walked her out as all the party girls watched from the windows. Her herringbone bracelet twinkled on her wrist as Marcus opened the door for her, shook her father's hand, went back inside, and got the party started. Inside, Jamal drank eggnog until I didn't seem like his sister anymore. "You still on the Pill?" Yes, yes, yes.

An hour is a long time to sit in a car, even if it is the good Lincoln. I switched on the heater to knock the chill off the air, but then we were too warm. I opened the window and hard-bodied insects invaded the car, crawling over our bare shoulders.

"This is terrible," Dana said. "This is a disaster."

"It's not a big deal," I said. "Next year you'll be in Massachusetts going to real college parties and I'll be stuck here, living at home, washing hair."

"Can you please call your father and tell him not to come?" Dana said. "My mama is already on her way. We could both ride with her."

I shook my head. "My dad is going to want to see about the Lincoln."

She opened the door, stepping onto the asphalt parking lot. It was late now, nearly ten. The clerk with the home perm was busy tidying up the store and glancing at her watch. "Come on, Daddy," I said under my breath. "Come on, Raleigh."

Dana entered the convenience store again, speaking to the clerk, moving her hands too much. Maybe she was on drugs or something. She was like a pinball machine — all energy, lights, and percussion. She zigzagged out of the store holding a silver key bolted to a wooden block. I watched her zip over to the pay phone, pick it up, and then place the receiver back, like she had changed her mind.

She Morse-coded the window with her fist. "I'm going to the ladies'. If your dad shows up, just go on home without me. My mama is on the way."

"My dad won't be here for another fifteen, twenty minutes," I told her. "You've got time."

"Okay. But just in case my mama gets here first, tell her where I am."

"How will I know her?"

"You can't miss her."

According to the clock on the car radio, Dana had been in the bathroom twenty-two minutes when Daddy and Raleigh rolled up in the limousine. They had been out in the yard pruning hedges. Wearing sweat-stained T-shirts and baggy gym shorts, they smelled like cigarettes and green stems.

"Madame," Uncle Raleigh said, opening my car door. I eased out, glancing over at my father, who was inspecting the damaged rim like he was deciding whether or not to give it CPR. "Chaurisse, James said you were out here with a girlfriend? Where is she?"

"She started freaking out, Uncle Raleigh. I don't know what's wrong with her."

"What's her name again, your friend?"

"Dana," I said.

Raleigh made a little *O* with his lips and squinted. "What does she look like?"

Now that everything is all said and done, what's obvious is obvious. But at the moment, it was only a little bit peculiar. "Brown-skinned, long hair. She's locked in the bathroom and she won't come out."

"Let me go help James with that tire," Uncle Raleigh said.

He and Daddy squatted by the fender and whispered together like mobsters. While they crouched there, dressed like boys, I went to the bathroom door.

"Dana," I said. "Dana, you okay?"

"Is my mama here?"

"No," I said, "But my dad and my uncle are here. Come on out."

"I can't," she said.

"Are you okay?"

"Just leave, all right. My mama is on her way. Please, Chaurisse, just get James and Raleigh to go." I could hear her crying though the door, belly sobs like my mama did at Grandma Bunny's funeral. She had laid out in the pew, kicking so hard, she lost her shoe. Raleigh and I searched on our hands and knees, but we never found it. Mama stood on the black ground in just her stockings while we put Grandma Bunny down.

I jogged back over to the car, where Daddy and Uncle Raleigh leaned against the hood of the hobbled Lincoln, smoking Kools. "W-w-what's the s-s-situation in there?"

"Daddy, something is seriously wrong. She's crying. Talking crazy."

"T-talking crazy? How crazy is crazy? What did she say?"

"Easy, Jim-Bo," Raleigh said.

"She said we should leave without her. That her mother is on the way. She wants to wait in the bathroom."

"Her mama?" Daddy said. "She said she called her mama?"

"Easy, Jim-Bo," Raleigh said.

The clerk stuck her head out of the door and I waved at her.

My father walked across the lot and knocked on the bathroom door with a delicate rap of knuckles, a habit he picked up after he'd walked in on me in the tub when I was about twelve. For weeks after, he'd knocked on every doorlike surface. I once caught him tapping on the cupboard door before reaching in for a bottle of tonic water.

"Dana," he said. "This is James Wither-spoon, Chaurisse's dad. Are you okay, young lady?"

"Yes, sir." Her voice was subdued as a whipped child's.

"Chaurisse says you're waiting for your m-mother. Is that correct?"

There was no response from the bath-room.

"Dana," Daddy said. "You mother is on the way? Confirm or deny."

There was still no response from the bathroom. This time Daddy gave a police knock.

"Dana, is your mother on her way? Con-firm or deny." When she wouldn't, he pounded on the door harder. "Confirm or deny, Dana. Confirm or deny." He beat on the door with his tight fist.

"James. Don't do her like that," Uncle Raleigh said.

Daddy hit the door one more time.

I said, "Daddy, quit before the white people call the police."

Meanwhile, the bathroom was quiet as a grave.

"Dana," I said. "You want me to wait with you until your mother comes?"

Uncle Raleigh said, "Chaurisse, you have

to come with us." He took me gently by the arm.

"We can't leave her. She could be sick. She could be dead in there."

"She's not dead," Uncle Raleigh said. "She's just scared."

"I can't believe you are siding with Daddy on this."

"We've got to hurry, Chaurisse," Uncle Raleigh said.

Daddy said, "You have to go." He walked toward the limo without looking to see if we were following.

Slipping Raleigh's careful grip, I stuck my face in the seam where the door met the jamb; I detected traces of bathroom smells, piss, and disinfectant cakes. "What's going on? Please come out."

"She's all right," Uncle Raleigh gripped me harder this time. "She's just upset."

As he led me toward the limousine, I let myself go limp, not even holding my head upright on my neck.

"Please don't make me drag you. Don't make this worse than it has to be." As he tugged me to the car, the asphalt scored the rubber toes of my spangled sneakers. My father was already installed in the driver's seat; the limo started with the music of a well-tuned engine.

Raleigh opened the door. "Just get in, Chaurisse. Just get in."

"No," I said. "We can't leave her."

"Her mother is coming; just trust me." Raleigh, still poised by the open door like a chauffeur, said, "Please."

My father opened the driver's door. "Move out the way, Raleigh." He stepped in front of me. "Chaurisse, get in the goddamn car right now. I don't have time to play with you. Get in." He put one hand on my shoulder and his other hand on the top of my head as he guided me into the backseat. "Don't question me."

My father has never laid a hand on me in anger. Although all he did was literally lay his hand, rage traveled from his skin to mine. I folded myself onto the backseat, compliant as a dog.

"Don't cry," Raleigh said. "We love you. We all three love you. Me, your daddy, Laverne, we love you more than anybody in the world."

"Raleigh," Daddy said. "Get in the fucking car."

Uncle Raleigh hurried around the back of the limo to take his place beside my father.

Daddy gently pressed the accelerator. Limousines are supposed to seem to float;

luxury is never even noticing that the car is moving. I hooked my fingers in the door handle and leaned my weight against it. There must have been only seconds between the click as the door opened under my wayward hand and my tumble to the pavement, but in that moment, I felt a zing of regret. As my body connected with the blacktop, I knew I was ridiculous. The rough surface scrubbed a patch of skin from my bare shoulder. My fall was at most a foot, maybe eighteen inches, but it felt like a free fall from the Chattahoochee Bridge. My life didn't flash before my eyes, but the events of the past couple hours passed like a ticker tape moving too fast for me to read it, though my desperate eyes scanned it anyway, longing to understand.

22
SKIN PAIN

When we got home, my mother was waiting in the doorway, filling the space with her broadness. With her blue robe tied hard across her middle, she stretched her arms like "suffer the little children."

"What happened?" she asked my father. "What happened to her shoulder?"

"She fell out of the car," my daddy said. "She was l-leaning on the door and fell out. Flesh wound, that's all. Just a little skin pain."

"Baby," my mother said to me. "What happened?"

"I don't know."

"What do you mean you don't know?"

I was about two or three inches taller than Mama, and this was made worse since she was barefoot and I stood in thick-soled sneakers. She hugged me, but I had to crouch to make myself short enough to fit her embrace. My mother smelled of relaxed hair and peaches. She tightened her arms around me, pressing hard on the sore places.

What *had* happened? On a bare-bones level, I fell out of the car and scraped the skin from my shoulder. Daddy stepped on the brake, Raleigh jumped out of the car, but Daddy didn't cut the engine. He sat still behind the wheel as Uncle Raleigh knelt beside me on the asphalt.

But before bare bones is skin, muscle, and blood. I pushed out of the car, clawed my way free. I landed on the pavement altered and confused. I left blood on that parking lot, and some skin, too, although it was probably invisible against the dark asphalt.

Uncle Raleigh said, "Are you okay? Did you hit your head?"

I said no and touched my shoulder; my hand came away damp. My father still did not kill the engine. He did not get out of the car.

"Why do you want to leave Dana?" I asked my uncle.

Raleigh said, "We're not leaving her. She said her mother's on the way."

"Something's happening," I said.

"Chaurisse."

"Confirm or deny, Raleigh."

I lay down on the asphalt, flat on my back. My scraped shoulder smarted against the rough pavement, but this seemed like the only thing to do. I lay on that dirty pavement, putting my body in between knowing and not.

Uncle Raleigh was getting old. His face was a little bit baggy and his stubborn beard that had to be shaved twice a day was coming in white along his jaw. "What's going on?" I asked him.

"Nothing that has to do with you."

"How come you never had any kids? How come you never had your own wife? Just tell me. I won't get mad. I just need to know."

"Come on, Chaurisse," Uncle Raleigh said. "Get up. Let's get you on home so we can take care of that shoulder. Your mama is going to have to pick the gravel out with tweezers."

My dad honked the horn, twice.

Raleigh muttered under his breath, "Don't do her like this, Jim-Bo." Then he said, "Come on, Dana."

"I'm Chaurisse," I said. "Dana is my friend locked up in the bathroom, who you and Daddy are trying to leave out here. Please, Uncle Raleigh. Just tell me what's going on."

Uncle Raleigh stood himself up and pulled me into a standing position. Raleigh said, "Chaurisse, we have all given up so much

384

for you. I would think you would have a little bit more faith in us. Can't you just walk out on it a little bit?"

He sounded so patient, Uncle Raleigh did. His voice was calm, as though he were asking me to hand him a flat-head screwdriver, but his face was creased and tight, as though he were negotiating for a hostage. My dad honked the horn again and Raleigh beat on the trunk with his fist. He turned his face to me, offering his hand, and it seemed only fair that I would get in the car. It was true. Uncle Raleigh had never asked me for anything.

I looked up into his gentle, patient face. "Okay."

Uncle Raleigh said, "We love you, Chaurisse. You are the reason for everything."

Raleigh smelled like sweat and something I would later think of as fear. "Please don't fight your daddy and me, okay?"

Daddy lay on the horn. "Raleigh," he called, "we got to get going."

"Take it easy, Jim-Bo," he said.

Opening the door, he helped me in like he would a high-paying customer. He shut the door, and tested it to make sure.

"Daddy," I said.

"I don't want to talk out here," he said. "I'll talk to you when we get home. Let me concentrate on the road."

Before he could pull away, a compact car, Ford Escort, manual transmission, made a sharp turn into the parking lot. The driver turned directly into our path. A woman jumped out; she was dark, smooth black like Cicely Tyson with long hair, held back with a rhinestone headband.

"God damn it," my father said.

"Easy," Raleigh said.

The woman strode to my father's window. "Where is she?"

"She's locked in the bathroom," said Raleigh.

"What did you do to her?"

"Nothing," Raleigh said. "She was locked in the bathroom when we got here."

"I wasn't talking to you; I was speaking to Mr. Witherspoon. Tell me you were not going to just leave her out here." The lady bent so she could look into the small slit where my father had opened the window. "You were! You were going to just leave my child stranded out here in the middle of nowhere." She moved her hand like she was going to slap my father, but the window wasn't open far enough.

"Calm down," my father said. "She told us that she had called her mother, and we assumed you were on the way."

"Did you even check to make sure she was okay?" She peered in the window. "You in on this, too, Raleigh? I would have figured that you were better than this."

She looked, finally, into the backseat at me. This was the woman I had seen Raleigh with at the park that time. She looked different now, her face was wild and creased. But she smiled at me, and it was a cold smile, more chain-gang than the man on the chain gang's. "My name is Gwendolyn," she said. "I'm Dana's mother. Will you please tell me what the hell happened? Will you please tell me what you have done to my child?"

"I didn't do anything," I said.

"Why are you wearing her top?"

"She gave this to me."

"Gwen, stop talking to her. Leave my daughter out of this."

"Oh, that's funny," Gwendolyn said. "That's really funny."

My father blew the horn. "Go take care of your child, Gwen. Tell Willie Mae to move her car so I can get by."

She hit the glass beside my father's face with the heel of her hand, leaving an oily spot. Raleigh opened his car door and my father and Gwen spoke at once: "Sit down,

Raleigh."

When Gwendolyn moved down the length of the Lincoln, my father pressed the lever to make sure the doors and the windows were locked. She tapped on my window with a dainty click of fingernails. In the front seat, my father turned on the stereo, flooding the car with Beethoven, turned up so high that the symphony was like the screech of dying rabbits. Gwendolyn's lipsticked mouth moved, but I couldn't hear her over the music. She kicked the door before heading to the bathroom.

My father blew the horn at the Escort, but the lady in the driver's seat didn't budge. I couldn't really see her face, but she wore a blue bandanna tied around her head. Daddy blew and she blew back. For a little car, it had a lot of horn on it.

At the bathroom door, Gwen spoke, but we were too far away to hear what she said. The door opened a crack, and then wider. Gwen disappeared into the small room. I could imagine how close they must be, jammed into such a cramped space. What were they saying to each other?

By now, my father was out of the car, arguing with the woman driving the Escort. Raleigh was stiff in his seat. He reached over and turned off the Beethoven.

"Uncle Raleigh," I said, "that lady is your girlfriend, isn't she?"

"She is dear to me, Dana. I'll say that much."

"Stop calling me Dana," I said. "I'm Chaurisse."

"Sorry, Chaurisse," he said. "I have a lot to keep an eye on here."

His voice sounded thick and I wondered if he was going to cry. "This is terrible."

The bathroom door finally opened. Dana leaned her weight on her mother like she was an earthquake victim being tugged from the wreckage. She turned and looked at my father and said the strangest thing. She looked at his short pants and said, "I've never seen your legs before."

23
TARA

One week after Dana and her mother disappeared into the Forsyth County night, my parents sent out two hundred double-enveloped invitations to the anniversary party. The guest list was essentially their combined client rosters, which had a lot of overlap. My mother gave me three cards to send to whomever I wanted, but I only wanted Dana, and she was gone. I never had her phone number, so I couldn't call her. I only knew that she lived somewhere in the vast Continental Colony apartment complex. Once she had mentioned her mother being "upstairs," so at least I knew that she lived in one of the town houses, but there were so many, and they all looked alike. I knew that my mother liked Dana, cared about her even, so I asked her to drive me to Continental Colony to look for the mailbox labeled Yarboro, but she shut me down. "James and Raleigh told me that

Dana was clearly strung out on something, and the mother, too. I knew something was wrong with that girl. I just hate that I didn't see how bad it all was."

"But Dana and her mother knew Daddy and Raleigh already. Don't you think that's weird?"

She sighed and spoke in the Mother Voice. "Just let it go, baby. I think Raleigh was involved with the mom, a long time ago. Maybe Dana was hoping that she could get him to be her father. So many kids, black kids especially, are hungry in their hearts for a daddy. You don't know how blessed you are."

"But it was weirder than that," I told her.

"Chaurisse, just try and put it out of your mind. I know you miss your friend, but that girl has serious emotional problems. You don't want to get mixed up with that."

"Emotional problems" was my mother's catch-all term for anybody who wasn't quite right in the head. The neighbor kid who climbed a hickory nut tree in his birthday suit — emotional problems. When Monroe Bills shot his ex-wife when she was walking out of Mary Mack's, my mother said, "Why couldn't anyone see that he had serious emotional problems?"

"Why won't you listen to me? Dana

doesn't have emotional problems. She just has regular problems."

"I am listening to you," Mama said. *"You are the one who is not listening to me."*

This was not a day to fight. We were in the Honda on the way to Virginia Highlands, a historic neighborhood in northeast Atlanta. Nowadays, you can take the freeway almost the whole way from southwest, but when we went shopping for my mother's party dress, we took the surface streets the full fifteen miles. We drove east on MLK, passed by Alex's Barbecue, which used to have the best ribs on the planet. A mile or so later, we passed Friendship, where we sometimes went to church. After that, we cut through downtown on a series of one-ways. The gleaming gold roof of the capitol reflected in my mother's sunglasses. On Ponce de Leon, we traveled east, past Daddy's IHOP and Fellini's, where you could get pizza one slice at a time. Finally we made the left onto North Highlands and the trees seemed to bloom all at once and the streets were clean and bright.

Virginia Highlands is one of Atlanta's oldest neighborhoods. The homes aren't columned like over in Druid Hills, but they're gorgeous Victorians and the side streets are cobblestoned. We drove all the way out here because my mother had her heart set on buying a dress from Antoinette's, which apparently is an Atlanta institution, although I had never heard of it.

Strangely enough, it turned out that my mother and father had similar taste in dresses after all. Who knew that my mother, who was extravagant only from her hairline upward, secretly dreamed of Tara? "Your father and I went to see that movie three times. It was beautiful."

I'd never actually seen *Gone with the Wind,* because a ninth-grade trip to the Turner Center was canceled because of a complaint from some of the black parents. Still, I found my mother's Scarlett-dreams to be plenty weird.

After we parallel-parked on St. Charles, Mama craned to read a street sign and then pointed that we should go right. "Vivien Leigh was so gorgeous. And that accent. It was Southern but not country. Elegant. I'll remember those dresses — even the one she made out of a curtain — I'll remember that for the rest of my life. That little waist!"

I turned my face away, embarrassed, but also not wanting to fall down her rabbit hole. "There's the shop," I said, pointing out the painted sign hanging from a purple awning.

It figured that if you wanted a white-girl dress, you had to go to a white-girl store. Antoinette's, the sign announced, had been doing business with Virginia Highlands' brides for more than a century. As we walked in the door, we were greeted with the delicate odor of jasmine potpourri and "Good morning, ladies. May I help you?" spoken like sweet tea. The owner of this accent was a white girl, about my age. She was so thin that the armholes of her sleeveless dress gaped, revealing a turquoise slip. The boy's class ring around her neck was so huge it could have been a bracelet.

"Yes." My mother shifted into professional mode, which basically meant she took special care to pronounce the letter *t*. "I am looking to purchase — today — a bridal-inspired special-occasion gown. I am hoping to make the purchase today."

"I see," the salesgirl said, doing a little double take because my mother's chestnut pageboy matched her own, in both color and style. "Is this for yourself or for your daughter?"

"For myself," my mother said.

"Well," the salesgirl said uneasily, and we could feel her sizing us up, "you just look around and let me know if there is something I can help you with."

The shop was small, but my mother and I were the only customers on this Sunday afternoon. If this store was such an institution, why wasn't anyone here? The salesgirl, as if reading my mind, offered, "Most people make an appointment, but you're in luck."

We were not in luck. My mother pulled a couple of dresses from the racks, frowned, and patted her wig. A cream-colored corset dress caught my eye and I turned over the tag. It was a good thing Daddy said the sky was the limit.

"Excuse me," I said to the salesgirl who was red-faced as she watched me. "What size do you go up to?"

She bit her lip and winced. "Ten?"

My mother returned three dresses to their racks. "Okay, Chaurisse. Let's go."

I turned to the salesgirl. Surely, somewhere out there, there were white girls with meat on their bones, and surely these chunky white girls went to prom, were introduced at cotillions, and got married at Callanwolde. "Where do they have the kind of dresses we are looking for in our sizes?"

The salesgirl flushed again. "There's the catalog store called the Forgotten Woman —"

My mother said, "I am not buying my

dress at a store called the Forgotten Woman."

The salesgirl said, "It's not a good name, but they have really nice things."

My mother shook her head.

"Let me call my mama," the salesgirl said. We must have looked confused, because she added, "It's a family business," before disappearing to the back.

Mama and I sat on an upholstered bench, not sure exactly what we were waiting for. Across from us stood a three-way mirror, and I saw what we must look like to the salesgirl. We didn't belong here — my mother in her embellished tracksuit and me in Dana's rainbow tube top. Mama reached over and plucked a lace garter from a table of frilly underthings. "Do you think I could get this thing to stretch enough to get around my toe?" She laughed, but her face was half anger and half sadness. "Before I got married, I had a teeny waist. I wasn't a pretty girl, but I was nice-looking."

I wanted to say "You are nice-looking now," but looking in the three-way mirror it was clear that neither of us was much to look at. We were both too fat, our faces round. Mine was threatened by a double chin and my mother's had already reached that point. She didn't have to worry about acne scars like I did, but unlike me, she hadn't had the benefits of orthodontia. As I leaned my head on her soft shoulder, the doll-baby fibers of her wig tickled my nose.

The salesgirl popped from the mysterious back room, fresh and bright. "It is your lucky day, after all. We had a special order that was returned. There's nothing sadder than ringing up a return on a bridal. But this is a happy ending. Do you want to see it? It's up-sized."

We agreed but without much enthusiasm. My mother and I were not lucky people.

"I think you'll like it," she said, unzipping the vinyl garment carrier.

It was perfect enough to make you believe that God really keeps his eyes on sparrows and overweight colored women alike. The dress wasn't pure white, but it wasn't that self-conscious beige that brides wear when they want to make it clear that they are not passing themselves off as virgins. This dress, more *A Midsummer Night's Dream* than *Gone with the Wind,* was a lush cream color, the same shade as the pale flesh of almonds.

"Try it on?"

The pale almond gown may have been up-sized, but it was still a bit snug for Mama. Later, back at the Pink Fox, she made the episode into a funny story, joking, "It took

Chaurisse, a ninety-pound white girl, and a crowbar, but they got me into it." Mama had been up against the dressing room wall, hands splayed against the wall like she was getting patted down by the cops. I pushed the sides of the dress together, using my index fingers to poke down the rebellious flesh, while the salesgirl coached, "Empty out your lungs. Shallow breaths! Shallow breaths!"

The plan was that Mama would lose a pound and a half each week until the soiree. In addition, she would wear a serious long-line girdle and a pair of control-top Hanes. And last but not least, neither Daddy nor Uncle Raleigh could see the dress until the special day.

"Mama," I said, "it's not a wedding dress."

"Stop being so negative," she said.

When teenagers throw parties, much of the thrill comes from deciding who to invite and who to ignore, but for my mother the delight was in including everyone she knew. The party was the only conversation in the Pink Fox ever since the double-enveloped eagles had landed. At dinner, my father patted himself on the back. "Looka there, Buttercup. I forgot that the ladies going to the party were going to have to pay your mama to get them ready to go! This thing is going to pay for itself!" It was a happy time in our household, even though Raleigh was a little down in the mouth when he thought nobody was watching him. He and Daddy had recently stopped working Wednesday nights, so we gathered together and watched *Hill Street Blues.* We passed the bowl of popcorn, popped without butter to respect Mama's diet, but Raleigh never ate any of it.

Mama said she thought his mopiness was because all the party talk reminded him that he didn't have a wife or kids of his own. He didn't even have a date to bring, saying he would just escort me. I told her that I thought that he was still shook up about the scene at the gas station. Dana's mama had cursed him to his face. Mama said, "Missing Dana is what's got *you* turned around. Raleigh's got problems of his own."

Three weeks in, my mama had dropped five and a quarter pounds. To celebrate, she had me heft a sack of onions. "Imagine this much lard, removed from my behind." It had been tough going. For two days, she consumed nothing but lemonade sweetened with maple syrup, made even more disgusting by a dose of cayenne pepper. One week, she ate turkey slices rolled in lettuce as lunch, but by bedtime she'd convinced herself that a little frozen pizza wouldn't hurt anything. She didn't ask the ladies at the Pink Fox to tote around a bag of onions, but she worked one finger, then two, into her waistband to show her progress.

"Show us the dress," said Mrs. Grant, mother of Ruth Nicole Elizabeth. She was getting her roots done.

"I'm not even halfway to my goal," Mama said.

"Just try it on," said Mrs. Grant. "We know you are a work in progress. We can use our imagination. Am I right, ladies?" She clapped her hands, nodding at the women sitting in chair no. 1 and chair no. 2, asking for their support. They waited a moment and then started clapping, too. Mama looked at me. "What do you think, Chaurisse?"

"Go for it," I said.

While Mama was gone, the Pink Fox was quiet. The TV, mounted on the wall like in a hospital, was broken, so there was nothing to distract us from each other. In chair no. 1, one person was ready for a relaxer. The lady in chair no. 2 waited for her curls to be combed out. Mrs. Grant, under the dryer, called out to me. "Are you looking forward to graduation?" Ruth Nicole Elizabeth had been given an honors scholarship to Emory University.

"I guess so," I said, busying myself organizing the hard-sided rollers.

"Plans?"

"Probably Georgia State."

Mrs. Grant's voice was loud because she was under the hair dryer. "I know Laverne is really proud of you."

"Yeah," I said. "I probably need to go help her."

I opened the back door and started up the concrete steps. No doubt my mother was upstairs. It seemed that $750 was a lot to pay for a dress that was still so much trouble. Like Grandma Bunny used to say, "Pretty ain't easy." Well, unattractive and unmotivated wasn't easy, either. I knew Mrs. Grant had asked about my plans to be kind. Going to Georgia State was what I would probably end up doing, but it wasn't a *plan.* I hadn't been accepted to any of the Sisters. Even the stepsister turned me down.

I thought about my flute and picolo, snug in their velvet-lined case. I'd lost interest even before I discovered that I wasn't any good at it. Blowing a flute could never get you anywhere. There is not one flautist in the whole world that anyone has ever heard of. Every boy that plays the trumpet dreams of being Miles Davis, but the flute is something you take up because you couldn't think of anything better to do.

I crossed through the den, passed the kitchen, and entered my parents' bedroom, following the crisp swish of crinoline. I found my mother, struggling beneath her wig-heads, contorting herself to reach the zipper in the middle of her back. "Help me," she said. Her face had grown damp with the strain of it. I tugged the tiny zipper up its track, sealing her soft brown body into a casing of silk and whalebone. A flush of tenderness overcame me and I pressed my lips to the spot just above the hook and eye. "I love you, Mama," I said as she stepped toward the mirror and reached down her front and lifted each of her breasts and settled them into the sweetheart neckline.

The women in the shop were a well-behaved audience. Mrs. Grant, who seemed to enjoy clapping her hands, led them in applause as my mother entered through the back door. They marveled over the detailing at the sleeves, the embroidered bodice, the tiny seed pearls, obviously attached by hand. My mother waved off the praise, apologizing for her bulging waist. She explained that she was going to wear Grandma Bunny's 1950s girdle. "That will be my something old," she said. Catching her own eye in the mirror, she added, "I guess my own self is my something old. I'm forty-three this year." Everyone protested that she was not old at all, and no one pointed out to her that this was just a party, not a wedding.

I'd been carrying her train like a lady-in-waiting, but I dropped to my knees to demonstrate how it could be gathered into a bustle, earning me one of Mrs. Grant's rounds of applause. While I was on the floor, matching satin loops to tiny pearl buttons, there was a jangle of bass bells as someone entered the Pink Fox. My mother's voice was thin as plastic wrap. "Hello there, Dana."

I pushed the dress aside like a heavy curtain to see my lost friend standing beside her mother. They were both dressed like schoolteachers — pencil skirts, button-down tops. If I didn't know them, I would think they were missionaries for some sort of strict religion. "Dana!"

"Dana!" her mother mocked.

"Finish what you're doing," my mother said when I started to rise from my crouched position at her feet. Although my mother was wrapped in layers of expensive cloth, I could feel her body tense, sheltering me. My hands were unsteady, but I stayed on my knees and matched each button with its loop until the bustle was tucked below her waist. Mama stood still until I finished and Dana and her mother waited, too. Looking back, I can see this little pause as a courtesy.

Mama took two steps in the direction of Dana and her mother, extending her hand. "I am Mrs. Witherspoon. You must be Dana's mother."

"I am," Dana's mother said. "I am Mrs. Gwendolyn Yarboro."

I could see that Dana was a younger, more frightened version of her mother. The corners of her mouth twitched every few seconds as she tried hard not to look at me. With the toe of her pump, she scratched her leg, running her hose.

"I need to speak with you," Gwendolyn said to my mother.

"I'll be with you in a moment," Mama said. "Just let me go and change out of this dress." She put her hands on her stomach where the dress was tightest. Then her hand drifted up to hide the plumped cleavage.

"Is your husband here?"

"He's working," my mother said. "Is there something I can help you with?"

"Mama," Dana said, "let's just come back later."

Gwendolyn looked at her daughter. "We have to see this through."

The customers were uneasy in their seats. Mrs. Grant offered to leave even though she was still wet under the dryer. My mother waved her hand. "No, stay. There's nothing happening here." She picked up a blow-dryer and turned it on even though she was still in the party dress. "Miss Yarboro is going to come back later."

"You can't turn me away," Gwendolyn said, reaching to take the roaring dryer away from my mother. "Turn that thing off and listen to me."

"Hey," I said. "Don't touch my mother." My voice, feeble in my own ears, gave away how afraid I was. In Gwendolyn's hands, the blow-dryer may as well have been a pistol.

"I'm a missus, too," she said. "You are not the only one. I may not live in as fine a house, but I am a missus, too."

My mother looked around like she was looking for a place to sit, but every chair was occupied and every eye in the room was on Gwendolyn, who held a sheet of paper folded in two. She thrust it toward my mother like a subpoena. I looked to Dana, who studied her shoes. Whatever that paper was, it was something bad. Mama refused to take it.

"Get out of my shop," my mother said. "Get out of my shop. This is my place. Get out."

Mrs. Grant, under the dryer, began to applaud, looking to the other women to join her in this odd banging together of hands, but they didn't. Like me, they couldn't stop looking at the folded page.

"Get out," my mother said. "I don't care what you got in your hand. You don't have any paper that has anything to do with me."

"Take it," Gwendolyn said. "Take it before I have to read it aloud."

My mother's breasts heaved over the sweetheart neckline. She didn't seem to know what to do with her hands. At her sides, they pumped like a pair of hearts. Gwendolyn opened the paper. She looked at it slowly before glancing up and taking a breath, surveying the room before touching her hair. Gwendolyn licked her lips and although she meant her face to be rigid and stern, I know I saw a flicker of delight tickle her cheeks as she prepared to read. Whatever she had in store, she had been waiting for a long time. I took three steps forward, tripping over Mrs. Grant's ankles a bit, but I managed to pull the page from Gwendolyn's hand.

"Good girl," Mrs. Grant said, like I was a pet.

I unfolded the page. It was a Xerox copy; I could still smell the chemicals. I was looking at a wedding license issued to James Lee Witherspoon and Gwendolyn Beatrice Yarboro in the state of Alabama the year after I was born.

"This is bullshit," I said, not to Gwendolyn but to Dana. Gwendolyn kept her arms crossed over her chest and Dana held her hands at her sides like a church usher. Gwendolyn said to my mother, "I am so sorry to have to tell you like this."

The truth is a strange thing. Like pornography, you know it when you see it. Dana, silvery Dana, was my flesh-and-blood sister. James, my ordinary daddy with his Coke bottle glasses was nothing but a dog. And what did that make me? A fool. I'd invited Dana into my house. Every time I wanted to hang out, she made me beg. And I did. Every single time. "You're not sorry," I was speaking to Dana, but I couldn't look away from the paper in my hands.

"I didn't send her over here. That's between the two of you," Gwendolyn said. "What's on that document is between your mother and me."

"Give it here, Chaurisse," my mother said. I handed her the page and she looked it over. She crumpled the Alabama license and tossed it on the floor. "You think I'm scared of a piece of paper?"

Gwendolyn looked a little confused, like we had fallen off the script. Supporting her large patent-leather handbag with her left hand, she began to rifle through it with her right. With a distressed glance at Dana, she dropped to one knee and rummaged through the bag. "I have something else," she said to my mother.

"You don't have anything I need to see," my mother said. "So take your little raggedy pocketbook and your raggedy little daughter and get out here."

At this, Mrs. Grant pulled up the top of the dryer and started a standing ovation. The clipped noises of her hand bounced off the tension in the room.

"What is wrong with you?" Dana said to Mrs. Grant. "This is not a TV show. This is our life."

"I have it right here," Gwendolyn said. "What is done in the dark will come to the light. That's what the Bible says."

"Don't you even try to confuse me with scripture." My mother nudged the patent-leather purse with her bare foot darting out from under the white gown. Gwendolyn scooted her bag back in front of her, pouring the contents of her handbag on the tiled floor of the Pink Fox. There were the usual purse contents — lipstick, chewing gum, emery boards, and a hank of keys. In addition, there was a compass, the kind you use to draw circles. She then shook the purse. "It's in here." Dana got down beside her and helped repack. Gwendolyn had lost that triumphant look and seemed a little lost, the way Grandma Bunny had when she was on a medication that made her forget who we were.

"I have it, Mama," Dana said, quietly, but not so soft as a whisper.

"Well, give it here," Gwendolyn said. "Why did you make me get on my knees before these people?" She waved her arms to take in not just me and Mama but the customers, maybe especially Mrs. Grant, who was still standing, as though this were a basketball game in the final seconds.

"Mama, don't do it. I have it, but don't do it."

"It has to be done," Gwendolyn said. "Give it here."

"Please," Dana said. "Don't make me."

"You started this," Gwendolyn said. "You

409

started this whole thing."

"Just go," Mrs. Grant said. "Take whatever you have and just go. It's not right, you coming. This is her *home.* You cannot come to her *home.*"

"Shut up," Dana said to Mrs. Grant. "You just shut the hell up. You don't know us."

Mrs. Grant straightened herself to her full height. She was gaunt, like she spent her whole life dining on nothing but chicken broth and saltine crackers. "I don't know you. But I know what you are."

"Give it here, Dana," Gwendolyn said. "These people don't care about you."

But I did care about her, and I cared about my mama. "Don't give it to her," I said to Dana. I couldn't imagine anything more devastating than the black-and-white document she had already given me, but just because I couldn't imagine it didn't mean that there was not a blow beyond my imagining. "Dana." She finally looked at me, and I hoped that there was something on my face that deserved mercy. I had never done anything to hurt her. I had scraped all the skin off my shoulder for her.

"Dana," said Gwendolyn. "Look at me."

Dana sighed and reached into her purse, the same fake LV she was carrying that day we met in the SupeRx. She looked exhausted. I couldn't believe that it had been only last summer that we were stealing from the drugstore. Fast friends is what they call it when you connect with someone like that. When you talk about it, you say you are like sisters.

She kept her fist closed tight around the object and passed it to her mother. Using her free hand, she tried to close Gwendolyn's fingers into a fist as well, postponing the moment that we would see the flush of aquamarine and flash of crystal. For a moment, I forgot how to breathe.

"No," my mama said.

"Miss Bunny left it to Dana."

"No," my mother said. "Miss Bunny would not do me like that. We buried Miss Bunny in her brooch."

I shook my head, remembering the day we prepared Miss Bunny and Raleigh took his awkward picture. I remembered my father's long hug and the star-shaped press against my cheek.

"No," my mother said. "No."

"Ask Raleigh," Gwendolyn said. "You know Raleigh can't tell a lie."

Mrs. Grant, still on her feet, walked toward Dana and Gwen wagging her finger. "You cannot do this."

I was close enough to Dana to touch her.

"Look at me. You are not my sister."

She turned and said, "Yes, I am."

Mrs. Grant said, "What's your last name, then?"

Gwendolyn said, "This isn't about names. It's about blood."

Cold as anything, Mrs. Grant said, "I didn't catch *your* family name, either."

Not for one second did I forget whose side I was on, but I felt a little ashamed for Dana and her mother. Every time Gwen went to speak, Mrs. Grant cut her off, asking again about her name, like it was an exorcism. Meanwhile, my mother, stuffed into her party dress, held her mouth open like she was singing a silent opera.

"Get out," I finally said.

Seeming exhausted and maybe even grateful to be dismissed, Gwen took a step toward the door, but Dana took a step in my direction. "Can I have it back?"

"What?"

"Miss Bunny's pin. It's the only thing I have."

I squeezed my hand around the brooch, letting the sharp pin press against my palm. "It's mine."

As they left, Dana looked over her shoulder mournfully and mouthed something that I

412

couldn't decipher. All my life, I'd wanted a sister. How many times had my mother said how sorry she was that I was an only child? That's what happened when you want something too much. Life, it seemed, was a long con, rotten with dirty tricks.

Near the door, Mrs. Grant knelt as my mother sank to the floor in her pale almond gown. I know I should have been at my mother's side, but I went to the glass door and watched Dana and her mother walk to the curb, struggling against the steep grade in their heels. Maybe I could have run after them, shoved Gwendolyn to the ground to defend my mother's honor. Perhaps I should have demanded some sort of truth from them, but at that moment I didn't want to know anything more.

24
A MIGHTY POOR RAT

My mother banished my father from 739 Lynhurst with nothing but the uniform on his back. Didn't even let him in the house. He didn't fight, didn't beg for forgiveness or for his toothbrush. He walked away at a quick clip, like an embarrassed deliveryman after knocking on the wrong door. Once we heard the quiet crank of his engine my mother said, "That wasn't so bad," but then she burst into tears and asked me to bring her a Tylenol PM. She was still mopping her face with a dishrag when the telephone mounted on the kitchen wall rang. Startled, I looked at my mother. "Answer it," she said. Although what happened that afternoon had made it clear to both of us that we didn't know anything at all about our own lives, we still had enough intuition to know that my father was on the other end of that jangling phone. "T-t-tell you m-m-mama that I understand that she doesn't want to talk to me. Tell her that I'm sleeping at Raleigh's. And t-tell her I love her."

I said, "Yes, sir. I will deliver that message."

"Chaur-r-rise," he said. "How can you be so cold? I'm still your daddy. This is between your mama and me."

"This is between all of us," I said, winding my fingers in the spiral cord, thinking of how many people made up the *us*. Gwen had left in our mailbox a fat envelope stuffed with all kinds of paperwork, including Dana's birth certificate. Negro female born alive four months before I was born and nearly died in the very same hospital. Raleigh's signature skimmed the line beside the word *father*. (Clipped to it was a ruled index card that said, *Do not be misled by this*.) And what about Dana and me? There was no scrap of paper making an official connection between us. I am not the one to believe that our shared blood made us sisters, but having shared a father gave us something in common that looped around our ankles and pulled tight around our wrists. This was between all of us. The six of us were hog-tied, fastened in place by different knots.

"Bye, Daddy," I said, so he couldn't say that I hung up on him.

415

It went on like this for two weeks, going on three. Mama refused to answer the telephone but also refused to take it off the hook. Phones back then were built with bells inside, so the ringing was like a fire alarm until I finally picked up. "Just put your mama on the phone," Daddy said, his voice unstable like an eighth-grade boy's. "Tell her I'm at Raleigh's. She can call back at Raleigh's number if she don't believe me."

Right before Johnny Carson's monologue, Raleigh would call himself. "My mama doesn't want to talk to you, either," I told him before I even said hello.

"What about you, Chaurisse?" Uncle Raleigh said. "Can you find it in your heart to talk to ole Raleigh?"

I wasn't sure what was in my heart. I went to school every day as usual. I scored C's on my tests, performed passable arpeggios on my flute, as average and as invisible as before Dana Yarboro bulled our china shop. For the first time in years, I was grateful that my father encouraged me to attend Northside, so far from my neighborhood — the ride to school was about twenty-five minutes by car and forty-five if I took MARTA. Dana was over at Mays High, just down the street. The word had no doubt trickled down a generation from Mrs. Grant to Ruth Nicole Elizabeth and outward from there. Even if she never heard the whispers, Dana was likely on edge like Mama and me as we kept on working in relaxers, scrunching in finger waves, and sewing in weaves. There was no way to know for sure who had heard what, so all you could do was live your life like no one knew anything while being scared that everyone knew everything.

During the seventeen days and eighteen nights of my father's absence, my mother slept beside me in my canopy bed. It wasn't my idea, but on the second night she tapped on the door frame, boozy-peachy and pleading. I rolled over until my backside bumped the wall. The bed sank a little under her weight. "You awake, Chaurisse? I can't sleep." She rolled over on her side, arranging herself around me. My mother's body was soft and warm, smelling of schnapps and the oily silk wrap wound around her head. "You're all I have now," she said.

"No," I said. "That can't be right. You still have the Pink Fox."

"Maybe. If I divorce your father, all of our stuff will be split up. He could buy me out. Him and Raleigh could together, and then they could move that lady and her daughter right in here."

"Daddy and Raleigh wouldn't do that."

"There's no telling what they might do, Chaurisse. Don't you get it? Anybody could be doing anything at any time."

I couldn't picture Daddy and Raleigh kicking my mama out of her own home, closing the Pink Fox and sending her back to renting a chair in another woman's shop. But then again, two weeks ago, I wouldn't have pictured them enjoying a whole second family, eating dinner twice on Wednesdays. When I didn't work hard to keep my mind on its chain, I could picture my daddy, naked but for his glasses, draped in a chenille bedspread, a churning mound over Dana's pretty mother, her hair spread over a satin pillowcase.

I gave my mother ten days for her hard mourning. My thinking was that people generally got a week off of work when someone actually died. During this set-aside time, I comforted her as she mooned over old photo albums. I knelt beside her as she turned out my father's top dresser drawer, sending change, matchbooks, prophylactics, and even a tiny jar containing my baby teeth crashing to the carpet. When her nervous stomach stole her appetite, I didn't force her to eat the meals I prepared. When her appetite returned, I didn't stop her from eating cans of cake icing, one buttery spoonful at a time. I figured it was her right. On the tenth night, I started what they used to call "tough love." At the first sound of her sniffling, I hardened myself and said, "Don't be so sad. You need to be angry, pissed off. If I was you, I'd be in the kitchen boiling up a pan of grits."

Mama tightened her arm around me under the sheet. "Don't play like that."

I was kidding, but then again, I wasn't. It seemed that there should be some sort of consequences for what my father had done.

"Even if he threw me out of this house," Mama said, "I wouldn't do what Mary done."

"At least Mary's famous. Everybody in the whole world knows what she did. And besides, we are not going to get thrown out of this house," I said.

"Let's say I file for divorce and we get a good judge that says I can stay in this house. You know James is going to just move in with them. When I was coming up, people used to say 'It's a mighty poor rat ain't got but one hole.' "

Crowding me in my own bed, my mother talked her greatest fears aloud. Did I think that Miss Bunny knew all along? I said that

419

Daddy was probably the one who gave Gwendolyn the brooch, not Miss Bunny herself. Mama said then she was glad that Miss Bunny was gone to glory before she could see all of us shamed like this. I said that yes, that was probably a blessing. In a drowsy voice, Mama pointed out that full-time students could finish beauty school in a year. Dana and her mama could get certified and take over the Pink Fox. I said, "Dana doesn't want to do hair; she's going to Mount Holyoke. She is going to be a doctor." My mother turned herself over and caught me again in a tight spoon. "Your father's going to pay for that. There won't be anything left."

She gave her little sigh that signaled that the schnapps and Tylenol had finally gotten the best of her and she was drifting to sleep. The clock on my bed table glowed 2:13 a.m. "Good night, Mama."

"Chaurisse?" she said.

"Ma'am?"

"Do you think he did it because I'm not pretty? You know, I wasn't yet fifteen when we got married. Gwen, she probably knows how to do things that I never heard of. She probably reads *Cosmo* magazine. And look how she keeps herself up. She looks like a dark-skinned Lena Horne."

While my mother was competing for the title of Most Brokenhearted Person Ever, I kept retracing my steps, trying to figure when I came to a crossroads and took the wrong turn. When it came to parents, I was a mighty poor rat. It's not like I could have chosen a spare set in case my folks went crazy on me. Mama and Raleigh got lucky. When their biological situation didn't work out, they ran over to Grandma Bunny. I didn't have anyone except James and Laverne.

My mother's body was heavy as a sandbag; my arm pinned under her was starting to hurt. I twisted free of her. It had been ten long days.

"Mama," I snapped, flexing my tingling arm. "Stop whining. Stand up for yourself. Grab a broom. Put sugar in his gas tank. Something."

My mother sat up, turned on the bedside lamp, kicked off the covers, and climbed out of my bed. The skin on the undersides of her arms shook as she jabbed her finger in my direction.

"Don't you turn against me, Bunny Chaurisse."

"I didn't mean it like that," I said. "I just want you to be more . . ." The word that came to mind was *black*. My mother's crying sadness reminded me of white women in movies, the kind who are liable to faint if something happens that they can't handle. "I want to see you fight back. If there was ever a time to boil up some grits, it's now."

Mama balled her hands on her hips. "Let me tell you what you don't understand. Al Green got out of that bathtub and Mary almost killed him with those grits. I heard he had to get skin from his back stitched onto his privates. Is that what you are telling me to do to your daddy, Chaurisse?"

"No," I said. "I was just trying to say that you should —"

"Al Green's privates aren't even half of this story. While he was lying there naked, burnt up with blisters, she took a pistol out of her purse, pressed it to her chest, and blew it wide open. Mary died right on top of him." My mother's breasts heaved under her worn nightgown. "Don't talk about what you don't know about. It wasn't the grits that made him get right with God. It was her blood."

My mother heaved herself out of my bedroom, leaving me squinting in the lamplight. I lay in my bed for another hour imagining the four of us — me, Daddy, Raleigh, and Mama — in our separate rooms staring at our own separate ceilings.

I didn't sleep again that night. At a quarter to six, I found my mother sitting at the kitchen table peeling a mountain of potatoes. Some had turned brown with the air, but the one in her hand was white and wet.

"Did you sleep, Mama?"

"No," she said. "I thought I would make a potato soup. I would make a lot, so we could freeze it."

"Mama," I said. "Go lay down."

"I don't want to sleep in my bed."

"Go sleep in my room."

"You put me out," she said, looking up from the potato. She had cut the peel so thick that there was hardly any vegetable left.

"No, Mama," I said. "I'll lie down with you."

We went back to my bedroom. I held the covers back and followed behind her. This time, I was the one who curved my body around hers.

Mama said. "Let me finish telling you about Mary. She left a note. They found it when they came for her body. It said, *'The more I'm trusting you, the more you're letting me down.'*"

I knew by then that I would never have my mother back, not in the way I had known her all my life. When you have seen your mother shattered, there's no putting her back together. There will always be seams, chipped edges, and clumps of dried glue. Even if you could get her to where she looks the same, she will never be stronger than a cracked plate. I climbed in bed beside her and closed my eyes, but I never relaxed enough to forget who I was and what had happened to us. At seven thirty, the old ladies showed up, ready for their clips and dips. It was a miracle that she hadn't missed a single appointment up until then. My father may have taken a wrecking ball to our lives, but not a single nap in southwest Atlanta went unstraightened. This is why I let my mother pretend to sleep as I eased myself out of bed and down the back steps to open up the shop. I let the old ladies in, explaining that my mother was feeling poorly this morning. I opened her heavy appointment book, rescheduled the clients, and then called the other ladies on the page. I blamed it on a virus and everyone clucked that it was going around. Then I called my high school, pretended to be my mother, and explained that I was the one feeling poorly. I blamed it on the same virus and no one seemed to care. Then I phoned Witherspoon Sedans and explained to the answering machine that I hated my father and I never wanted to see him again.

Daddy and Uncle Raleigh were just guys, like Jamal and Marcus, loyal only to each other. I thought the whole point of growing up was that you got to be somebody's wife, that you weren't caught up in some man's crazy games. And here I was, this only child, told all my life that I was a miracle. I may have been my mother's miracle, but I was my father's other daughter. His not-silver girl. My mother wasn't the only person in this house who had been cheated on.

I don't know how much my mother slept, but she got out of bed when she heard the mailman putter by in his little jeep. The RSVPs for the anniversary soiree had been arriving daily. Despite everything, she used an ivory letter opener to open the little envelopes, like she was shucking oysters looking for pearls. Then she stacked the reply cards in two stacks on her dresser. One for yes and one for no. Two days earlier, I had asked her what she planned to do about the soiree and she said it was my father's problem, not hers.

In the kitchen, the starchy scent of the peeled potatoes was suddenly stifling. It's strange how a smell that has been there all along can suddenly slam you, like a memory. Waiting for my mother to handle her odd business at the mailbox, I remembered myself at the science fair, wearing a rabbit-fur jacket. I remember the other girl in an identical coat, a silver girl, with dark skin and hair hanging to the middle of her back. I'd seen her in front of the Civic Center and again when I stopped by the ladies' room. I remembered the smell of the blue toilet water. It was Dana. Of course it was. I remember thinking, "This girl wants to hurt me." How old had I been? Thirteen? Something like that. I ran out of the bathroom like I was running for my life. The roots of my hair tingled. My bladder had been so full that I unhooked the button on my waistband. When I finally made it home, the pee had leaked a little bit and I washed my panties out in the sink, so Mama wouldn't know. Dana. How long had she been nibbling at the edges of my life? When I saw Raleigh and Gwen in the park that day, was it really a coincidence? I put my face into the cradle of my arms and inhaled my own scent, which was Dana's smell, too. I couldn't escape the odor of her because she smelled just like me and just like my mother and my father and this house. Anaïs Anaïs, White Shoulders, menthol cigarettes.

426

This is what made up the air of our lives, and theirs, too.

My mother finally returned from the mailbox. "Anything good in the mail? Anything besides RSVPs? We are going to have to decide how to handle the party thing, you know. It's only three weeks away." She didn't say anything, and I worried that I shouldn't have mentioned the party and her strange obsession with who planned to come to a soiree that was never going to happen. She fanned herself with a postcard. "What?" I said, trying to read her face, to figure out if what she had in her hand was good news or bad. I reached for the card the way you might try and take a sharp object away from a baby, but she jerked her hand back.

"You will not believe this. You will not fucking believe this." She smacked the postcard on the table like it was the high joker. The edge of cardboard got wet with potato juice.

I picked up the dry corner and held the card to my face. The front of the card featured a photo of a giant smiling peanut that resembled Jimmy Carter. "Howdy!" I frowned and flipped it over. The message on the back was written in block letters that I imagine you would find on a ransom note

— anonymous and menacing at the same time.

BIGAMY IS A CLASS C FELONY. IN JAIL YOU WILL NOT BE A ENTREPRENEUR. YOU WILL BE JUST ANOTHER NIGGER.

"Wow," I said, running my fingers over the card. The words were written so hard that you could feel the imprint of the words across President Peanut's front teeth. "Is this good or bad?"

My mother looked at me like I was the one who had gone crazy. "Bunny Chaurisse Witherspoon, whose side are you on? That bitch is trying to destroy our family. You see she addressed the card to James and sent it over here, to this house." My mother nodded her head with something that looked like satisfaction. "If she's sending mail over *here,* it's because he ain't sleeping over *there.*"

I swear to God that she smiled for the first time in two weeks. "But Mama —"

"Listen to me. That bitch is just jealous, and she will not be satisfied until she has destroyed everything I have worked for. This is serious now."

"Mama, it was serious the whole time."

"Don't use that tone of voice with me. I

am still your mother." I regret not turning my eyes away, because she looked in my face and saw that this wasn't true in the same way that it had been two weeks ago.

"Mama," I said, "what Daddy did is against the law."

"Statutory rape is against the law," my mother said, and softened her tone at my kicked-dog yelp. "Baby, I am not saying this to be hurtful. I am just saying that I could have called the police on Jamal Dixon. You were what, fourteen? But I knew that wasn't the best way to handle it. Yes, men do things that are illegal, but calling the law is not the way to handle private, family business. It's entrapment, anyway. And she knows it. You know she forced him to marry her. And now she wants to press charges. Crazy heifer."

"Mama!" I said, no longer using that careful voice you use when talking to babies and alcoholics. "Gwen might not be the only crazy person in the equation. Daddy was with her for almost twenty years. Dana is their kid. Don't you think he should, I don't know, suffer?" It wasn't the right word, it sounded too biblical, but it was all I could come up with.

"I'm the one that's suffering, Chaurisse." She walked across the linoleum of the kitchen and dragged the trash can to the corner of the table. Using her forearms, she raked the potatoes into the trash, soiling the sleeves of her sweatshirt. "You and me, we are the only ones that didn't do anything wrong. We were just living our lives, thinking we were normal people. We are the only people who deserve a say in this."

"What do you want to happen?"

She tied off the trash liner with a twist tie and sat down in my father's chair. "I want our life back like it was."

"Mama," I said. "You can't put the rain back in the sky."

She drew her hand back as if to slap me. I turned my good shoulder to catch the blow, but it never came. My mother took her hand down and held it in front of her face like a mirror. "No, no, no," she said talking to her hand like it was a small child in need of a little discipline. "I am not going to let that whore make a barbarian of me. She is not going to take my dignity. I am a wife. I will act like a wife."

"Mama, sit down. Do you want your Tylenol PM?"

My mother paced around the kitchen, still holding her right hand by the wrist like she didn't trust it to be free. "No," she said. "You asked me what I want and I told you."

"I want to move to Massachusetts," I said.

My mother looked puzzled and I can't blame her. The impulse came from out of nowhere, but what I wanted more than anything was to be far away from both my parents. "I want a divorce," I said.

It was too much for me. I should have been preparing for graduation, looking for a white dress to wear under my robe. I told my mother that I wasn't going to march for commencement and she said, "It doesn't matter, as long as you get your paper." We were in deep water, my mother and me. Mama needed help — probably professional help but at least the help of somebody who knew her better than I did. If there was someone else I could have called, I would have. Women on television have friends they can count on. My mother's favorite TV show was *The Golden Girls,* about these four old ladies that live together in an apartment, solving each other's problems, being each other's bridge over troubled water. With Grandma Bunny a year in the ground, my mama didn't have anybody but me.

25
QUIZ SHOW

Miss Bunny's brooch sat in my mostly empty jewelry box. It was an old-fashioned case, one of the things my mother bought me when she started wishing for her own lost childhood. A tinny version of Für Elise plinked out when I lifted the lid. I held the brooch in my hand, proof that my father was somehow living two lives at once. Everyone had been in on this scam, even Grandma Bunny, closed up in her casket.

Is it safe to say that we all went a little crazy in May of 1987? It was like our lives turned into a movie — not the blockbusters you have to go to the theater to see but the ones you catch on television in the middle of the night. Once our lives began to seem made for TV, we all started acting like characters. Who could blame us? There were no real life models for our new reality.

For my part, I acted the role of girl detective. I handled the postcard only by its edges, so I wouldn't get my fingerprints on it. I tricked my mother into taking a double dose of Tylenol PM, so she wouldn't stir as I eased her keys from a hook and took the car out in the middle of the day. Nervously scanning the lanes behind me in the rearview mirror, I made my way to the airport.

Uncle Raleigh was sitting in the blue Lincoln, reading a photography magazine when I tapped on the window. He smiled to see me and I could see how old he had gotten in just a few weeks.

"Chaurisse," he said, unlocking the door, "come and sit with me."

I opened the door, and sat on the familiar seat. "Hey, Uncle Raleigh."

"Aren't you supposed to be in school?" he asked.

I shrugged. "It doesn't matter. I'll graduate, regardless."

"You want me to turn on the air conditioner?"

Overhead I could hear the high-pitched noise of airplanes cutting through the sky. Just under it, there was the smooth crooning of Al Green, talking about he was tired of being alone.

"Daddy couldn't have done it without you," I said.

"I figured you would get around to that,"

Raleigh said.

"That doesn't answer my question."

"You didn't ask me a question. What is it that you want to know?"

I was stumped. What did I want to know? I was already aware of more than I wanted to be.

"Daddy is really married to that lady?"

Raleigh nodded. "He did stand up in front of a judge."

"And you were there?"

Raleigh nodded.

"You signed the paper. I saw your name."

"This I did do."

"Why did you help him?"

My uncle shifted in his seat so I could see his face. "I called myself helping Gwen." Raleigh's face burned red when he talked, like he was on fire.

He said, "You can't know Gwen until you see her in a photo. In person, all that pretty is a parlor trick, a distraction, really. But when I get her in a photograph, you can see her entire life just in the way she holds her jaw. Even if the roll isn't finished, I develop it right then. I don't care."

"What about us?" I asked him. "You take our picture all the time."

"With you, Chaurisse, what you see is what you get. When you were a little girl, you were just that, a little girl. Even Laverne, for what she has been through, she is exactly who she is, all the time. It's good. That's where your beauty comes from."

I knew he was trying to compliment me, but it felt like an insult. The way people tell a fat girl that she has "a pretty face." I reached for the door to let myself out, but Raleigh asked me to wait.

"Gwen didn't do any of this on purpose. You have to take my word on it. I'm telling you because I don't want you to think that your daddy would do this for some two-dollar whore, because that's not what Gwen is. In her way, she's a lady."

I made a pillow of my hands and leaned on the dashboard. Every day this situation got crazier and crazier. "What is wrong with you people?" I asked. "Daddy got kids with this lady, you're talking like you're in love with her. What is it about them? Me and mama can be complicated. We can be interesting."

"It's not a competition," Raleigh said.

"That's easy for you to say."

Uncle Raleigh reminded me a lot of Jamal, the way those nice guys break your heart but manage to make you feel like they're the ones who have been done wrong. I got out of the car, walked around and stuck my face into the crack where Uncle Raleigh had his window open.

"One more question," I said. "What's their apartment number?"

Continental Colony was set up to look like something from Europe, maybe a ski lodge or something — cream-colored buildings with black shutters. The town homes were shaped sort of like stop signs on the top. Their building, 2412, was in the middle of a row of identical houses. I stopped in front, checked my purse to make sure that I still had the postcard. The edges were buckled from potato juice. I checked my look in the rearview. Mama was in no condition to tighten up my augmentation, so I'd made a headband from a purple scarf to hide the rough edges. I licked my fingers, pushed back a few kinky strands and opened the car door.

The pathway to their home was warped by grass pushing through the concrete. I took some pleasure from this. Our yard was neat and orderly. The azaleas were in bloom and Daddy had recently painted our mailbox with a fresh coat of white. I stood before the door with my hand on the knocker, trying to decide what I was going to say. I wanted to know why Dana had elbowed her way into our lives. Did she want to know me, or did she want to hurt me? Was it all done under her mother's orders? What did they want from us? I had no idea how I could extract this information. If there was anything the last few weeks had taught me, it was that people only told you what they wanted you to know. Asking a straight question didn't necessarily get you a straight answer.

I'd taken my hand down from the knocker and turned toward the car, when the door swept open. Standing there was Gwendolyn wearing a white nurse's uniform. "Yes?" She looked like Dana's Ghost of Christmas Future. She wasn't all glammed up the way she had been when she invaded the Pink Fox. Her pretty hair was bound behind her head and her face was creased around her mouth. "Are you looking for me?"

"I'm looking for Dana," I said.

Gwen smiled. "Dana is at school. And, if I may be so bold, what are you doing here in the middle of the day? Don't they have truant officers anymore?"

Her manner was hard to read. It was as though she was amused, like I was a little kid who had done something grown, like order lobster at a restaurant.

"I'm taking care of my mother," I said.

"Don't you think your mother has enough people to take care of her?" She kept that tickled-adult tone and invited me in.

Her living room seemed to be set up to honor Dana and Swarovski crystal. On every flat surface rested glass figures atop mirrored coasters. The walls were crowded with photos of Dana. Some were school portraits and these seemed to be arranged chronologically and there were others that looked like Uncle Raleigh's work. She waved her arm and I sat down on a leather couch. Although a chenille throw covered the cushions, I could feel the cracks in the leather against my thighs.

"May I get you something to drink?" Gwen asked.

"No," I said.

"No?" she said with a question at the end like I was being prompted to remember my manners. Something in me almost corrected myself and said "No, ma'am," but I instead said, "No, I don't want anything to drink."

"Very well," Gwen said. "Did you mother caution you not to drink from my glasses? Does she think I am going to put some root on you? Is that what she thinks happened?" Gwen laughed a little. "It's warm in here. Should I turn on the fan, or did she warn you against breathing my air, too?"

"My mother doesn't even know I'm here," I said. "And I would appreciate it if you would stop talking about her."

"You and your sister are so much alike," Gwen said. "I had no idea that my daughter was spending her time with you. Someone should write a book on the secret lives of girls."

"You should know about secret lives," I said.

Gwen turned in my direction. "All this back talk. You and Dana really are sisters."

Every time she said the word *sister,* it felt like a tease. I shifted on the couch.

"Would you rather sit here?" Gwen said, rising. "This is your father's chair."

"No," I said.

"So," Gwen said, "what can I help you with? I'm on my way to work, but I can make time for you."

"Don't call the police on my father," I said.

She smiled, a little. "Come again?"

I took the card out of my purse. I wanted to keep my tone level, like woman to woman. "You sent this to my mother. Don't you think my mother has suffered enough?"

Gwendolyn picked the card up and held it away from her like she didn't want it to stain her white uniform. "Little girl," she said, "while this card does make a good point, I did not send this." She flipped the card over to the smiling peanut on the front. "Jimmy Carter?"

"You're lying," I said. "You and Dana just lie and lie and lie."

Gwen's mood shifted and she leaned forward. "Do not speak ill of my daughter. She has done more for you than you will ever know. Both of us have lived our entire lives in order for you to be comfortable. Nobody that lives in this house ever lied to you."

"You're not all that innocent."

"You are not, either," Gwen said. "Everything you have, you have at the expense of my daughter. Just because you were ignorant doesn't make you innocent."

I stood up from the raggedy couch and Gwen stood up, too. It was as though we were either going to fight or embrace. "Stay away from my mother," I said. "And my father."

Gwendolyn said, "Listen to me. Sit back down. You came here because you want to know something, so let me tell you something."

I sat back down, because Gwen was right. Wasn't whole point to find things out?

"First, what you are asking of me is

440

unreasonable. I exist; Dana exists. You can't ask us to pretend that we don't. When I came to the Pink Fox that day, I did not ask Laverne to leave her husband. I did not ask you to live without your father. I just came to the shop and showed myself. You have been showing yourself to me for every day of your life. I can't believe how arrogant you are, Chaurisse. I have been good to you your entire life, so give me some respect."

Gwen crossed her white-stockinged legs and bounced her shoe up and down. "Don't cry," she said.

I wasn't crying. I felt my face to make sure. She spoke with a grand tone, like there was someone watching. I swiveled to see the whole room, but there was no one else there except the pictures of Dana.

"Now I want to ask you something," Gwen said. "Okay? We're civilized here."

"I'm not telling you anything," I said.

"Oh," Gwen said. "I know everything already. You are the one who needs to know things. I want to ask you for a small favor."

"A favor?"

"Yes," Gwen said. "I want to ask you to give Dana back her grandmother's brooch. It's all she had."

"Hell no," I said.

"Why not?" Gwen wanted to know. "You

have everything. My Dana has fed herself on your crumbs her whole life. Why can't you just share this one thing?"

"Sorry," I said standing up, feeling a bit prideful. "It's mine. She was my grandmother. My daddy stole the brooch from her dress when she was in the casket."

"Don't be so selfish. My daughter has never asked for anything. I never asked for anything. You see me in this uniform? I work every day. I pay my own bills."

"I don't care," I said.

Gwen stood up. "I asked you nicely. I tried to talk to you like an adult. You have forced me to tell you this. Listen here, young lady. When you go home, look at the marriage license. Look at it carefully. Dana, your sister, the one who you think you hate so much, she changed it with a ballpoint pen. I didn't marry your father one year after you were born. He married me when you were three days old, still in the hospital, still in the incubator. Dana changed the date because she didn't want to hurt your little feelings. How about that?"

"That's not true," I said.

She shook her head.

"You are such a liar," I said.

"No," Gwen said. "The devil is a lie, just like your Daddy."

She led me to the door, as though I was just a normal guest. I squinted across the room at a photo of my mother preparing Grandma Bunny for the grave. I was stunned to see it there, as though we were part of her family. Gwen followed my eyes and looked into my astonished face. "It was a gift."

Since I was the one who called my father and told him to come to the house, it would have made sense for me to unlock the door and let him in. Maybe I would have been more cooperative if he had rung the door like a guest, instead of trying to use his key like he still lived here, like everything was okay, like my mother was his only wife and I was his only daughter. His key slid in the lock but wouldn't turn. I stood on the other side of the door and let him try three times until it dawned on him that the locks had been changed. My mother had done it on the first day, before she turned into a sodden mess, when she was still singing "I Will Survive." Before she started wishing he would come home.

When he rang the bell, I opened the wood door, undid the bolt, but I left the glass door locked. He wore his dress uniform, clutching his hat under his arm. If the outfit was red, he would have looked like an organ grinder's monkey.

"Ch-chaurisse," he said. "Thank you for calling me. Is your Mama all right?"

"How can she be all right?" I said.

"None of us is all right," he said. "This has been hard on everybody."

"Daddy," I said, "how could you do this to us?"

"Open the d-d-door."

My mother was asleep on the couch, dead from Tylenol PM. I didn't think she would wake up, but I kept my voice low. "Explain it to me."

"Don't make me talk through the door." My father was so close to the glass that I could make out his chapped lips. I took a small step away; it wasn't much of a move, but he saw it.

"That's how it is, Chaurisse?" he said. "You are afraid of your father? Your mama being mad at me, I can see. What I did was a sin against her. Look at me and see I've been laid low. But I never did you nothing, Chaurisse. I'm still your daddy, nothing can change that."

"You did do me something," I said.

"What have I done you?" he said, like he really wanted to know.

It was hard to explain this thing I felt. It

wasn't like daughters are supposed to expect some sort of exclusive relationship from their fathers, but what he had with Dana was an infidelity. "We didn't even know you," I said.

"You know me, Chaurisse. How can you say you don't know me. When have you ever needed a daddy and I wasn't there? Half of your friends don't even have a daddy. Tell me if I'm lying."

He wasn't.

"Now open the door, Buttercup. Don't leave me standing out here in the street. You said your mama wanted to talk to me."

"No, I said I wanted you to talk to her. She didn't tell me to call you."

"I want to talk to her, too. I've talked to your mama every day of my life since I was sixteen years old. Two weeks away from her liked to kill me."

"What about two weeks away from me?" I said. "You talk to me every day, too."

"Oh, Buttercup," he said, "Don't be like that. Of course I miss you."

"Do you love me?" I asked him.

"Of c-c-ourse, I love you. Your uncle Raleigh loves you, too."

"But do you love me better?"

"Better than your Mama? What kind of question is that?"

"No," I said. "Do you love me better than Dana?"

Now, it was his turn to back away from the glass. "What's the p-p-point of asking that?"

I didn't want him to leave. Not yet. I needed to ask him when exactly he had taken Gwendolyn Yarboro to be his "lawfully wedded wife." Had he really done it when I was in the hospital, underweight, and stuck through with all those tubes? I'd snuck into my mother's drawer and looked at the marriage license, but I wasn't quite sure. If Gwen was telling the truth, I had a problem because I could never tell my mother and I didn't want to join the party of people who loved my mother and lied to her.

"Y-you know, Chaurisse," he said. "Open up this door. You are trying my patience. When you act like this, people grow calluses on their heart. I don't want any calluses on my heart when it comes to you."

Hearing the threat in his voice, I put my hand on the knob to let him in. "Do you love me?"

"Of course I do."

"Then why did you marry Gwen when I was still in the incubator?"

"Who said I d-d-did that?"

"Gwen," I said.

"I wouldn't do that," my father said, "I wouldn't do that to you."

It was easy to take him at his word, as easy as taking off a heavy pack, as easy as falling down a flight of stairs, as easy as shutting my eyes at bedtime.

26

EPITHALAMIUM

She took him back. Was there ever any question? Of course I had doubt at the time, but I wasn't old enough to know anything about the how the world works. When my mother asked me to join her at the kitchen table, she looked like herself again. She wore a green spangled warm-up suit and her hairpiece hung over her shoulders in optimistic ribbon twists. When she spoke, I concentrated on her mouth, her teeth stained by her lipstick.

"Your father never meant for this to happen. He is a good man at his very heart. When we got married, he came forward on his own. There were a dozen wrong things he could have done and only one right thing. We were just children. Chaurisse, when I was your age, I was three years married, had buried a child. Well, that's not fully true. There's nothing under that headstone in the churchyard next to your Grandma

Bunny. By the time I got two feet on the floor, the people at the hospital had already put his little body through the furnace. Nothing was left. No ashes, no nothing. He was so teensy that he just evaporated. All this happened before I was your age now, and your daddy wasn't much older. And that was his baby, too, turned into nothing but smoke and air.

"Nobody turned me away. No matter what is happening in this house today, I can't forget that. Your daddy married me because I was having his baby, and even when I didn't have no baby to show for myself, he allowed me to stay and be part of his family. That's history. That's solid, and there is no changing that. No matter how mad I am, how hurt, no matter what may be going on in your head, there's no undoing that kindness."

"But what about me," I asked her, feeling small even to ask.

"What about you, honey?"

"What about what I want?"

"This is all about you, baby. We are a family. This is about making our family whole. Isn't that what everybody wants?" She smiled at me. "This is the third time the world tried to make an orphan of me. The first was when I got pregnant and my mama put me out. But then Miss Bunny saved me. After that, your brother died, but you saved my marriage. This is the third time. God didn't mean for us to be alone. Can't you see that?"

I crossed my arms and made a nest for my head on the kitchen table. I breathed in my own smell. Life was turning into a quiz show, full of trick questions, and wagers. "I don't know what I see," I said to her.

"You just have to trust," my mother said. "Trust and believe."

EPILOGUE
DANA LYNN YARBORO

My daughter, Flora, looks just like me and I am sorry for this. It's not that I have any quarrel with my own appearance, but I would have liked to give her a face of her own. In so many ways, you can't choose what you give to your daughter, you just give her what you have.

Flora is four years old, born in 1996, the year that Atlanta hosted the Olympics and the whole world came to our country town. I was in labor during the opening ceremonies, but I heard the fireworks as my bones shifted to make way for this new life. My mother was beside me, speaking my name. Flora's father was there, too, but we are not together as couple. He's not married to me, but he's not married to anyone else, either, so I suppose that counts as progress. She doesn't have his last name, but he picks her up on some Sundays and he loves her in public.

She and I live in a town house on Cascade Road, across from John A. White Park. You can't say it's a far cry from Continental Colony, but it's my own home. I pay the mortgage each month and it feels good even without covered parking. It also feels good to send her to the same kindergarten where I first saw Chaurisse so many years ago. My daughter is smart. The teachers love her.

This is the year 2000. In high school, Ronalda and I were convinced that the world was going to end at the start of the new millennium. Part of it was the round number, 2000, and the other part of it was that I couldn't imagine having survived to be thirty-one, but here I am. I don't have much hair these days, I keep it Caesar shorn and brushed flat, but there are silver strands there. I'm not aging as beautifully as my mother, but she works a lot harder at it than I do.

On the Wednesday before Thanksgiving, Flora's school lets the children out early. I was there even earlier — I never want her to wonder where I am. She and I were headed toward the car, when I noticed a blue Lincoln in the space beside mine. I held Flora's hand tighter and ignored the itching in my throat. My mother and I joke

452

that there should be a medical term for the condition we have, the irrational fear of Town Cars.

As I got closer to my car, the driver's door of the Lincoln opened, and Chaurisse Witherspoon stepped out wearing a uniform that was tailored for a man. It had been twelve years, but I would have known my sister anywhere. She looked like her mother from her dull figure to the silly mop of fake hair.

"Hey, Dana," she said.

I suppose the real question was what was she doing here, but I have always known I would see her again.

"Hey, Chaurisse," I said. "What's up?"

She shrugged. "I just wanted to see you. I was driving by the other day and I saw your daughter playing outside. She looks just like you."

Flora liked it when people talked abut her, so she smiled.

"What's her name," Chaurisse wanted to know.

"Flora," my daughter piped up.

The small parking lot was busy with parents and little children. All the kids carried cardboard cutouts of their hands decorated to look like turkeys. I waved at some of the mothers. I hoped I looked

453

normal, well adjusted, and happy. I leaned against the side of my car. "Well? Is somebody dying?" I said it with a sort of flippant attitude, but I really wanted to know. All these years later my mother still scanned the obituary page every Sunday. If James Witherspoon died, she would be there in widow's black.

"Nobody's dying," she said. "I just saw your girl and I wanted to say hello and see how you are."

"I'm fine," I said. "How are you?"

She sighed and leaned on the car next to me. As we talked, we watched the cars fly down Cascade Road. "I'm okay."

"How are your parents?" I asked.

"Still together," she said.

"Figures."

She shifted her weight to her other side and took a really deliberate breath. "You ever see him?"

I could have laughed at her. After all these years, she couldn't quite believe that she and her mother had won.

I hadn't seen my father since the day he and Laverne renewed their vows at the big party at the Hilton twelve years ago. I had gone on my own and spent most of my time riding the glass elevator all the way to the twenty-third floor and then back down again. Looking at the city lights, I wondered if James had other children like me. I had gone to the soiree, not looking for my father, not trying to spoil anything, but hoping to see Chaurisse. I was going to ask her if maybe we could be sisters. It wasn't our fault what our parents had done to each other.

They called it a "recommitment ceremony" and held it in the Magnolia Room, the same space where Ruth Nicole Elizabeth had her Sweet Sixteen. When the elevator stopped at the twenty-third floor, I was too afraid to step out. The ceremony was under way behind a pair of closed doors decorated with bunting. I could imagine Mrs. Grant, silently applauding with her satin gloved hands as Chaurisse pranced down the aisle clutching a bouquet of calla lilies. Behind her would be Raleigh and Laverne in her almond-meat dress. I could see Raleigh bending to kiss her cheek before handing her over to James.

My mother had taken to her bed and I didn't like leaving her alone, but I allowed myself an hour more. I took the elevator underground and walked the aisles of the parking ramp until I found the Lincoln. I sat on the hood as the engine beneath me ticked like a patient bomb.

My father approached the car at quarter after eight. He had to smoke. I may not have been his "legitimate" daughter, but I knew him well enough to anticipate his cravings.

I said, "Hey, James."

He said, "You can't be here."

I said, "I know."

"Then how c-c-come y-y-you're out here."

I told him the truth, that I wasn't sure. I think I wanted him to hug me and tell me that I was still his daughter, that blood meant something. Yes, he could walk away from my mother, but could he walk away from me? My mother could find another man, but there wasn't any way for me to replace my father.

"Don't you love me?" I asked him.

"It's not about loving people," he said. "You have to go home now. I've m-m-made my choice, just like you made your choice when you went bothering Ch-Chaurisse. You almost took my whole life away from me."

"What did you think was going to happen?" I asked him. Did he think that I could live my entire life tucked away a dirty photograph? "I'm your daughter."

"Everybody knows that now," James said. "That's what you wanted. You got it."

■ ■ ■ ■

Even now, I cringe to remember it. I fought
him. I threw myself at my father, fighting
like a girl, all windmilling arms and shriek-
ing. My voice bounced off the concrete
walls, but no one came to stop us. No one
helped even when he shoved me away like I
was a grown man. I didn't fall. I didn't
crumple. And I am proud of this small moment of dignity.

"You made me do that," he said. "You and
Gwen have turned me into an animal."

"No," I said to my sister. "I haven't seen
him."

"Would you lie to me?" she asked.

"You only lie to people you love," I said.

Chaurisse left then and Flora and I walked
toward my car. I was shaken, but I hid this
from my daughter. She recited her -*at*
words, then sang a song in French. I gripped
the steering wheel hard to keep my hands
steady. I spoke my daughter's name over
and over in my head to keep my soul from
shattering. Finally, I pulled the car into the
parking lot of a large church. I went to the
backseat and unhooked Flora from her

safety seat. I knelt beside her and hugged her tight, the way my mother used to hug me, the way that I promised that I would never grip my child. I used to swear that I would never be a desperate mother, that I would always respect the line between Flora and me. But I squeezed her hard and asked more than once, "Do you love your mommy? Do you love me, baby?"

After some minutes, the moment passed. I put my girl back in her seat and drove in the direction of home.

People say, That which doesn't kill you makes you stronger. But they are wrong. What doesn't kill you, doesn't kill you. That's all you get. Sometimes, you just have to hope that's enough.

ACKNOWLEDGMENTS

Thanks first to Team T, who read this story before it was a book, back when I was still afraid of it: Sarah Schulman, Nichelle Tramble, Allison Clark, Joy Castro, Renee Simms, Bryn Chancellor, Alesia Parker, and Virginia Fowler. My sister, Maxine Kennedy, is my whole entire heart.

The United States Artists Foundation and the Collins Family came through when I was just about ready to give up. The family of Jenny McKean Moore and George Washington University granted me a year to write and to work with DC's finest writers. Rutgers-Newark University, the MacDowell Colony, the Corporation of Yaddo, Blue Mountain Center, and the Virginia Center for the Arts provided generous support. Thanks, as well, to Dianne Marie Pinderhughes, who sheltered me during the home stretch.

My aces: Rigoberto, Natasha, Kiyana Sakena, Jafari, Nichelle, Jeree, Lauren, Jaci, Alice, Jim, Evie, Anne, Deborah, Jayne Anne, Cozbi, Dolen, Aisha, and Uncle Ricky held me down when I was in real danger of flying away. Dr. June MacDonald Aldridge taught me how to keep it classy, and Pearl Cleage showed me how to keep it real.

For my fairy godmother, Judy Blume, I have astonished gratitude. My agents Jane Dystel and Miriam Goderich are the very best in the business. Algonquin Books and I have been making eyes at each other for a decade. Thank you, Elisabeth Scharlatt, for making it happen. My editor, Andra Miller, cares about this story as much as I do. You will see her careful attention on every page.